The Astronomic

– JAMES TURNER –

An environmentally friendly book printed and bound in England by
www.printondemand-worldwide.com

FSC
Mixed Sources
Product group from well-managed
forests, and other controlled sources
www.fsc.org Cert no. TT-COC-002641
© 1996 Forest Stewardship Council

PEFC
PEFC/16-33-476

PEFC Certified
This product is
from sustainably
managed forests
and controlled
sources
www.pefc.org

This book is made entirely of chain-of-custody materials

www.fast-print.net/store.php

Astronomic
Copyright © James Turner 2011

All characters are fictional.
Any similarity to any actual person is purely coincidental.

ISBN 978-178035-213-8

FASTPRINT PUBLISHING
Peterborough, England.

For family, friends and those who have offered support

THE ASTRONOMIC

By James J. Turner

Welcome, vital reader, to this collection of short stories set entirely in the future. The tales take in everything from robot politicians to time travelling students and plenty of creatures that I would be unable to describe fully in this small space, some of them human. As a first time writer my influences may seem quite obvious and indeed I wouldn't have been inspired to write such stories if it wasn't for the incredibly vivid and memorable writings of authors such as Brian Aldiss, Isaac Asimov, Stephen King and Phillip K. Dick. They have formed just some of the influences to many of the stories here that you are hopefully about to read. Some stories are allegorical, some are political whilst others are simply quick yarns; I will allow you, the reader, to totally define which stories fit these categories if indeed any. The stories here also fit a particular time line of events; so whilst you don't need to read all of the stories in order to understand each individual story, most of the tales are all interconnected by a certain history of events. The influence of the Venusian War, the advancement of robot spies and the importance of the Sphere should hopefully become clear in a few hours! So now I leave you to hopefully enjoy some of these stories and to hopefully show you a future we may all one day experience…

BEYOND MARS

Following the colonization of the moon in 2067, Man truly felt like he owned space. Human ownership of the moon had seemed like another triumphant leap forward for the species. Gone were the days of just looking up at the stars; wondering what lay out there. Man had been out there and now had a vantage point from the Moon. Humanity had gained a better angle on God's creation. Indeed the more vainglorious individuals that went to live on the now conquered Moon now truly believed they were looking down from the High Chair above all creation. Spacecrafts and oxygen-regenerators had furthered the 21st Century philosophy that Mankind now owned God. The initial mission to establish living stations on the surface of the Moon went flawlessly. The subsequent trips that involving the installation of networks of tunnels establishing both living and industrial sectors had also gone without problem. Soon after a basic working infrastructure was established, commercial areas began to crop up as well. Shopping malls, supermarkets and eventually boutiques came to be seen in the more populace living sectors. Life on Earth had indeed been transposed with minimal fuss in all it's glory. The large Lunar building authorities were even eventually able to create man-made lakes, man-made parks and man-made nature reserves in different sectors of the Moon. There were also two churches, one mosque and one synagogue for legal worshipping regulations. If you travelled far enough and paid enough, you could definitely visit lions and pandas on the zoos there. The finest restaurants were now being founded on the Moon rather than New York, Beijing or London. The leading fashion designers were paid millions to open exhibits and catwalk shows, and of course the latest bands were playing all over the best spots on the Moon. The citizens who had moved to the moon were initially from the elite social strata. To begin with people were excited by the chance of living in a place that made Earth seem passé. The option was taken up by thousands of couples and families, not to mention scores of celebrities, actors, politicians and billionaires. New economic opportunities had presented themselves on the moon, particularly following the mineral bonanza during the 2080's. The economic success of the Moon had developed concurrently. Besides, it was only an 18-hour journey to Lunar-Port 1, and space travel had been made fully safe following the development of the X-Class World Space Association (WSA) Crafts. It was becoming cheaper and more accessible to move there by the year.

Theodore Backus was a 34 year old space craft pilot. He was a tall guy, standing comfortably at 6"3. He was reasonably good looking and had no trouble finding action whilst stationed on the Moon. He knew that his wife wouldn't find out about his playing away because she was always too busy looking after their kid, Peter. Thankfully she was not the type of woman to marry and then break those vows. He was a damn lucky guy in that respect. Sure he still loved the pair of them, but man oh man, the advantages offered from living in a decent sector of the Moon whilst having a good job and plenty of disposable income meant he could almost take his pick from the bars he frequented. Let there be no doubts, Ted Backus was an immoral man. He had convinced his family that he had to work overtime on a frequent basis to cover the Earthly mortgage of their 3 bedroom house he had briefly lived in during his early piloting career. Theodore had been a long-term resident on the Moon now; despite the occasional flights home his family were becoming a bit of a distant memory. He had been living there on and off since 2081. His career had seen him inducted as one of the first commercially licensed pilots taking ships full of tourists to the Moon. He had liked the place so much he decided to prolong his stay there. He kept in contact of course with Anna and Peter through Vid-Screens and the Sphere, but his responses to their calls was nearly always along the lines of "Great to hear from you two, I'm missing you so much on this dustbowl". He probably over played the hardship angle. The pair of them saw enough on the news to know that life in any sector of the Moon really wasn't a hardship. The place offered everything to anyone. The pressure and responsibility of being a family man had probably lead to his decision to spend the majority of his time literally on another planet from his family. The Dad job had been alright when the child was just a fleshy bump his wife had, but the business of reading bedtime stories, changing nappies, heating bottles, not having sex and so on had really changed the positive dynamic he previously had with Anne. The interplanetary nature of his work was a good excuse he felt for being a total failure as a parent.

His job had also defined him more than his family did. The journeys he had to control were relatively simple in the X-Class crafts, and his main concern was simply to ensure the right co-ordinates to and from Earth.

Most major cities had developed space-ports. Indeed it was only rational really. Fossil Fuels had actually become more efficient than any government had dared initially dream. It seriously took him only about 10 gallons of ionized petroleum to power his craft for the journey from Dallas SP to Lunar-Port 1. The additional, and technically vital kinetic energy used was derived from reversing the force of gravity and gaining positive motion via a very complex Nano-Engine system. All crafts when damaged were assessed and fixed by the Robots of course. He could explain the science behind his X-Class craft maybe with a guide and definitely with assistance from some of the techs at the WSA, but it would certainly take a while. These were the good days for Mankind indeed, before any major intergalactic conflict involving alien races and their armed forces. The days had genuinely seemed to show Earth conquering space. To master it's forces and to control it's atmosphere with advanced technology. They had developed space suits with self replenishing oxygen for goodness sake, a man could practically live on an asteroid if he wanted. Theodore Backus was just one of the other billions of people who were wrong about how dangerous space could prove to be.

The brown official looking envelope that was resting on the hallway floor of his apartment appeared innocuous enough. Theodore examined it closely; indeed it was from the WSA as he had suspected. Would today finally be the day? He tore open the ridged end of the envelope messily and quickly. He read the contents eagerly…
"Mr. Backus,
First may we thank you for your application to join the first manned mission to Mars. There were thousands of applicants from both Earth and the Moon, and we obviously are not required to inform you about the highest quality of all candidates. We are delighted to inform you however that you have been chosen by the WSA as part of the first manned mission to Mars. You will be serving the ship as both reserve pilot and ongoing logistical officer"
Theodore read eagerly on…
"May we offer you our proud congratulations. We must legally remind you however Mr. Backus of the specific terms regarding your employment. You may inform no press, no media from the Sphere and no individuals beyond your immediate family of your appointment to the crew of the Nexus-XII Craft. The privacy agreement is equally pertinent to your

11

family and I think we need not remind you that if they endanger the mission in any way as well by publicly revealing your role, then you will be removed from the crew, denied your license and imprisoned. As per the application we recommend you fully minimise the details of what you inform even your closest family members. A high end WSA official will collect you from your home and take you to a secret location outside of Lunar-Port 2.

Congratulations and good luck"

The Moon was old news, he was going to Mars baby! The Red Planet itself. He would be travelling further through space than any other man up until now. Adding up the miles of this trip with the hundreds of journeys he had made between Earth and the Moon Theodore realised that he would have to be amongst the highest individuals on the hypothetical list of furthest travellers. He would be a billionaire, in miles at least. His wife and child knew that a promotion at work could be a possibility; he didn't tell either Anne, or Pete (his ten year old son) about anything to do with Mars however. They both wouldn't mind he realised. They understood that a lot of travel was part of Ted's job. It always disappointed him when Pete called him Ted. It was always a sharp but innocently made reminder that he wasn't always around for either of them. Having said that it was more heartbreaking for him when Pete was actually looking up to him. The pressure of his kid thinking the world of him was really tough. Knowing that he would be having an affair at some point after checking into Lunar1 made his kid's admiration more heartbreaking. His conscious had finally got to him though. He had sent a clear Vid-Screen message to his most frequent Lunar squeeze, Cheyenne, and committed himself to the upcoming life of monogamy. Getting back to the right state of being called Dad rather than Ted. Through this job he knew that the journey to Mars would finally mean he would be able to afford a big enough apartment in the affluent sector of the Moon for all of them. They would be a family together. A well off one to boot. Something still existed inside him, badly wanting to be there when his kid was growing up. He had certainly missed Anne and the regular, less expensive variant of love making. It was time for him to grow up he realised; to commit his life to his family rather than just random women and long glass cocktails. At this point Theodore Backus was still unaware of the terror and danger that would present itself on the journey to the Red Planet. His innocence and ignorance of genuine fear would be a much lamented state of affairs.

Theodore looked up from the WSA hover cruiser he had been travelling in. He craned his neck to partially take in a gigantic example of a space craft. He doubted that he would ever see another object so unquestionably massive ever again. As a craft loving man he had to take a moment to really appreciate such a fine piece of work. The guy beside him noticed his fascination…

"Beautiful piece of work ain't it?"

"Yeah it sure is" he replied, almost instantaneously.

He had hardly spoken to this chap since leaving sector-4 together, but at least he appreciated fine craftsmanship.

"It's Ted, isn't it?"

"Sure, what's your name again"

"'Eddy. The maintenance officer on board that ship my friend. Hired externally by the WSA like yourself"

"Right, of course", they had briefly and inanely spoken earlier during the journey.

"Man, I cannot wait to get back out into distant space again. Travelling further than any other damn craft ever on record. It is going to be freaking phenomenal!

"Yeah of course man", he could only bother to reply quickly and simply. He looked out to the craft again. He was starting to get the jitters. The task really was enormous.

"Do you think we'll find real, intelligent life?"

"Maybe" he hadn't really thought about that. "Doubt it though".

"I think there'll be creatures like land turtles or something. Animals you know?"

"I guess so"

"Doubt there'll be anything like us there! I mean the planet is so dry obviously. I'd heard rumours about caves though, you know like the catacombs in Paris or whatever"

"Right, underground maybe"

Thankfully the driver turned round to inform us we were only about two minutes away. There were so many entrances and gates it was impossible to tell where they would need to go and debrief. Gate 4993 turned out to be the answer.

The man addressing the group of the 7 hired WSA crew was a huge, hulking and impressive looking guy. He was a General Major in the Space Division of the US Army and looked like the toughest bastard in the known universe. He was muscular like a professional boxer or lumberjack maybe and had the booming voice of the hardest drill master. When he was talking, the crew fully listened and appeared scared to even blink.

"Right, so you individuals have all been chosen to serve on this WSA craft on the first manned mission to Mars" he rhetorically put. Somehow emphasizing the word individuals like he was referring to a bunch of Nazi war criminals.

"You have been deemed worthy, not be me I might add, of representing Earth and in particular the United States of America as an intergalactic presence. As per your agreements you must remain disciplined at all times both on board the ship, and off board. John and Marie, you will be the first faces that will meet any inhabitants of Mars. You have been well trained to be both friendly or hostile and I am confident you will do your duty"

"Thank you sir" both replied in unison.

Theodore was beginning to feel nervous and hugely out of place. He was becoming sweaty and twitchy. He hoped the Major wasn't aware of his right foot tapping the ground consistently like some sort of pneumatic drill. He was also praying that he wouldn't have to answer any questions in front of these people. They were very much a random assortment of individuals; Jack and Maria obviously looked and acted like G.I. Joe and Jane whilst the rest were an odd mix. The talkative guy in the cab, Eddy, looked as terrified as he felt. The stern looking officer had addressed him whilst the poor guy was shaking. Despite being a tall guy with a beefy structure, he still looked like a rabbit in headlights.

"Mr. Kovacs, you have been appointed as a result of being the leading private craft maintenance man available. We did have a military man arranged and appointed, but let us just say he failed certain tests that you did not".

That explained the Eddy's presence and job thankfully. Another guy to his left looked intelligent, kind of like a scientist or something. To his right there was an attractive middle aged man who looked very stern and serious. He was paying close attention to the Major General and must have been another military figure. Whilst the last individual he noticed in the briefing was an attractive lady that didn't appear overly fascinated by the team talk. He guessed she was private and commercial too, like him and Kovacs.

"Dr. Anders…" he was clearly referring to the scientist looking guy, it wasn't some sort of ESP from his part, the guy was wearing a lab coat he realised on second glance.

"You will be required to analyse any unusual samples we find on Mars. You will also be required to vid-scan any seemingly intelligent life forms apparent, to give Sergeants Smithson and Rawley the fullest preparation". Theodore guessed he would have to refer to each of that couple now as Sergeant.

"Right, Captain Davis you have been chosen and closely trained to pilot the X-II Class Craft. We have full faith in your abilities."

Davis was the stern looking guy evidently.

"Thank you sir"

The Major continued, unfortunately with him.

"Mr. Backus you are actually the most successful commercial pilot available. As a non military figure we couldn't inform you of the additional tasks you may have to undertake up until now. You are indeed a last reserve to cover Captain Davis, but will also be required to pilot the escape pod should any emergencies happen. Needless to say Mr. Backus, you are not briefed to leave the X-Class craft"

That surprise from the Major General was not altogether welcome. He had been looking forward to stepping out on the Red Planet itself.

"Finally Ms. Phillips, you will be on board as the ship's psychotherapist"

He knew there would be one on-board somehow.

"That is everyone introduced then crew. Know one another. This is only the initial briefing of course, and some socializing between yourselves has been scheduled to enable effective integration of your personalities. It is fair to say you have all been pysche-scanned and equally safe to say that you all passed the rigorous tests. This intergalactic mission should be no harder than most of the journeys you have all undertaken at some point. I wish you all a safe and successful mission".

So these were the people he would have to spend two months with then, great. The ladies were attractive thankfully, though he guessed that the sexual tension between the military pair would prevent any action with Sergeant Rawley. Focus man! his brain reminded him. The psychotherapist, Phillips, was a very attractive lady too. She looked sexy in her black smart glasses and had bright alluring eyes. He remembered his pledge to be a better family man though. Besides, travelling through deep space in a confined craft wasn't going to be good for his mojo. Then a worrying thought struck Theodore like a personalized bolt of lighting; if we are all so sane according to the pysche-scans than why do we need a psychotherapist? He guessed it was jut a precaution, a fail-safe. But for such a small crew she seemed a luxury. Yeah, like a reserve escape pod pilot he thought. Any crew member, especially from the army, could be trained fast enough with take-off and landings for basic jet powered craft, which the pods would undoubtedly be. Still they had wanted him, and with the money involved he had no complaints.

The socializing section of pre-mission training actually went better than he thought. The military people obviously congregated more with one another than the civilians, but still he didn't feel totally ostracised by the military professionals. Eddy Kovacs, when not shitting himself or blabbing away was actually a nice guy. A real future drinking buddy, should they both survive the mission he thought. Dr. Kathy Phillips, as her full name was, introduced herself calmly and carefully to all of the crew. She had a real air of confidence about her, gliding from person to person making them feel individually very important. He met her more fully when walking down the main unit corridor, heading to get a hot drink.
Her opening statement totally startled Theodore.
"I know you Mr. Backus"
"Ah, how would that be then?" Theodore was racking his brain, until he remembered the worrying truth.
"We slept together on Earth about 12 years ago"
"Shit! Of course, Oh my God of course you, Kathy, damn"
"Well, I remembered it as being better than that; to be honest I don't remember you as being my finest hour either. Still time doesn't always guarantee accuracy" she replied, laughing quietly.
"No, of course. I mean it was great obviously"
"You didn't tell me you were married"
"I wasn't married at that time"
"No but you had a partner"
"How did you know that?
"Psychological profiling of all crew members Mr. Backus. I cross referenced the time we were together after recognizing your profile. If I had known of your partner then I would not have chanced such a relationship"

Theodore felt a flash of guilt before replying.

"Hey, you weren't asking any questions of me that night…Kathy…right"?

"Yes, that was before I fully knew you"

He laughed at her reply, some lame excuse for doing the horizontal mambo with him. It takes two to tango he thought.

"Yeah, fully knew, good one Kathy"

"It's Ms. Phillips now please Mr. Backus"

"You didn't seem to mind darling the last time we met" Theodore replied, guilty of bringing up their past liaison. He couldn't fully get rid of the playboy part of his mind however. He slept with her because he wanted to. Man, she looked just as good now as she did then.

"They were distinctly different circumstances Mr. Backus"

" What as compared to now? Shit, why did it have to be you on board?"

"Because of my full training in deep space psychological conditions Mr. Backus"

He began to worry about spending some time confined with this lady.

"Oh come off it, Ms Phillips there are about a hundred other professionals like yourself who could have taken the job. Surely if they knew about our past relations together they wouldn't have let me or you on board. Come on what's going on, why are you torturing me?"

"I don't want to torture you Theodore, I know about your family man plans after this mission, it is all in your pysche-scan results after all"

"Sure I believe that. But I didn't think you could even risk a dormant sexual dynamic being allowed on board. I'd have been replaced if they had any idea about us. Man it must be too late now, it would cost billions upon billions for any delays. What were you thinking approving me after our time together?"

"They could replace you easily Mr. Backus and besides they don't know about any potential problems between us, because I didn't tell them about how I had slept with you 12 years ago. It's all in the past now"

"Well that's just great Dr. Phillips. Now we have to pretend we don't know each other on board. That's great, I'm only human, now I have to put up with the ghost of a sexual relationship on board. Nothing can happen between us of course, I mean I still hardly know you"

She replied defensively, "I realise that. We have socialized together during preparation training however and I know you probably better than you know me"

"True but if anyone asks whether we have slept together, maybe you can just lie again".

"That isn't fair Theodore"

"No, you're right I'm sorry. Look we'll just react normally to one another. If you want to flirt with me, play with your hair, stuff like that because I'm so irresistibly attractive that's ok" he was exuding his complacent confidence side again. It had helped work like a charm quite a few times. "Mr. Backus you are the third most attractive man on board, and the most stupid. If I do any flirting, you won't be on the agenda".

"Fine, then I wish you a good night"

As he was walking back down the corridor to his sleeping quarters, the reality of the situation came clear to him. Great he thought, an old flame who has it in for me. She'll probably diagnose me as mad and leave me to rot on Mars with just space turtles or bacteria for company, I better not have slept with G.I Jane too, Theodore thought, her husband will kill me.

Strapped down preparing for take-off, Theodore felt like a prime cow waiting to visit the abattoir for the first and final time. Every inch of him was sweating profusely, the fluid stinging his eyes, which were still trying to search their take-off cabin for any hypothetical radiation leaks that could enter and slowly kill them. Or worse gas leaks that could lead to an initial explosion in the crew section of the ship, setting off a chain reaction that would eventually blow the Nexus X-II silently to smithereens before even leaving the Lunar-Port. He didn't want to look at any of the others to see how comparably comfortable or terrified they were. It disturbed him no end to see the scientist, Dr. Anders praying to God. Great, even the experts are fearing for their lives he thought. His eyes wandered to Dr. Phillips as well, the sex pot come psychotherapist; she appeared to be repeating some sort of mantra. The G.I. couple were busy staring into one another's eyes, like they were on a damn picnic or something. Kovacs was unsurprisingly mumbling and swearing to himself nervously. Ted could only make out "shit…deep space…no oxygen…old parts…no spare Nano-Engine", he decided to ignore the madman in case his insanity spread into his conscious as well. Oh that's no problem he thought, I've got a part time call girl who hates me to offer psychological advice.

Following 30 minutes of excruciating tension whilst the gigantic craft rocketed out of the Lunar-Port vertically a voice came through the main intercom, "You have passed through the initial problem stage guys, congratulations. The Nano-Engine is firing well and the co-ordinates have been well set by the Captain"

"Roger, WSA" Davis replied confidently. He was the only one not presently strapped in, and was sitting comfortably at the control panel. It was now travelling at a more reassuring angle. There could be no turning back he realised; Mars lay ahead.

Looking out absently from the far side view-point, Theodore was completely immersed visually and possibly even spiritually with the blackness of space, waiting blankly on the other side. The sight, if you could call it that, was truly mesmerizing. Outside was genuine and total darkness. Looking out from the view point was like squinting into an abyss. The massed nothing out there had evidently been there for light-years, existing as it always had and always would do. Apart from feeling this craft of course, he reminded himself. These were still exciting times for the progression of humanity, and despite the seemingly impending boredom of such a long journey, the crew had remained upbeat and talkative about the potential findings on Mars. I mean everyone on Earth had known for a very long time that the Moon would be uninhabited. We had been there for centuries, it was almost like another part of Earth, even in the ancient 20th Century. Dr. Anders, the scientist, kept talking away at length to everyone on-board about what could potentially be out there on that planet, and indeed what he expected to see.

"Just think about the possibilities of seeing genuinely new creatures!" he kept exclaiming.

"There could be life out there shaped like nothing we have ever seen before. Just envisage the situation if bacteria itself were to evolve" Dr. Phillips interjected herself.

"But it has done Dr. Anders. Over centuries and probably millennia on Earth. Just think of Spanish flu, or the plague, or smallpox. Bacteria has indeed always reacted to changing conditions on Earth. What would be so special about a flu virus on Mars?"

"You aren't thinking laterally Dr. Phillips. I am referring to bacteria not a flu virus per se. Imagine if a huge collection of bacteria, billions upon billions of large cells collecting, morphing and evolving together, consider how it would appear. Now this may seem far fetched but I believe we could encounter floating creatures of some sort, created from hugely massed bacteria"

"That seems rather far fetched Dr. Anders"

"No hear me out please Dr. Phillips; I refer not to just clouds of bacteria but rather to literally complete creatures akin to Jellyfish, sentient beings that thrive on the atmosphere as opposed to the conditions of the sea"
Sergeant Smithson joined in, "Well I guess that may be plausible. After all we have received no visual reconnaissance about any large life forms on Mars, maybe some could be different to what we expect.".
His partner joined in "Besides, jellyfish should be easier to kill than the aliens in movies"
"Good one babe" he returned.
Eddy joined in the conversation, "I still think they would be large, and sturdy creatures to survive on that place. I mean there is no water we can see. They would have to be alien camel types or something to live on the surface. You know they could be roaming around on there, we just haven't scanned any yet".
Dr. Anders began to control the conversation again.
"People, you are also forgetting about how we expect to find an underground ecosystem. Literally we have only scratched the surface of Mars and we expect to find out far more now than in any previous unmanned missions to Mars combined. We have infinitely greater resources", Dr. Anders was sounding far bolder than he did when they were taking off.
"What do you think Theodore?" Dr. Phillips kindly asked him,
"I don't know. I mean I probably think we won't find anything out there. Like on the Moon you know."
Eddy looked like he was going to intervene. Theodore continued however.
"These places you know, they just don't seem to offer the conditions for any kind of life. That bacteria idea is interesting Dr. Anders, but I mean I just don't believe it".
"I don't either" Eddy agreed .
"I think you guys should trust our scientific advisor" Sergeant Smithson intervened.
Theodore was compelled to reply, "Hey just because Dr. Anders is a scientist, doesn't guarantee he knows about what life on Mars will be like, Sergeant. No offence Doc"
"None taken Mr. Backus"

"I mean we are still millions of light years away at this point anyway. We have no idea at all what could be there as of yet, the previous unmanned missions didn't show us anything as you know. I think we'll just be the same, you know?"

"I have no ownership on the truth Mr. Backus, and indeed you may be right. Who knows, maybe Mr. Kovacs could be right with his, what was it, camel theory?".

Kovacs replied excitedly "Yeah true doc. I'm telling you alien camels or something like that will be there waiting there"

Dr. Phillips started laughing quietly

Theodore turned to her, and talked to her quietly

"Hey, Dr. Phillips shouldn't you be supportive of us normal crew members"

"I am Theodore. Come on, alien camels? It just isn't going to happen. That guy Eddy, is practically a sub-norm"

"Hey give him a break, what do you know about Mars anyway? There could be a tribe of Machu Picchu banditos waiting there having travelled through time you know?"

She didn't have time to speak but looked at Theodore the same way she had done with Eddy; Dr, Anders turned his attention to the pair of them,

"Hey you two, have you got anything important to share?"

"No, not at all Dr. Anders" Theodore calmly replied, "We were just talking about deep space psychosis and how to manage it"

"Right yes I understand, we've had that talk" he replied smiling at Dr. Phillips in an overly friendly manner.

Theodore enjoyed it. "She is great huh, Dr?" He enquired knowing it would infuriate Kathy.

"Of course, she is wonderful and may I also say beautiful"

Having said this his expression turned bashful and he turned his attention back to the others, going on again and about his theories for the evolution of bacterial life.

Phillips then whispered back to him,

"Theodore Backus, I think I can safely diagnose you as an intelligent idiot"

He laughed quietly, keeping a low radar from the others

"Well you chose at some point to be intimate with me, Dr. Phillips, so I guess we aren't too dissimilar".

"That was just a one-off bad decision. You are a bit more continuously idiotic"

"Hey thanks" she was right of course.

"You are scheduled for a session with me early next week too by the way"

"Great, I knew it would come at some point".

"It's standard. You won't get any special treatment for me"

"I definitely know that"

"Excuse me?"

"Nothing Doc. Sure I'll attend your powwow and unload all my big psychological defects to you. You manage to fit a leather couch in here?" She smiled. "No couch. Look it will do you good. Didn't you see how much more relaxed Dr. Anders has been?"

"That your handiwork again?"

"Not like that Mr. Backus"

"Sure"

Anders had glanced upon picking up his name, but was now busy talking to Kovacs about why alien camels would be unlikely to live on Mars.

"I'm going to enjoy analysing you Mr. Backus"

He knew she would. Theodore began to worry more about his mind being shown up rather than the dark reaches of outer space. It was another irrational fear of his.

The loud startling alarm made Theodore leap up from his bed. What the hell was this about? He made his way instinctively to the entrance to the escape pod. Dr. Phillips and Dr. Anders were waiting there, the others were still in the main technical areas evidently stupidly trying to sort out the situation, whatever it was. There had not been the time the appropriate conditions to practice emergency drills so far and the alarm had shocked Theodore. He calmed himself though; there was a general procedure to follow and he thought all crew had to follow it. He was annoyed not all of them went to the escape pod immediately, he would hate to have the decision of leaving people if there was a genuine disaster. Thankfully after another thirty seconds the alarm stopped.

Dr. Phillips asked him excitedly "Do you think it's over? Do you think that the military guys stopped it?"

It was actually Eddy who came down to the three of them waiting desperately by the escape pod. Theodore actually felt a bit ashamed he was so quick to get to the escape pod really, despite being the escape pod pilot; surely he should have helped the others? What if there had been an internal fire or someone had been seriously injured? He felt a bit impotent and was reminded of his limitations on this mission.

"It's okay guys, no problems now. I didn't know what was wrong at first, but it turned out the mainframe system had fully shut down briefly"

"Fully shut down? What; you've got to be kidding me?" Dr Anders enquired

"No I'm not Anders, we got back online okay though. That isn't the problem. I'm not meant to tell you this, but they have lost the saved co-ordinates to the landing area of Mars"

"What?!" Dr. Anders appeared apoplectic.

"Calm down Howard" Kathy calmly informed him. She turned to Kovacs…

"These things can happen, I was informed during my training. You were right to inform us of the situation Eddy. I also know that Captain Davis almost knows the co-ordinates to Mars by heart. He has simulated this mission to a frankly unhealthy degree. These types of problems have been hypothesized, entered into the simulator and worked on. Captain Davis will know which backup files to search for, do not worry." She was addressing Dr. Anders more than Eddy.

Sergeant Rawley came down the corridor looking terrified.

"What is wrong, Maria?" Dr. Phillips instinctively and kindly asked.

"It…It's John."

"Okay, calm down Sergeant Rawley. What is wrong with John?"

"He has…I mean we can't…."

"Come on Sergeant tell us damn it!" Dr. Anders was lacking compassion and patience under stress, Phillips knew if anyone would begin to crack it would be Dr. Howard Anders.

"He's disappeared"

Theodore soon gathered that there was bad news when he met Kovacs in his sleeping quarters. The guy looked more pale faced and terrified than any one else he had ever seen in his life. This was no mean feat either, having piloted some of the earliest and bumpiest journeys from Earth to the main Lunar-Ports. Hell Eddy looked even more terrified than the man who actually died of a heart attack on one of his more turbulent flights had.

He decided to try and politely probe the guy though, try and get an idea of what was going on before hearing it from Dr. Phillips.

23

"You aren't going to believe this Ted, but Smithson, the Sergeant…he's disappeared".

"What? That's impossible Eddy, the escape pod is still there and we haven't had any holes blown into the side of this thing, so he hasn't gone anywhere. He may have got scared too and gone to where he's hidden some booze, or maybe where he has an excess of mood pills you know?"

"They've searched everywhere. Besides, everyone had a chip inserted into their arm during the medical, so the maintenance team, in other words me and ironically Sergeant Smithson could know roughly were everyone was on the ship".

"Woah, hang on then Kovacs, surely when the mainframe went down the programme running the location of our microchips went down"

"Maybe initially, for like half an hour or something, but the programme is back online now. Everyone else is registered and clearly in the right place. It's just, you know Smithson who's disappeared".

"Okay" Theodore thought things over, trying to stay calm and rationalise. "Maybe, Eddy, Sergeant Smithson knew about where his microchip was planted…"

"I guess he did, sure he was more briefed than I was being military. He was actually the one that told me all about the microchips and how we would need to monitor where everyone was. Kind of ironic really"

"Sure, sure. Anyway, so you know personally that he was already aware of these microchips. Now, I don't want to think the worst, but if he didn't want to be seen when avoiding duty on the craft or be seen because he was having a breakdown on his own an argument with his wife, then maybe he could have physically remove the chip and destroyed it".

"Maybe. He wasn't a guy who would betray the crew though I know that. Those things are so tiny Ted, it would be impossible"

"Come on Kovacs, somewhere in the lab there must be an incredibly powerful microscope, you know for all the germ monsters we are going to meet"

Eddy quietly laughed at that; thankfully he was looking a bit more relaxed and nodded.

"Then you know he could find where this device is and remove it. I'll ask him to do it for us too when he returns huh? Maybe then us guys can all try and find a bar or some alien hookers, sound good Kovacs?"

He chuckled again, "Sure maybe. Guess you're right, man. It's just the pressure, you know, of being out here with so much darkness all around".

24

He knew where Eddy Kovacs was coming from. After calming the one maintenance man apparently left there on the ship, he decided to search everywhere on the ship, praying that he would find Sergeant Smithson.

When he finally found Sergeant John Smithson after four hours of continued searching, he definitely wished he hadn't. He was there in one of the loading bays, lying face down, shaped like a man who had been made of pipe wire and subsequently formed into a grotesque statue. He was definitely dead; that much was clear before he even checked for any signs of a pulse. Damn, Kathy would have a hell of a task explaining this to Rawley, he didn't envy her job at this moment. Kovacs had explained to the rest of the crew that Ted was looking for the location of Sergeant Smithson. He had relayed to all the remaining living members of the ship the theories that Theodore had wrongly developed about the location of Smithson. Hopefully most of the crew would still think that Smithson was simply drunk or something, or that in the worse case scenario he was involved in an accident or something. Yeah, an accident involving a deadly alien chiropractor he thought. Unfortunately Ted knew he had too quickly come to believe his hopelessly optimistic point that Sergeant Smithson somehow removed his tiny microchip that told the mainframe where he was. He knew his stupid optimism would spread and that the impact of the mangled dead body would increase the upset to already delicate minds. When Dr. Phillips came down to see what Theodore was doing, (his pulse on the mainframe having been motionless in a land craft loading bay and thus causing concern as well), she had gasped in shock and horror at the startlingly dead form of Sergeant Smithson. If he hadn't been there, Ted was certain that the good doctor would have screamed out loud in the large craft and beyond the thick steel structure into the void of space. He was close to doing so himself when first seeing that damn body.
After a pause that seemed to last an eon, Dr. Phillips finally addressed him.
"When did you discover him like this? "
"About half an hour ago. I was… I guess I was looking around the room for clues you know"
"Right. I understand if you are in shock"
"No, no, I'm not in shock. I mean, I was scared initially you know, just in case he was killed and mutilated like that by some sort of atmosphere leak or something in this bay"
"Understandable Mr. Backus"

"But you know after about twenty minutes or so I discounted that"

"What do you think happened Mr. Backus?" for the first time since he had known her, she sounded anxious

"I don't know Doctor, I mean we can be fairly sure it isn't murder. Maybe one of those bacterial creatures Dr. Anders was going on about came onto the craft and killed him"

"Whatever you do, don't tell Howard that" she replied looking a bit more stable.

"Yeah, he'd be both elated and terrified", Theodore wanted to calm her, and himself down a bit.

She smiled briefly "Indeed, that would not be a helpful psychological mix under the current circumstances"

"True, I guess those emotions aren't so different really"

"Look Mr. Backus, you do know you're going to need an extensive mental assessment after witnessing such a traumatic event don't you?"

"I didn't see him die Kathy, it wasn't me undergoing the trauma"

"I know that Mr. Backus, but I must inform you that you will also require psychological assessment. It will be a comparable treatment to his wife"

"Shit, I bet she hasn't heard the news about the body yet. She's going to be devastated"

"I realise. Look I was sent down to see you here by the others. They, and I to be honest, had assumed you were having some sort of nervous breakdown"

"Hey, thanks, I'm that mentally unstable huh?"

"It's not a personal insult Mr. Backus"

"Theodore please"

"Right, well it wasn't a personal insult Theodore"

"It is now, considering we're on first name terms" he replied, looking mischievous.

She smiled at one of his silly, convoluted jokes. He wasn't totally mad at least; maybe a bit infuriating but probably not insane. Kathy Phillips worried that wouldn't be the case with Sergeant Rawley.

"What had happened to Sergeant Smithson, Theodore? Come on, I know that you found something important by that loading bay. Tell us the truth." Dr. Anders sounded and looked desperately worried.

"I'm sorry Dr. Anders I can only tell you that the Sergeant was dead when I looked in loading bay B."

"I want to see the body, Dr. Phillips"

"Sorry, no can do Howard. You know that if any fatalities take place on board the Nexus then the body is placed in the on-board morgue, awaiting an autopsy back on the Moon or on Earth in an emergency"

"I would say that losing a key member of staff was an emergency Dr. Phillips, I think we should head back to the Moon, right away. I mean has the Captain even reprogrammed the co-ordinates yet?"

"Look calm down please Dr. Anders. I have spoken to the Captain and we will not be turning the craft back any time soon; as I have mentioned the body will have an autopsy when we reconnect with either home base"

"It's interesting though, Kathy, that you already knew that dead bodies can't be examined here on the craft"

"I don't know what you are referring to Dr. Anders. I need to know many protocols for emergencies"

"You should know what I refer to Dr. Phillips. Another medical professional with more experience dealing with human corpses should have been called on. The situation should have demanded a second opinion prior to the movement of the body to the morgue, I know certain protocols as well"

"Please Dr. Anders calm down. I understand the many psychological and personal reasons for your paranoia Howard I really do. Your mind state is totally understandable. You should know, paranoia is one of the main side-effects of isolation in confined areas over a period of time, as opposed to just being anything wrong with you. Please don't feel personally about it.

"Come off it Doctor, you are being presumptive and unprofessional. So for wanting to know how a colleague died, I've been branded as paranoid"

"Come on that isn't the case Dr. Anders. Look, please speak more to Mr. Backus; he discovered the body and knows about as much I do. I should also not need to remind you either Dr. Anders that you were with me during a pysche-discussion when the body was found. Neither of us are suspects".

"Suspects? You think Smithson was murdered?"

"Please calm down Howard. Nobody is certain about how he died. Tensions are high on such a ship. Please talk to Theodore, you'll thank me now if maybe not later"

Theodore knew that as Dr. Anders approached him whilst he was drinking a stale coffee, that the doc was going to question him at length about

Smithson's death. He let the cogs in his brain whir round until they resembled a state reasonably ready to deal with the onslaught of questions he probably wouldn't have the answer to.

"He was murdered wasn't he Theodore? Come on you should tell me now"

Great start, what do you want me to tell you he thought.

"Have you found any evidence? You know, any knives, any spots of blood that we can test, any fingerprints you've dusted? You should really tell me Mr. Backus, I am the leading doctor in terms of physical diagnosis"

"Come on, calm down a bit Dr. Anders. Sure there is a chance that Sergeant Smithson was murdered…"

"I knew it!"

"Hear me out… but the murderer definitely couldn't have come from this ship. Or at least, he wasn't one of the crew"

"What makes you think it was a he?"

Anders made a good point amongst the babble.

"Look, the body when it was found was grotesquely positioned. Like he'd had a massive, full body seizure. The damage just couldn't have been done by any human, or any machine I know of either"

"You do know Theodore that those types of convulsions can be created with the right, or should I say, wrong medication"

He unfortunately didn't. Damn questions began to start on his own comprehension of the death of Sergeant Smithson.

"Look, I hear what you're saying doc, but I just know it wasn't anyone on board, don't ask me why"

"Well that's the case settled with" he sarcastically retorted.

"I didn't say that doc. Like I told Dr. Phillips, your fellow medically qualified buddy, maybe it was an advanced creature from beyond our knowledge killing him… like maybe a bacterial being"

"Ha, I didn't think anyone was listening to me then"

"Come on, I wasn't fully doc, it's just there could be much more to this one death than plain old murder. If you'd have seen the body like me then you'd be agreeing"

"Maybe Mr. Backus, but need I remind you I have seen more dead bodies than you will ever hopefully witness. Not too much would surprise me on the matter. Maybe homicidal bacterial jellyfish though" he smiled and looked a bit more relaxed. Theodore guessed he was on the cusp of saying something important. He was also certain that Dr. Anders wouldn't have been so blasé had he seen that broken human puppet lying there, it's limp form looking like Geppeto had never existed. He should have seen it; legally as well as morally really. Maybe the slightly unstable Dr. Anders did have a point about rushing the body off to the morgue. Was it really due to regulations? Dr. Phillips hadn't even told the Captain before sending the body to the morgue.

"You should know I've had dealings with Dr. Kathy Phillips in the past Mr. Backus",

"What, really?" somehow Theodore guessed that was it.

"That sounds rather ominous doc, you're worrying me"

"Well, it was only really very brief dealings. It wasn't even a personal encounter. It certainly wouldn't show up in my pysche-scan analysis or personal data search"

"Oh come on, spit it out man, what do you know about the good doctor?"

"During the initial briefing I had thought that her face looked familiar..."

"Right"

"So, during a quiet moment in the socializing session we so painfully had to endure, I thought I'd check the Medi-Sphere archived news network on my mobile vid-screen"

"They still let you keep that? Mine was taken"

"I had hidden mine in my shoe. Can't be without the thing for too long! They were monitoring our thoughts with a basic scanner anyway I should inform you Mr. Backus"

"Guessed so. That's why they didn't mind the mobile vid-screen unit you had then?"

"Yes indeed. The military couple had theirs too during the session and were making calls to their family or whatever"

"Come on doc, tell me more about Phillips", Theodore really was getting impatient to know more details. He had slept with her after all, and he had unloaded some close secrets to her during one of the on board pysche-evaluations.

"Get this" Dr. Anders was sounding like the biggest gossip in the universe, let alone WSA Nexus X-II; "the innocent and lovely Dr. Kathy Phillips has previously been arrested on suspicion of... murder"

"What? You are joking" He thought someone like Kathy Phillips would prefer to diagnose a fly of it's problems rather than try and hurt it.

"No unfortunately not; there hasn't been an appropriate moment to inform anyone I trust"

"This is ridiculous Doc; any charges of murder must discount her from

29

being a suitable psychotherapist at any time, let alone on a deep space high pressure mission involving the US Military?"

"Yes, it sounds somewhat bad. She was cleared of all charges I guess"

"Oh right, then she's totally innocent. Damn, I slept with that woman, sheesh I'm lucky to be alive"

"Sorry, what did you say Theodore"

"Oh, nothing doc. Come on, what can you tell me about the case"

"Well, the man who died was one of her patients"

"Sounds familiar"

"Yes, and well this individual was found hung in his room. He had used a length of rope"

"That doesn't sound like a murder scenario doc"

"You haven't heard the good bit yet... On the man's body were, oh what to call them, I guess love bites"

"Ok" again that sounded scarily familiar again.

"And in his blood stream were high amounts of the drug Difapium"

"Difapium, what? Come on you've got to give me info doc, I'm not a fellow scientist what does this stuff do?"

"The drug is used to release all inhibitions. It leaves the individual massively suggestive and vulnerable. The drug is only subscribed to bedridden M.E. patients or those with previously incurable agoraphobia"

"Which presumably our innocent victim suffered from neither?"

"True".

"So they think she gave it to him?"

"Well put it this way, the police knew that she was with the victim the evening of his death, they knew that she was carrying a quantity of Difapium and that, oh you've got to get this, that she had a history of dating vulnerable patients"

"You've got to be kidding me" suddenly he felt like she had hunted him down at that bar and not vice versa. His sense of pride was stung yet again by Dr. Phillips.

"Can you see why I have been so suspicious of her Mr. Backus?"

"Well yeah certainly now doc".

"Yes. I would prefer it if you did not inform the captain, and without question not Sergeant Rawley of this information"

Shit, indeed the now ex-wife of Sergeant Smithson. She may completely lose it and give her own judgement on Dr. Phillips. The captain too may put them in the quarantined area, which had been earmarked as a cool down cell, or in this case a makeshift prison. Theodore decided to head back to his room, and try and calm down. Two hours later nothing had changed.

Three hours later however another major incident happened. The intercom situated just above his head on the bunk bed loudly informed him of the Captain's request for all 'available' crew members to attend to the Captain's area. Having stuck on the nearest pair of trousers and the uniform shirt, Theodore walked as quickly as his lanky legs would carry him to the main piloting quarters presided over by Captain Davis. He was already addressing most of the crew when Theodore joined what was left of the group. Something was up, immediately he could tell, when he turned to see the Captain speak he had unfortunately already worked out the problem.

"I must report to you crew, that unfortunately at present Mr. Edward Kovacs has become M.I.A"

"What? Not him as well, we're running out of crew captain" Sergeant Rawley sounded fearful, the thought of her husband's very recent death and disappearance still prominent within her mind.

Dr. Phillips, the once suspected murderer Theodore thought, replied quickly to Rawley.

"Please calm down Sergeant Rawley. I totally understand your tension, I think the whole crew does" the crew were all nodding in unison, most of them looking slightly confused and terrified as well bar the Captain, who gave nothing away.

Theodore began thinking to himself. Another crew member disappearing was very bad news. If Kovacs couldn't be found, there would be no-one able to effectively repair the mainframe system that really controlled everything from the intercom to oxygen levels then disaster could strike from countless bloody problems. He somehow felt thoroughly redundant. Great, he thought, two available pilots and only one technician. The problem somehow seemed familiar. He began to seriously panic upon realising that another mainframe shut-down akin to the last one could mean either permanent or catastrophic potential loss of co-ordinates to either Mars or the home bases; not to mention the loss of some or all Nano-Engines. Sure some back up generators could cover the oxygen levels at least for about a week, and lighting on the craft would stay on for about a month after full mainframe shut-down which was great design he

31

thought. Plenty of lights to show aliens where any dead bodies where. If another disaster struck and they were still without Eddy, the ship could theoretically travel through space until the end of eternity, with all crew members on board either disappeared, killed by a murderous psychotherapist or devoured by the bacterial jellyfish that had been sailing the seven seas of outer space looking to pillage any passing intergalactic crafts. Theodore put that thought aside, knowing now was not the time to even think about joking. He was calm somehow despite fully knowing the fact that if Eddy Kovacs was either not discovered or found seriously injured in any way, shape or form, then the mission to Mars would probably be thoroughly screwed,

The loud, long and painful scream that echoed throughout the ship came from Sergeant Rawley, who had gone back to investigate the loading bay where her once husband and now infamously deformed corpse, Sergeant John Smithson, had been found. Theodore obviously realised that Eddy Kovacs had been found in a similar circumstance to the recently deceased Sergeant. Without thinking, Theodore decided to go down there again to see what scenario had happened this time. He hoped that the body didn't look the same, the scream from Maria indicated otherwise however. He approached the loading bay with a fair degree more trepidation this time. He was simultaneously scared and disappointed in himself for finding the place so vaguely horrifying. One body was an accident, two were suspicious he thought. Especially if those two bodies were found on a space craft containing just seven crew members and in the very same area to boot. His suspicions and fears were high. Could Dr. Phillips really be involved in these deaths? Could Dr. Anders be fully trusted? Was the Captain a problem, or maybe the bereaved former wife and current Sergeant Maria Rawley was to blame? He felt ashamed of himself for suspecting all of the crew members however briefly. He was fairly certain however that neither death was the result of assisted suicide, which probably ruled out Dr. Phillips.

When he got there, Sergeant Rawley had Dr. Anders pinned against the wall.

"Why did you let him die?" She was clearly beyond emotional.

"Please, Sergeant Rawley, Maria, I didn't let anyone die. Mr. Kovacs was found by yourself in the same condition as your husband, I do appreciate that. The stress and worry you are experiencing must be considerable. But

I let neither of them die. Had I witnessed, their seizures I would have endeavoured to intervene with the full range of medical options I have available"

He had gained a sudden calmness in disaster, Dr. Phillips however was quietly beginning to unravel.

"We don't have enough crew. The damn WSA were wrong about minimizing group dynamics, they were bloody wrong!"

Theodore decided to intervene and pulled Dr. Phillips quietly aside. Thankfully Dr. Anders remained busy, briefing both the Captain and Sergeant Rawley on what he knew about the Kovacs body and the information regarding Smithson. Theodore waited until he and Dr. Phillips were out of sight of the others before addressing the once composed health professional in front of him.

"Please calm down Kathy. Now isn't the time to lose your composure. Sergeant Rawley is suffering from both some sort of extreme guilt and maybe post stress syndrome"

"Post traumatic stress syndrome"

"Yes, that's the one. She may be suffering from that. You of all people need to have a clear mind to be able to speak to her and ensure that she will be ready for arriving on the surface of Mars"

"But, what if I can't keep my thoughts together Theodore? What if I can't do? Maybe I can't calm her down."

"You will be fine Dr, Phillips"

"But what if we don't make it to Mars? I mean Sergeant Smithson is dead, Eddy Kovacs is dead, people keep dying on me! What if I'm next? What then?"

"Calm down, you won't be. No one else is going to die. I have already decided to stay here in the loading bay until we reach Mars"

"What you're insane? They were both discovered there, dead, and you know in what sort of condition, why do you want to die like that?"

"Hey, you know I don't want to die like that. Please calm down; look if there is something there, living in that loading bay busy picking off crew members, then I'm going to be the person that hunts it down"

"It killed the Sergeant and Eddy, Theodore. They were bigger men than yourself.

"Agreed, but neither of them were ready to face an enemy. This time I will be"

"You are insane Theodore"

33

"I'm sure my records show that" he had made his mind up. He tried to calm Dr. Phillips down anyway, for good relations long-term.

"Anyway, I'm really tired now of people dying here on board, so I won't move from that place until I find out who or what has been killing our people"

"And kill it?"

"Well stop it at least Dr. Phillips, I may not be able to kill it. Go and tell the others I've decided to keep guard. As you probably know, only Eddy could get hold of the security vids for the loading bay. However if you want to keep yourself busy, may I suggest you try and find the video for when both of these men were killed. Then come back to me with what you know"

"Will do, Theodore"

"Good, now go and give a pysche-evaluation to Sergeant Rawley, she clearly needs it. I'm going to sit here and wait for whatever is out there"

He had only been in the loading bay twenty minutes when then there was the flash. Theodore had no idea about what had just happened to him. One moment he was sitting on a makeshift stool in the loading bay area and the next his life literally flashed before his eyes. He witnessed his infancy, pre school years, adolescent years, pilot training years, meeting his wife, his child being born, getting the letter about the Mars trip, and then briefly nothing. It was an instantaneous moment of pure nothing. For one millisecond it felt to Theodore like he had never existed. One second he had seen his entire life, the next he felt as if that life were not his own and he did not truly exist as himself or indeed as any other entity in the universe. The sensation was strange but also transcendental; like he had glimpsed the true meaning of existence but had then seconds later been made to forget it. What was going on? he thought upon reconfiguring his thoughts. He guessed he wasn't dead like the others, and he could still strangely perceive his body which was clearly and seriously damaged. Sprawled wildly like the others, There was just one more small problematic detail with situation he realised, in addition to the mauling. He was floating on his own in outer space. When he realised the fullness of the situation, which came about a millisecond after his life had been shown, Theodore began to panic insanely. He thought he wasn't breathing for one moment, like he couldn't breath, like he had never been taught how to and was simply going to die for the damn stupid reason of not learning

34

how to breathe. It was then that the voice came to him; calmly and with authority it reminded him, 'you know how to breathe Theodore".

Floating in the pure air of space, the once massive ship was now just another lost dream. Theodore felt certain that he had died. This wasn't possible; there was no air to breathe out in space, out here, in the vast wastes of deepest nothing. The voice returned jolting him briefly from another existential stupor.

"Theodore, you should know that your crew mates have not died. They still live and exist as you know them"

But they were so badly mangled he thought, they looked like still, motionless human puppets, waiting for strings to be added and movement given to their pliant limbs. What was happening?

"You should know that on the ship, you will be in the same condition as the others. This will last until the Captain turns away from Mars"

What he thought, so I'm dead too? He decided to try and communicate with this entity, angry that it had appeared to take the lives of two fellow crew members and was now instructing them to turn away from their destination.

"You, Theodore, will tell the Captain and Dr. Anders that both Sergeant John Smithson and Edward Kovacs are still alive. You will inform them that they had suffered toxic shock, upon dealing with the micro particle remnants of ionized fuel that had been left following a tiny leak in one of your land cruisers. You will be out of the state by the time anyone comes to find you. You are required to bring the two of them out of the morgue and to get the Captain to reprogramme the co-ordinates for the Moon"

Theodore was still shocked. He had no idea what this voice was, what it was instructing. Were the two dead crew members really still alive? Had this creature bought them back to life itself, in the same way it evidently killed them?

"Theodore, you must know that the Captain will not be able to take this craft any further towards Mars"

"What, why? Why are you interfering with this mission? I need to know why you are messing with our lives, killing people and then just bringing them back. What are you? What do you want?"

"I do not want Mr. Backus. All I can inform you of my actions is that I have the knowledge that man is not yet ready to truly know beyond himself. Perhaps the mysteries of the universe will one day become

35

apparent or available to your species but for now they will remain unknown".

Are you God, he asked the voice.

"No. I am not Theodore. If I was God talking directly to you, you would have ceased to conceive of yourself and would be an abstract being.

He didn't understand the voice. He didn't understand anything of what had just happened. He tried to speak to the voice again,

"Look Mr. not God, if you are not the main man himself, what we know of as the Prime Lord, which I'm guessing your at least partly omnipresent brain is aware of, then who are you?"

"I am the beginning of the unknown. As you would put it, I am 'partly omnipresent'

Then you can tell me why we cannot travel to Mars then, since countless thousands of billions have been spent.

"You, as a species, are not yet ready to fully know the further opportunities and dangers that will be available should on and beyond Mars"

What, this is ridiculous Theodore thought. No 'partly omnipresent' voice had damn well interfered when they colonised the moon. It hadn't interfered when America was being discovered, yeah unless you count the Mormons his brain briefly chuckled, and hey it certainly didn't intervene when the Nazis were killing thousands upon thousands of innocent Jewish people so why now? Why now should the big man, Yahweh, Allah, Buddha, the damn Prime Lord himself, why has he now intervened to stop mankind actually progressing?

The voice inevitably replied.

"As you know Theodore, I am not God. I can tell you though that I was unable to communicate with the other two as I have done with yourself. They were not able to believe"

So then you killed them he thought, angrily.

"Please calm down Mr. Backus, as you know they are still alive"

Why have you engaged with me, like this? he began to consider. Why not the Captain or the troubled psychotherapist, why not them?

"You have provided the answers we were looking for"

What answers? he thought. Surely it couldn't judge the human race on the basis of engagement with just him and a couple of other crew members from the damn Nexus X-II. It wasn't right. It wasn't fair. He began to think maybe they should have had a priest on board; scientific calculations however had shown that with the psychotherapist, it wouldn't be

36

necessary. They got that bit wrong too. The voice then intervened mid thought…

"Do you truly believe Mr. Backus, that the mysteries of space, of myself and of the unknown to your species would be revealed through a priest?" No, he didn't think that either.

"As I have mentioned, your species is not ready for such knowledge. It may come when you stop to rely upon machines in the manner you do; I can inform you that at least".

"But without 'machines', neither I nor the other two crew members could have contacted yourself, we wouldn't damn well be in space at all. We would be in the dust and the dirt of Earth again, simply looking up to the heavens. We would not be able to speak to an advanced creature, or spirit, whatever this voice was.

"That you believe this to be so represents the limitations of your species Mr. Backus. I shall remain in contact with the Earth and the Moon, waiting and hoping for the day of your true enlightenment. You are a well designed and technically very capable race; yet you remain unable to truly consider the unknown itself. As such I cannot allow you to engage with the world as it exists beyond yourself and Mars".

With that, Theodore was transported back into loading bay B. He knew that he would have to inform the crew slowly and carefully that Sergeant Smithson and Eddy Kovacs were actually still alive albeit unconscious in their new and narrow morgue homes. He would give the others the apparently true reason about the ionized leak that would claim to have cleared whilst wearing a chem-suit. He would also have to explain to the Captain about the need to turn back to home base. His reason would be simple; due to the mainframe system going off line calculations had changed and we would now not be able to make it to Mars due incorrect fuel limits. Later he would find out that the Captain had apparently confided in to Dr. Phillips that this was his greatest fear for the journey. It was as good as an excuse as any thankfully. No-one apart from himself would recall the contact with a being of the truly unknown. No-one would know the first and possibly last time that Man had communicated with space. Theodore began to ready himself for the journey back; he was ready to believe in his family this time.

WHATEVER HAPPENED TO TED JOHNSON ?

"Hello… Yes, we got the order you mentioned… right… yeah it's already been sent there…Thursday, sure… Thanks, bye".
Graham Hadley sat bored at his desk, and put down the tiny receiver. He was thoroughly tired and thoroughly unmotivated Graham was a middle aged and typically middle status office worker. Successful enough to keep a job, but not interesting or corporate enough to be given any sort of promotion above his standing. Sure he was getting paid enough to cover his flat and to keep him in Indian takeaways, but he had reached the non-glass ceiling of this company and was more than happy to stick to it. Graham always made an effort to appear smart, in all aspects. He wore wire frame glasses and always had a suit with a tie that matched company colours on. If other workers actually looked at him closely, they could never tell he couldn't give a shit about any of his tedious work load. He felt there weren't too many employees at his level who were concerned about their fellow workers though, which gave him yet more breathing space. The floor he worked on, six incidentally, was a firmly clock in, answer Vid-Screen calls, clock out kind of place. He liked it, it felt like home. Today, Tuesday, was just another day at Nano-Tech Enterprise and he knew it. Despite the great advancements in the World in relation to "big important things", like the advancement of democracy to counteract the problems of nationalism and the formation of the Central Religious Network of course to help with the problems of organized religion, life at work was still a dull and repetitive environment.

On the Vid-Screen he kept seeing the same unchanged spreadsheet. Numbers and letters blurred into a mess of cells. They were something to do with orders for the company, he knew that at least. Tiredness had slowly gripped his mind this afternoon and he had forgotten the point again of starring at that damn Vid-Screen. Ah, that was it! He was meant to be conferring with head office throughout he day by using the Sphere, but obviously his mind was absent. Shit! It was 4.30 now and he probably wouldn't be able to contact them again at this time in the afternoon. Thankfully he had done enough work earlier in the week to lessen any criticism that would come his way. Hey, if anyone looked over to see him or Prime Lord forbid, any mind scanners went past, he would invariably start working once more. They would see him typing away, filling the screen briefly with some more numbers, any numbers. The appearance of work was vital to him.

He stared across at the desk opposite him. Man-oh-man was that Sophia a magnificent specimen of woman. She was ergonomically spectacular with wonderful curves, beautiful breasts, as revealed through her cleavage on show in that black blouse, and had a beautiful face to match. Graham had never dare enquire as to her status, although he was fairly certain a woman that attractive would be partnered with some sort of millionaire, and probably a publicly famous guy too. Lucky bastard, whoever that gut was. It had been four years since any intercourse and at some points in his life, I.e. about twice a day he lamented being so single, middle aged and alone. Thirty-Five certainly didn't mean the end of the road. He had a good job, a hover car and a nice apartment but still nice ladies didn't take his offer up. Maybe it's my stink he thought? Crudely smelling his armpits, he thought no way, that is the scent of a successful man. This terrible sense of smell would prove to be the least of Graham Handley's worries. He could see the clock on the wall tick over to 4.55, so he grabbed his coat and went out into the lobby to wait for the elevator.

Graham slumped back on his white leather sofa, in his equally gauche but cosy one-bedroom flat. The place was in a nice area and he had made a slight effort to make to convey the appearance of middling success. He had a fine projector, a home Vid-Screen by the far wall and an excellent coffee machine. The overall stylistic impression of his life was good. Graham got up and went to the fridge for another drink. His thoughts went lazily to what had happened after work. Immediately after finishing at the office he had grabbed a couple of moderately expensive lagers in the pub across from road. He obviously shrank away when one of his area bosses from the floor above came into the place. He didn't want to be seen by them despite knowing that those guys would call in at some point. They were definitely heavier drinkers than he was. Being there was not so much of a problem, he thought. I have enough stats on my system so as not to be suspicious and obviously enough to not yet be fired by them. A couple of drinks in a pub wasn't a sack able offence anyway. Back in the flat he thought about what he had done at work. His sad conclusion of five cappuccinos and three phone calls was depressing enough for him to grab another beer.

When he arrived at his desk on Wednesday morning, precisely two minutes late, Graham saw a note on his desk. It was crudely written and just said "7th Floor- when you get in, JH". He gulped a large breath of air. This really wasn't good he thought, He knew that someone would be there to meet him and that they would be serious. Business actually took place there, he knew that. Money came and went through that office so people took their jobs more seriously than the pencil pushing likes of people such as myself. He fumbled in the lift to press the right button, and before he could even clear his throat he had arrived at the next floor. He continued quietly coughing when the doors opened to reveal John Howard, his area boss. Howard looked at Graham with a bit of contempt and suspicion when he had entered the seventh floor coughing and spluttering. The sturdy looking figure was quick to get to the point.

"Look do you know why you've been called up here Mr. Hadley?"

He honestly didn't.

"No, not really Mr. Howard"

"It isn't a great problem actually Handley, more of a promotion actually"

"What, a promotion?" Graham started laughing, attempting to make the involuntary laughter quiet but it still came out in a annoyingly boisterous fashion. He didn't want to appear as some sort of joker or fool to people on the Seventh Floor.

"We aren't joking with you Mr. Handley. Seriously, we are now looking to make contacts and expand our business of providing Nano-Technology to the intelligent species on Venus".

Ah, Graham stopped laughing.

"You want Nano-Tech to deal with Venus?" he enquired.

"No, we want you to deal with Venus Graham. Our records show that you have the best psychometric profile to deal with the - ahem - businessmen, shall we politely say of Venus".

He really didn't what to say, and certainly didn't know whether to take that as a compliment or an insult. Memories were still pretty raw regarding the destruction of so much of Earth following the Venetian War in the late 21st Century. Getting this job was like being charged with the job of helping directly to rebuild Nazi Germany.

"We can assure you great strides have been made to impose democracy on the planet, and we have taught them to appreciate monetary advancement in the way that they knew advancement through violence"

"Right" he absently replied. Graham really didn't know whether his last particular point was a good thing or a bad thing. Good Lord, some companies really did search for bloody money anywhere. Graham decided to find out more.

"How... how was my profile comparable to the Venetians?"

"You matched them for moral callousness, hesitancy to respect order and the need to express dissidence"

"Ah" he knowingly replied.

"The good news is that in addition to your promotion, you still certainly have a human mind overall. Particularly in regards to your lust levels and your low boredom threshold. Yes, you score on the human level about as well as anybody. You should be relieved".

"I am. It's just that some of my brain patterns are... Venetian?" he replied.

"Yes, well some of them".

Never mind he thought, some Venetian, some human what's the difference? We weren't so different he thought. Humans lusted after money, they lusted after destruction, some sort of dynamic could be reached he felt. It's a basic floor seven, floor six situation. One level is more serious about some things, the other level cares a bit more about other things. Graham felt his brain go slightly numb, as if he had been sitting on it. More had happened in this one morning than had seemingly happened in the last four years at this place! It bothered him that they psyche-monitored his neural activity, but still they did that to everyone these days he thought.

"Can I head back down now Mr. Hughes?" he quietly asked, still a bit overwhelmed by the new task that lay ahead.

"Yes sure Mr. Handley, go get yourself ready for this new job of yours".

He looked at the Vid-Screen and it no longer seemed so blank and oppressive . He knew the beginnings of serious economic trade agreements were stirring and through the company he worked at of all places! Nano-Tech would be the pioneers in beginning to help rebuild relations between Earth and Venus. It was really quite a task he had on his hands. The peace between the planets had been ensured only through treaties and summonary executions of leading 'war criminals' from individuals on both sides. There hadn't been any diplomatic or economic truce that was for sure. Earth had been given free reign to expand economically, whilst the ultimately defeated Venetians had to focus on building social and democratic order. This was necessary to "help" control their legally defined "evil" citizens. There was no denying he thought that the Venetians had got the rough end of the stick following settlements. They paid in all respects in the end. Earth on the other hand continued as before until some of the domestic pressures aiming to minimise all wars came into force. Thank the Prime Lord for that. Graham knew that the days would begin to feel shorter whilst he was preparing deals to be enacted with the telepaths of the Venetian world.

It was very early Wednesday morning and Graham was still awake. He as mentally pacing up and down in his brain. How should he word the agreements between the parties? Should he refer to them as "evil"? I mean, would he legally have to? Questions, questions, questions. They had kept him awake all night. Three times already he had gotten out of his bed to make a single cappuccino. His idea was that the milk content of the drink would make him tired. This ill-thought precept had come back to haunt him in the shape of thoughts travelling at about a hundred miles an hour. The milk centric thought he had was overridden by the caffeine. All positive thoughts start out milky he thought, then the reality kicks in. At some points during the night his brain randomly tried to remember some of the thirteen digit head office numbers he would need. At other times in the night his brain tried to tell him to relax, that this task was just another boring job really at work. He agreed with his later morning milky brain in the end. The arrange of orders with Venetian business would be no different really than making deals with companies in London. Yeah, his conscience thought, like making deals with Nazi funded companies in London. It had a point. The destruction of the Venetian War had undoubtedly changed the Earth, and just the word Venetian continued to retain a dirty influence in the minds of the public. He was surprised actually that Nano-Tech hadn't put some sort of gagging order on him. This information was very sensitive. Maybe they realised he had no friends and no-one to talk to he absently thought. It was early that Wednesday morning however, in a blurry midst of his caffeine induced state, that he watched an important news story.

He squinted at the large projected image on the far wall. He couldn't really see that clearly this early but he could hear the early morning announce clearly enough.

"Ted Johnson, a supposed citizen of London has today been simultaneously summoned and executed for war crimes during the failed Venetian campaign. We here at Network News can reveal that Mr. Johnson was aged 72 and had ad been living on Earth in the form of the originally murdered Mr. Johnson for 30 years. He was caught by chance following the work of an off duty police officer"

Graham was stunned and unnerved by the broadcast. He knew in many respects that the Venetians had more advanced technology but a full mind and body switch was a hell of a technique. Selfishly Graham began to worry. He didn't want to see any negative stories about Venus. He didn't want the Venetians to be on the defensive, and he didn't want the even remote possibility of being attacked due to dealing with what had been until that morning the old enemy. He had obviously never heard of this guy, Johnson. The man was old and lived in a care home in Zone 1. That wasn't the disturbing part. It was the fact that Venetians could be here and living amongst us. They weren't just a distant enemy. They could be anywhere, on any company floor. He assumed that they would chose to move to Zone 1 to arouse less suspicion, but maybe what if they moved there to try and initiate terrorist attacks? So many questions flowed through his brain. The Venetians were a violent race, they were looking for more ways to kill and destroy the people of Earth, surely that was it. They would initiate attacks in his zone, and kill him and thousands of other innocents! They would not stop into Earth was destroyed, damn Venetians! Calm down Graham. Deep breaths. He paused and regained his composure. The Venetian War was over thirty years ago, and he was only an infant when it had been going on. It was to be Graham Handley himself who was to begin to initiate measures that would lead to increased peace and shared prosperity between the planets. There shouldn't eventually be any need for an infiltrated terrorist attack now. Beside this guy mentioned, Johnson, he was 72 anyway and was old and decrepit there were no other signs of infiltrated ex-VF members. This guy Johnson clearly posed no apparent harm to the people in his care home or elsewhere. He wasn't caught by pulling out a laser pistol when they served the trifle, he was caught by an off duty body scanner that a police officer had (illegally) driven past in whilst travelling off his patrol route. He was in the district in order to visit an elderly relative of his. Evidently his law enforcement instincts still came into play even when visiting gramps. Graham knew though that the message had resonance. He would certainly decline to tell

43

people that he was selling robots to the Venetians. And he definitely wouldn't mention that part of his brain had been shown itself to be Venetian.

When getting in to his office that morning, early this time, actually by about fifteen minutes, Graham found another scrawled letter on his desk "Don't worry about Johnson, it doesn't concern us JH". He was simultaneously relieved and disturbed by the message. They were obviously being careful with the regards to the potentially explosive Earth-Venus relations. So they should he thought, hundreds of placard waving peaceniks and headline hunting news crews would do nothing to help the image of Nano-Tech Enterprises. First things first, Graham thought, he went over to the coffee machine and ordered a strong double espresso with a splash of milk. Sitting down at his desk, he checked the Sphere for any messages, and after reading the usual early morning updates he leant back and guzzled his strong morning boost. After the coffee Graham left his coat at the desk and went to the lift. There was no one about the office on his floor at least. He felt a brief and smug flash of contempt, Ha! Those average floor six workers beavering away like the robots we build on endless and aimless record keeping tasks. He was feeling more confident in himself than he had done for years. Maybe he would ask Sophia out for a drink at some point? Yeah, he'd let her know his status as an official diplomat. A vital figure in defusing tensions following the last devastating intergalactic war. She would have to be a bit impressed by that! He was hoping too that the job would lead to a salary increase, Graham had certainly had his eye on a newer, flashier motor and this promotion would have to help. When Graham looked up he could see that the lift had accidentally gone up to level ten. It was only sheer horror that made him get out on that floor…

Surrounding the body were five huge and well armoured police men and a few office workers. They scarcely looked up when he got out of the lift. Graham found himself standing in the middle of the lift doors gawping, like the classic rubber necking drivers heading past a motor zone pile up. What was going on here he thought? The atmosphere of death hung heavy in the air. Floor ten had the feeling of a battlefield morgue. Instinctively Graham looked around for someone to gain information. He tried to speak to one of the workers who was chatting quietly to one of the larger police officers but all blank faced guy said to him was, "John Howard, it's terrible isn't it? I mean this guy was godfather to my kids. He was just a nice guy you know?"

He didn't know that, but looked empathetic whilst the guy unloaded his emotions about John Howard. Graham suddenly felt very awkward and out of place. Thankfully another floor ten office worker calmly guided Graham to the side. The man was a small and compact guy. He was neat and efficient in nearly every aspect. His being was perfectly suited to calmly dispensing information on any matter. Anything ranging from orders to Zone 3, sudden gangland style executions of fellow office workers, things like that.

"Ah, Mr. Handley, I'm sorry you have had to see this. We didn't expect to be able to tell you the bad news until a quieter period during the day". Graham was still shocked, his mind wasn't working. Was John Howard from floor seven really dead? Was the very real, very dead body lying there limp and rag doll-esque really that polite guy who had only just started leaving him notes on Tuesday this week? The same guy who was going to get him promoted? The neat chap continued proffering information…

"It is terrible news, unfortunately for John of course and actually for yourself Mr. Handley. The promotion that was offered to you has necessarily been removed, we apologise".

Somehow he had guess that would happen.

"Can you tell me how he was killed please" morbid curiosity got the better of him.

"He was shot and murdered, a hit and run job. It could be the government, it could even be someone from the Central Religious Network, we don't know yet. Don't tell anyone else that view though"

"So he was assassinated?" Graham was stunned and shocked. "Why?"

"I'm sorry to tell you this, but they believe that Mr. Hughes was a Venetian spy like that fellow at the old people's home, Ted Johnson"

"What?" Graham didn't want to believe that.

"There was evidence that he had been sending messages from public Vid-Screens to leading figures in the Venetian Forces. He was another war criminal Graham, like that other fellow summoned and executed".

There was obviously no public jury this time he thought, things had evidently become suddenly very sour and very serious. The seemingly great world diplomatic progress that the two of them were on the brink of was turning to be just another loose and meaningless dream. The economic truce planned was simply a set up after all. Hughes had been a spy and was sending the Venetian's knowledge of our war technology. That was just great. Why did this Howard have to start sending him notes? Why did he have to be a damn accomplice to a Venetian spy? His dreams of an intergalactic truce seemed like a bit of an insult now in the cold light of a new day. Truce? His conscious mind laughed callously. There cannot be a truce between a morally superior and a morally inferior planet. The scoffing sound of disdain came from the more annoying part of his brain he normally kept silent. Disappointment and shock however had reinvigorated it. Earth was sorting itself out, but any dreams that it would export these values to the rest of the vastly different planets of the universe seemed fairly fatuous now. The Prime Lord and his virtues were still owned by Earth apparently. Stupid utopian ideals he thought, they just get people murdered. He was annoyed at Howard for dying and briefly spoiling his chances of helping to seal the rift between at least one planet in this universe and Earth. Stupid virtues denying me a new hover car. Then his active mind, the supposedly practical bit then told Graham pertinent news. The good part of the brain told him that the police would soon start following up leads in the company soon and they would quickly lead to him. Graham Handley would be a bloody suspect in an assassination case. Fantastic. Even though he was probably taking a dump or drinking a coffee when the man was killed he would almost certainly have to head down to the station and answer a whole manner of questions probably whilst being mind scanned. Great, a police record. That will really help me if I get fired after all this.

The neat man that introduced him to level ten began speaking again, maybe he had been talking for a while. Stupid interrupting brain, he thought. Without his good brain's permission.

"Ahem. You should know Mr. Graham that we were developing top secret military technology on this floor. Much like yourself, John Howard came to this floor by accident a couple of weeks ago. Unlike yourself however he left a small but very real mobile vidi-unit to try and get information about the latest military secrets going on here at Nano-Tech Enterprises". The news was still rushing through his head. He felt bitter still, despite these latest espionage findings about that Howard guy. There was genuinely going to be peaceful agreements made! He would have been involved in something globally important as opposed to the standard

46

monumentally dull. All parts of his brain were selfishly feeling quietly devastated.

"So my work with regards to Venetian orders is off" Graham asked the floor ten rep, despite knowing the answer.

"They are certainly off Mr. Handley, for an indefinite period that could turn out in fact to be hundreds of years, with any luck. The Venetians may have to be given some more very serious economic sanctions. The use of spies by such a destructive species was obviously outlawed following the post war settlements".

"Yes of course." He felt a strange sense of disappointment that the chance for integrated economic trade was slipping away.

When he asked the next question he felt the continuation of that prophetic feeling he had developed.

"Couldn't we just sell them military hardware as well? Who is to say they would use it against us? It may just be self defence"

The answer was straight from the pre-knowledge text book.

"Really Mr. Handley, they were certainly right when scanning your brain weren't they?".

Despite knowing the answer he still felt bothered by the response. So humans really know everything about the universe then? He let the thought go, calmly and without any struggle.

The tenth floor figure guided Graham back to the lift. The chap obviously had some sympathy for the office drone from level six standing despondently in front of him. Still remaining on a higher level stunned by involvement that day with both death and disappointment.

"Look, I'm sorry you had to see the body. You can take the rest of the day off Mr. Handley"

He didn't argue. Handley left the large tinted-glass high-rise building of Nano-Tech Enterprises and went across to the pub.

Graham arrived forty-five minutes late on Thursday morning. He hoped it was still morning, at least officially. Driving early whilst having a large hangover was harder work than he anticipated. Mid journey he managed to get the auto route programmed, just in time probably. The night had been an indulgent blur of expensive lagers and shots at the pub. He knew that there would be the inevitable consequences and that work would still be there. Great he thought, another morning of looking at the same, now permanently meaningless, Vid-Screen. He got to his desk and forgot about the need for getting a coffee. Part of his brain knew he needed one, but another more influential part said 'Just sit down Graham, you are here'. He tried to open his early morning messages, to look to see if he had to reply to anyone quickly to apologise for being late. Before he was able to check these messages however his eyes caught a news broadcast that was playing in the corner of his and all other standard Vid-Screens. The stern, brown haired human automaton began authoritatively reading the new news…

"Police have now caught the two individuals who we believe are the only two spies working for the Venetian Forces. In the spirit of intergalactic diplomacy and following the spirit of the Prime Lord, no reciprocal strikes will be aimed by crafts into Venetian cities or even at Venetian factories. The forces at the World Government and Central Religious Network have made clear today that they genuinely aim to end war as we have known it". Graham felt a wave of relief go over him. Maybe peace and trade would be possible again between the two planets again at some point. Maybe after known spies have been killed, he sadly and cynically thought.

There was actually one real message on the Sphere for him. It read "Go to level ten for police questions." There was no name given. There didn't really need to be one with that type of request. Great he thought, time to give a profile of a guy I had just met who happened to be a Venetian spy. Maybe they would like me to talk about Hitler's favourite breakfast whilst I'm there, or more accurately why this guy Hughes seemed to behave like a spy. Not that his opinion mattered to whoever had killed Hughes. He doubted it would matter to the police much either.

He got to the tenth floor and waited in the immediate corridor. The same neat man met him.

"Yes, hello again Mr. Handley. I see you look a bit worse for wear. Never mind, eh? The questions will be routine, they just want a simple statement about what Howard had said to you in person".

He got to the desks where the police where sitting and mentally prepared for the pending questions.

"He seemed like a good guy" Graham found himself saying

"He was pleasant and seemed to want to help out with things".

The police officer to the right of him interrupted…

"Did you ever think he was working for the Venetians? Did he give you any clues"

"Lord, not that I can think of. I guess…"

48

"Go on, Mr. Handley"

"I guess… Well maybe, he described the Venetians as 'businessmen now' I think. He seemed to believe that trade between us and Venus would be easy. I guess I got carried away with the whole possibility of it all as well. I mean I guess he felt that the Venetians were badly treated by the post-war settlements"

"Right, I see" the burly officer replied.

"He was keen to pick you because you were, or are, we should say… workably malleable?"

"Who said that?" Graham felt a surge of anger

"It was in his intercepted Vid-Screen messages to the VF. Look it's ok, it doesn't actually mean you are in trouble, it gets you out of trouble"

"That's good"

"Yes, indeed you were simply picked because you have arrived at work permanently, well until this morning, on time within five minutes of the clock"

"Right"

"Which we should tell you now is ten minutes early"

He had guessed that before.

"So, Howard really was a spy then?"

"Yes, I'm afraid so"

"And I'm going to be charged aren't I, as an accomplish?"

"No, you are actually free to go. Like I said, you weren't chosen because of any psyche-scan, that was totally made up by Howard, you were chosen as we said because you could be manipulated".

Graham slowly got up.

"Is it ok then now to leave?" he asked.

"Yes, sure you're free to go Mr. Handley".

Graham walked back past the desks the police were huddled around, he walked back down through the corridor and back into the lift down to the sixth floor.

After work, Graham decided to be more productive than getting hammered as he had done the previous night. He cleared the cans and bottles that had been left by his personal Vid-Screen and began to search the Sphere again for the original guy "Johnson", there was something about that name that bothered him. Despite it being early in the morning the last time he saw the image, Graham could have sworn that he had seen the old man before, possibly even at the pub outside his place of work. He put in the terms, JOHNSON<EXECUTION<VENUS and ten results came back. It was definitely the first that interested him. Some citizen journo from the comfort of his bedroom had written an exclusive piece, 'Old man wrongly executed! Blood on the hands of the World Government?' He scanned on further,

'Evidence we have exclusively uncovered her on this site has indicated that the man killed, Ted Johnson, was in fact not a veteran of the Venetian Forces but actually a veteran agent for Earth Zone 3 forces! Yes, indeed our research has shown the man may have in fact been a double agent who was involved with the Venetian's simply to ascertain whether they were or were not going to instigate any terrorist attacks on any Earth Zones. Evidently they were not since the guy had been retired for twenty years and we hear at Newsforce certainly haven't been aware of any Venetian ordered terrorist attacks on Earth! The rumours too on the Sphere are that the dead businessmen of Nano-Tech Enterprises was another suspect innocent of Venetian involvement! Is there a reason for this Venetian spy panic, Newsforce certainly thinks that the authorities are obviously worried about something emanating from Venus- maybe the gas of that giant war zone has become toxic and is heading back to Earth! This is Writer Zee signing off'

Graham decided to give searching a break for a while. The information found on this site had raised enough questions- maybe this idiot was right! Maybe the people killed, Ted Johnson and John Howard were killed by mistake. Howard was obviously a panic job and despite the legal jury, it seems that Johnson was too. Why had a war that had been dormant for thirty years with a now tamed planet suddenly become front page news? Why had John Howard really been killed. Then it struck him, quickly and viciously. Somebody doesn't want Earth and Venus to begin trading with one another.

Graham actually took Friday off work. He wanted to really get to the bottom of all this. After all he had known John Howard, and he couldn't shake the nagging suspicion that he knew Ted Johnson. He got himself a double espresso and sat down by the personal Vid-Screen. He decided to search the Sphere this time for VENUS<TRADE<AGREEMENTS and this time only three results came back. The first one seemed too vague and out of date to be interesting, "Earth plans interplanetary trade eventually"

the article was speculative stuff, the kind of drivel that was popular in the 21st Century. Well at least in the years before people began to get to know the harsher reality of outer-space and the differently modulated intergalactic species. The second piece was slightly more relevant "Venus: can investment help us stop future war?" it was dated from before the Venetian War. It was from the brief time when the World Government really thought they could sell the Venetians soft drinks and insurance. The manned probes there came back empty handed, but in the early days still alive.

It was the third piece given on the Sphere that really took Graham aback "Are the Venetians more brutal or more advanced than us?' It was certainly a question that wasn't often posed. Earthly superiority was grounded firmly in government and religion. Most assessments of foreign bodies almost certainly ended with disdainful analysis. Not here though, somehow. The article went on 'We believe at the University of Nairobi that the Venetian people are simply misunderstood. The violent tendencies that have been analysed were the result not of any psychosomatic problems from within the species, but were a natural and fair reaction to the alien (to them) bodies that were entering their vastly different atmosphere. They were reacting to forces armed with weapons to back their pre-supposed reason. They did not co-operate with us as we wanted them to not through belligerence or inferior values but as a result of already being perceived of as a threat. The principle of 'do unto others as they do unto you' was indeed realised following our earliest relations. Earth and the World Government in particular set the tone of destruction. War followed prolonged hostility and superior notions of the human intellect'.

Graham sat a bit stunned by the piece, thankfully freedom of speech, if not freedom of thought, had been prominent on Earth for centuries. Then he realised the meaning from these three articles, it struck him like a tiny meteorite. Ted Johnson and John Howard weren't killed because they were Venetians but actually because they were not! Both had involvement in dealing with Venus so they were proved guilty before innocent. The authorities obviously felt they were going to collude with the Venetians and so were killed before any tensions could increase again. Graham began to panic. Surely I would be next on this seemingly short list? I mean he had already sent one proposed order forms to the government of Venus. Sweat started to form at the base of his spine. What would his life be to the authorities? It was clear to him that the deaths of Johnson and Howard had sadly been accepted by the public as blood refreshing the tree of liberty. The dominance of humanity would be ensured by life and death apparently

The weekend passed like so many without real interest or incident and Graham got himself dressed and ready Monday morning in the same mechanical fashion he always did. Apart from in the those rare mornings you struggle with a hangover and with dealing with remnants of sick his conscious told him. Anyway, he soon arrived at work after programming a route that avoided the morning work traffic. He didn't feel like driving the route this morning for some reason. When he arrived at work for the first day of the week Graham had this horrid and unshakeable sensation that he would indeed be the next person ordered dead for dealing with the Venetians.

He went to the coffee machine first before his desk, collecting greedily two double espressos. Well, if it was to be the last day he was alive then muchos caffeine would be needed

He scanned his screen for any important messages again. Thankfully nothing from the Venetians yet. Thinking ahead for once, Graham went to his 'sent messages' and deleted both the template and the actual message to the Venetians. There were no messages to be deleted from John Howard. It was almost as if he had never existed. To be sure he scanned his desk for any of the notes Howard had left, thankfully though they had already been thrown into the bin. He checked the bin itself, which was empty. Surely the police or the killers on his case wouldn't be checking his personal bins for messages? Would they? There was a chance certainly, but he couldn't do anything about that now. Graham decided to busy himself with the task of looking like a real level six office worker and not some assailant in conspiratorial activities.

It was actually his co-worker and occasional drinker partner Gary that led to the arrest of Graham Handley. He had heard and reported on Graham after that drunken evening, where evidently he had been talking at length to everyone about how important he could be in the history of intergalactic relations. That evening he had arisen the suspicion of the passing thought scanners and half of the other people in the bar too. His situation was different from Ted Johnson and certainly John Howard though. Ted Johnson was certainly an ex zone service man, and he had certainly infiltrated Venus during the war years. He was wrongly tried by the jury for being a Venetian and he did indeed lose his life with the world seeing him as a traitor. John Howard on the other hand was a spy for the World Government, They knew about the military plans going on at level ten, but also about the proximity of Graham Handley himself to these prototypes. You see John Howard didn't send any vidi-scanners or any other spying equipment into level ten. He had been sent there three months ago by the Intelligence division of the Central Religious Network to monitor suspicious activity from a certain level six employee at Nano-Tech Enterprise aka Mr. Graham Handley. Graham knew that it was his thoughts betraying him. He thought about peace and trade between Venus and Earth more than most, or really any, normal human would. For the simple reason that as an infant at the start of the Venetian War he had been mind and body scanned into the newly born body of a zone 3 infant. He was of course a full and cold blooded Venetian at his core. The Venetians had helped to get him a job, and subtly intervened in his thoughts to try and get him in adulthood to get him a job at a major firm with intergalactic trade. The intention was to try in some small way to end the hostility between Venus and Earth. As telepaths you see, those high officials in the Venetian Forces were aware of certain defeat in the war with Earth. They simply didn't have the advanced nano-weapons of the combined World Government forces. The original, eventually altered intention had been to use Handley as an intergalactic spy. To force him to indeed go to level ten get a promotion at some point and to steal prototype nano-weapon technology at the very cutting edge used by Earth forces. Unfortunately Graham Handley had proved quite adept at reacting to conditions on Earth and become to all intents and purposes a human. Despite the continued subliminal telepathic messages sent to him, unknown by the thought scanners because of the different cerebral frequencies of the species, Handley went undetected and unchanged by Venetian orders. Ironically it was his human thoughts of attempted reconciliation and his damn praise of the Prime Lord that on the one hand pointed him out as a non-typical human (seeking reconciliation with a defined enemy, whatever next!) and on the other modulated his thoughts to force the Venetian high command to consider his placement to advance more peaceful means. The high command of the Venetian Forces were not fully distraught however when Graham was caught. His mission had failed and become potentially problematic. Indeed it was a relief that the authorities on Earth decided to do the judgemental killing for the Venetians. If only they knew, General

53

Philox thought, what destruction some of their warped ideals caused. That article Mr. Handley had found was certainly right. The Venetian Species was not inherently destructive, but they had to reply to conflict that was generated on Venus. They had to consider the continuation of their species via any means possible. Survival not war was their basic instinct. War had temporarily at least changed that, like it had with most other nations who suffered from righteous hostility. Peaceful reconciliation between the planets he realised would be impossible whilst such destructive processes of thought went on from within. Never mind though. Let them slowly undo the progress they have made. Then we will return with greater purpose, greater meaning and greater weapons. Indeed through Graham Handley they had began to comprehend and appreciate the meaning of the Prime Lord. This was a monumental discovery for the Venetian Forces, and they wanted to spread the findings to their people. God had finally found Venus. The Venetians had strongly come to fell that the human race, particularly as represented by the destructive Central Religious Network (which was ironically set up to minimise religious differences) could be a globally destructive presence in the liberation of other intergalactic species. The Venetians now too intended to spread the word of the Prime Lord. The Venetian High Command responded to the execution of jury of Graham Handley with plans and procedures to show Earth, by force, the true mental and spiritual liberation offered by the Prime Lord. General Philox felt charged with religious righteousness and set out to carefully plan a more effective war to wage with Earth.

MALFUNCTION OF THE DIVINE

Priest Bryan Connor finished off his nightly prayers and settled in to bed. It had been a long day; he was busy in the morning tending to the monastery garden, the afternoon was spent discussing multiple theologies with the newest intake of hopeful priests whilst finally the evening saw him spending time asking questions to what the general public referred to as 'the God Box'. This device, which Connor amongst other religious folks devoutly referred to as 'the Divine Invention' as opposed to the less reverential 'God Box' was a true work of technological genius re-appropriated by the Combined Church of the True God, founded in 2061. The device was a device of great knowledge; it was the single largest source of divine scripture and chronicled various events of engagement between man and God, The device was programmed by a collection of technologically sound religious followers; a team of modern monks as it were, which busily went over all forms of scripture from literally every sect, every faith and every news story to gain the most complete image of God possible. Where there were disagreements with the role of God between the programmers, all results were placed in anyway. The device worked by having the user ask the Divine Machine a question regarding faith or God. The answers would then be drawn from the entire cannon of man's knowledge of God. Priority of results was obviously given to the ancient and established faiths like Judaism, Islam, Catholicism and Christianity. The machine was purely used as a matter of faith, and to provide answers for troubled religious scholars. Most major churches or synagogues possessed a similar device, although they were not commercially available as of yet. The Combined Church of the True God whilst still relatively new in the grand scale of world religions was still devoutly followed by millions over the various world zones and by citizens stationed on the moon for over 30 years. The Church had been formed by a man called Robert Blume in 2029. He was a theological professor at Oxford University who claimed to have an intense and personal religious experience. The account goes that whilst working on a book that examined the major similarities between the major faiths in a room at the Oxford University Library a strong beam of light came through the small window of the study and illuminated the four major sources of religious knowledge he had in front of him; a Bible, Torah

Scroll, Koran and New Testament were all highlighted by a strong beam of light. Lore then has it that Blume heard the words of God briefly whilst fully illuminated by the light through the window which should barely have covered a page in the Bible. The voice is reported to have told Blume, 'You have been chosen, tell the people of the true word of God'. Then the voice and light left, and Robert Blume was left with the apparent words of The Lord ringing through his ears. He immediately leapt up from his chair, left the books in the library and literally ran back to his quarters to start writing down the major connections he had made that morning combining the scripture from the major religions. Blume spent years collating all accounts of the Word of God, and before he died he was able to produce a massive volume of work entitled 'The Divine Word'. Following the work of monks and scholars using future technology these words were then put into a computer which was then fully programmed with all knowledge of God. Priest Bryan Connor had certainly become an addict of asking the device questions. The answers always reassured him as to the true wisdom and beneficence of God. It was because he was always asking the right questions.

Bryan came down to the great hall having said his morning prayers and vows. He collected a bowl of muesli from the breakfast area and settled down to speak to some of the newer entrants to this monastery who had decided to study and learn here in Winchester City in Zone 2. Whilst he would never admit this himself, it was well known that many hopeful monks and promising religious scholars who wanted to dedicate their lives to God went to Winchester in order to learn from the wise and incredibly learned Priest Bryan Connor. He was well known and respected in public circles. He was pretty much alone in religious terms for having a Sphere page, and he was regularly called upon by the media to provide the Combined Church with a say on matters of public conscious. When he wasn't busy speaking to the new intake, or asking questions of scripture to the Divine Machine, Father Connor was often getting recognised. Rare trips out from the monastery were often hazardous, with some people politely addressing him and thanking him for some message other he had delivered on TV, whilst plenty of other times he would get accosted by youths shouting out fairly offensive obscenities such as 'there's that religious tosser' and other choice remarks. Leaving the quiet peaceful bounds of Winchester monastery was not something he choose to do lightly. Today however was certainly an occasion where he had deemed it necessary to intervene. A Justice Minister from Zone 3, Kenneth Wells, had decided to publicly make the argument that religions, no matter how inclusive, were no longer relevant in the maintenance of social order. Father Connor had obviously prepared numerous cautious replies to the main question; admittingly he had spent most of the last evening consulting the Divine Mechanism about how best to show religion in it's various forms is still very relevant with regards to social order. Bryan was convinced the bet immediate response was to focus on how our laws, and the foundation of 'society' as a nation was ultimately dependent on the laws God has given us. Through utilising quotes from Deuteronomy and Judges, Father Connor felt certain he would be able to reply the notion that somehow God wasn't relevant to the laws of society. He would make the claim that a basically lawful society, which was surely the bedrock of any society whether modern or ancient, depended upon certain laws and tenants. 'A society could not exist for example if murder was widespread on the streets for example', he would argue. A 'society' as this Minister had decided to focus upon, surely required some basic engagement with the laws of God in order to be viewed as viable. The main argument that Father Connor was going to present was that if you remove God as basically any faith conceived of him, then you would be living in a society that wasn't worth it's salt. This type of encounter wasn't rare for Father Connor; most years at some point he would be required to brush down the old crimson cloak and visit a TV station in order to counteract some upstart World Government official, seemingly heart-set on abandoning any form of religion or even acknowledgement of God. It saddened him at times to see the levels of bile on these politicians faces whilst they were spewing out often the same garbage trying to oppose the one being that is unquestionable in the universe. His match record had been flawless so far; nine encounters and unquestionably nine victories. His opponents so far had mostly been made to look stupid and ironically delusional in their secular veracity which was often painfully clear in their attempts to question the wisdom of the Combined Church of the True God. None had really challenged him, other than this particularly intelligent Senator from Zone 6. He had made the argument that if the God of Exodus and Genesis was still the operational deity that we know today, then why hadn't he intervened during the times of great struggle and starvation for the African Continent which now made up the majority of Zone 6? If God had intervened to destroy the Pharaohs, then why hadn't he defeated and drowned the individuals behind the similar repression of African citizens? Father Connor was very calm in his answers and reproach. He refrained from giving the old-fashioned and outmoded argument that somehow God as an entity 'became' kind through the life and death of Jesus Christ, but instead gave the counter argument that only after true repression could and would God intervene. He didn't intervene to prevent the death of Jesus, nor did he intervene to prevent those who followed Islam from entering into terrorism. The argument was made by Father Connor that the lack of intervention into certain terribly events shouldn't be blamed on God, but instead should be blamed on the failure of man. Absolute repression would and did result in Divine Intervention but failures in the operation of man were sadly left to be treated and slowly repaired by those that caused it. He made the argument that God is truly selfless and gives himself for our freedom and liberty; continuous intervention from the true being the Church of the True God believed was a singular deity could not be a common occurrence if we were to ever be truly free and liberated people. God did not intervene to stop the persecution of Job, nor that of the African people; the Israelites were different, possibly because the known deity of Yahweh is now different. Questions of course followed this point, but Father Connor was able to overall calmly explain the beneficence of God and his ultimate wisdom in minimally intervening. The Senator looked as if he wanted to disagree during the time of the interview, but afterwards when the cameras were off he went over to Priest Connor and calmly thanked him for his views on the matter. The Zone 6 Senator Mbuti was indeed a religious man also, albeit a Christian, and calmly agreed that he would no longer blame God for the problems that the people of Africa and Zone 6 had experienced. The personal resolution that the Senator offered reminded Father Connor why he was in this whole business in the first place. Most of the other candidates had offered basically the same staid arguments along the lines of 'why should a barely seen ancient entity have a direct influence on our now modern 21st Century daily lives?' The answer he gave was almost a cliché now, 'oxygen is fairly ancient but I'm still of the opinion that we require it'. Some continued in the same vein though, 'Well we used to need cauterisation and leeches, but I think we are coping better with science', this always prompted a more measured response 'True sir, but like the knowledge of science the knowledge of God continues to expand. Much as I'm sure you'd agree that the world isn't flat, we here at the Combined Church of the True God believe that God himself isn't actually a man in the sky with a grey beard. Indeed in the same way that the Muslims have always refused to depict the prophet Mohammed, we here at the Combined Church are very reluctant to use images to depict God himself. We believe that God himself is even more undoubted presence than established scientific tenants like gravity.' So far the eight people who had turned up for the televised interview went away slightly bruised by the encounter in least in egotistical terms. The main approach given that scientific knowledge is still relatively new whilst God is relatively ancient surely we should be following the more modern idea? This manner of thought made the job of Father Connor so much easier; rather than being challenged on matters of debatable scripture such as those lines that possibly acknowledged the legality of slavery, the acceptability of multiple murders or the cursing of infidels, he was simply challenged on grounds of context. God was somehow thought by certain politicians to be 'out of context' with the modern world. The existence of life meant that the context of God was always relevant he thought. This meeting with the Justice Minister of Zone 3 would prove to be hugely influential in changing Father Connor's thoughts and even his beliefs.

Father Connor was beginning to panic; it was already the day before the television interview with the chap from Zone 3. The new training priests had gathered outside of his doors when Father Connor emerged from his morning prayers. The small congregation outside were looking nervous; as was often the case before the Combined Church was represented on TV. Trainee Father Davies asked the first question of doubtlessly many.
'Have you heard Father Connor that Mr. Wells is a former member of the Combined Church? They re saying he is going reveal secrets about a monastery in Zone 1!'
He answered the young man in his same normal, well honed and calm manner.
'No I hadn't young father. Many people I have been interviewed with and have spoken to have been former members of our church and many others. It does not provide an immediate concern Father Davies'.
Another nervous looking young priest asked a question,
'Have you heard Father Connor that this man has met you before during his training? They say that he has secrets about you in particular and your beliefs'

'I would not want my beliefs to be secret, Father Jones. I think that this chap Mr. Wells I believe, will provide the normal level of difficulty in dealing with. I would imagine that he has similar questions to the other members of the World Government I have dealt with'.

The young trainee priest persisted though.

'This man is different though Father. They are saying he is the person that is going to start the downfall of our church, in the same way that the Christians and Catholics were challenged'

'We cannot avoid challenges if we wish to aid people and offer salvation to their lives Father Jones. Please, if you gentlemen will excuse me, I need to consult the Divine Mechanism this morning to fully prepare for this interview'.

The young men quickly parted, many offering warm words of encouragement to their most famous older Priest. He had trained most of them how to gain optimal use of the Divine Mechanism; something told him he would need to get the most out of the machine prior to meeting this man, Mr. Wells.

Father Connor arrived by the room storing the Divine Mechanism; the room was known by the priests as 'God's Bedroom'. He crossed himself and then entered, heading solemnly over to the very old looking computer situated by the back wall. He powered on the device by instigating a retina scan and soon enough the screen lightened up, offering a simple search box in which to scan for answers in scripture. The types of questions he would need to ask went rushing through his head; should he search for answers about the life of Jesus after the resurrection? Should he be checking for why Abraham was asked to sacrifice his son? Questions kept churning through his mind like clothes in a spin cycle. He decided upon the first question needed for interview preparation; 'Why is evil allowed to be more dominant than good?' - the machine internally went into full speed mode, nodules doubtlessly connecting with other nodules, microchips being scanned for tiny pieces of digital programming- when it had finished, about 0.3 seconds later the answer was left on the screen.

'Good is relative to man. Only God himself is truly good. Henceforth evil on Earth will always be more prominent. See New Testament, Book of Job and the satanic verses'

As usual, Father Connor felt a wave of relief upon receiving the answer. This time he decided to search the machine for a question that Mr. Wells would be more likely to ask himself.

'Why do natural disasters happen?'

'Who says they are natural'

The response left Father Connor feeling a bit shocked but somehow not surprised, the answer would somehow not be effective however he thought when responding to someone like Justice Minister Mr. Wells. He tried again following a similar vein of thought,

'Why does so much of the world have to suffer'

'No-one has to suffer' came the reply.

Strangely in that moment, Father Connor felt a wave of frustration at the Divine Mechanism; it vexed him to have to deal with cryptic impersonal responses to questions that greatly troubled the world. At that point he decided to switch off the ageing powerful device. For the first time since Father Connor had consulted the machine it had not given him comforting answers. By increasing his level of questioning in preparation for facing a potentially hostile opponent, he had only succeeded in increasing his own levels of personal doubt. The response to the question about natural disasters particularly troubled him; why did good people have to die in disasters and accidents such as floods, volcanoes, hurricanes and tsunamis. Perhaps the world as we know it hasn't moved on so much from Noah he absently though. The wrath of God would be unlikely to appear from a bearded fellow from the heavens he thought. As a member of the Combined Church of the True God the answers somehow troubled him more. Why would a God that would send down his son, the holy man Jesus Christ, to die for our sins and then punish us with literal waves of natural disasters? Despite so many questions about faith being answered by the Divine Mechanism, personal matters of faith remained pertinent to Father Connor. He felt frustration at the ultimate loneliness of conscious existence. Even a man of his faith and standing so often felt distant from God, if not more so than people who did not worship any form of faith. Being so close to a machine of such power only invariably raised questions as opposed to answering them. So often he just felt like asking, 'Lord can you solve my doubt', yet somehow he inherently suspected that the answer would be 'No'. It felt to Father Connor as if doubt were as vital to being a believer in God as proof was. If God were a certainty in his being and his actions surely we would not earn or be deserving of salvation? He felt like salvation was an important matter, something that was either learnt through close teachings of the Torah or through understanding the

61

limitations of the self through the love of Jesus Christ or indeed through comprehending the potential for joy or torture in the afterlife as shown through the Koran. God instructed us through many ways yet somehow Father Connor felt frustrated that their remained so much doubt. His recent answers from the Divine Mechanism, which although clearly designed by theologians and holy individuals was still the closest understanding to the mind of God known. Somehow knowing the mind of God was what began to trouble Father Connor. It was the understanding of likely realities that was proving more problematic to the Father than matters of faith. Faith as an agent alone was as insular as doubt, he realised that. He believed that simply acting on basic tenants from any religion and then depending on the notion of that faith would not necessarily bring salvation. In his heart of hearts he hoped eventually the questions and answers provided by the Divine Mechanism would eventually lead to a greater comprehension of the intentions and laws of God and thus a greater possibility for individuals to be saved. Heaven and Hell whilst widely believed in by members of most known religions including his own were not fully understood. Heaven and Hell existed as polar opposites of a nominal future. Potential destinies for the good and wicked alike. They were as instructive to Father Connor as the day's horoscopes. He didn't have a certain understanding with regards to either possibility or indeed any other potential futures. Heaven and Hell as ideas couldn't influence him when answering questions about faith or religion. Gone were the days when answers to questions about God and the church could be answered with a swift 'obey the church and you'll go to heaven, sin and you'll go to hell'. Matters had certainly progressed from the idea that simply building the right tabernacle, not drinking or gambling or believing in Jesus will get you into Heaven. The afterlife wasn't a tool Father Connor was prepared to readily yield. It was a last resort for dealing with questions. He didn't want to answer anyone on television with righteous rhetoric; it would not help spread his faith to say, 'look if you do this you will have the joys of heaven'. Engagement with God should never have a transactory feel to them; God's judgement whilst finally and unquestionable was also quite individual and fluent. A man who sinned in mind but in action praised the Lord could go to hell. Conventionally bad people certainly had the chance to go to heaven as well. The key aspect that Father Connor wanted to emphasise was that our judgements of righteousness as humans could not even dream to match those of God; even if as priests, we fully ascribed

Jesus with the ability to lift sin, it would not affect the true nature and judgement of God by a jot or tittle. Questioning matters of destiny and faith to a close degree in preparation for this interview had conversely increased his doubt. Doubt was something that had not often troubled Father Connor, or indeed as he once simply was Bryan Connor from Frilby, West County. Even as a young child of no more than five he had a set understanding of God; he felt he knew and understood God even from that age. For him it proved to be a gift; he was able to learn quickly from hymns and prayers, from priests and teachers. He understood that to be a boy of faith, you needed to trust God, to truly believe in his intention and love. He had felt that holy love through many different sources as a boy, and indeed growing up as a young trainee priest in Winchester he began to further understand that love through comprehending multiple sources of scripture. He felt the love from God through the Bible, the Torah, the Koran and the New Testament. He understood that none were perfect about the representation of God; the conflicts of meaning were not born from conflicts within God but problems created by man and his limited comprehension. This only served to increase Father Connor's frustration however; here he was presented with complete and unquestionable answers from scripture, yet somehow he had never felt more doubt about God in his life. He did not need to know the time to understand that the morning was over and he would need to get some lunch. Thankfully he possessed a key to the dining area; he arranged himself a sandwich and heated up a portion of pasta. Eagerly he gobbled the food. He had not had any breakfast such was his eagerness to consult the Divine Mechanism and had grown ravenous throughout the morning. Guiltily he put the plates back and prepared for an afternoon of reading, praying and thinking.

Time went by in a flash. Father Connor deeply engrossed himself with technical details and with key quotations of scripture. He did not want to be humiliated by anyone from the World Government. The questions of the morning were still lingering, yet somehow he felt far more sated having eaten. The food had helped to calm his troubled mind and hungry stomach. The troubling questions with regards to salvation and wrath had begin to ease. An afternoon of study and reading calmed him; the meek probably would inherit the Earth, David will eventually slay Goliath, the prophets of God let alone Elohim himself cannot really be conceived of as a notional identity per se and lastly rest really is possible eventually on the seventh day. The words of prophets like Elijah and Mohammed had eased his worries. The teachings and miracles of Jesus also helped remind him of the ultimately benevolent power of God. He remained aware of the questions that his opponent for the day Mr. Wells would ask, yet somehow he felt relaxed about the upcoming challenge. After all he had dealt with nine different other doubters of his faith; all of them had been dispatched with barely a second glance to any scripture required. Father Connor realised that the doubts he was having before dealing with this chap were roughly the same doubts he had always faced before embarking on an interview. When thinking about it, he realised that those feelings of doubt about God and about salvation and judgement were just the same as they were before facing Judge Curtis, Foreign Minister Dunn and even Deputy World President Clyne. He had dispatched them all with polite but forceful aplomb. Questions came and went about sin, evil and humanity. It was almost an honour to be questioned so vigorously by so many people; his television appearances and his minor fame with regards to the trainee priests at the monastery were gratefully and gracefully received by Father Connor. He had vowed not to be complacent about any of the advantages gained through minor notoriety. It would not be allowed to cloud his judgement; all questions regarding the teachings of the Combined Church of the True God would be treated with the same significance whether he was being asked the question on TV or by youngsters on the street. He felt the need to remain devout for he never hoped to feel truly satisfied on Earth. More than enough religious teachings had shown him that this life was just a step on the pathway of existence. The nature of being went beyond the needs and desires of human understanding he felt. Questions with regards to his faith and indeed his comprehension of God would always be treated significantly by him; never complacently and never dismissively. Even questions like, 'why can't we see God?' would be dealt with in a thoughtful manner. To that he believed that God was not seen by us regularly, as his power was a blessing to humanity rather than an instruction. If God ever wanted to be seen, Father Connor felt that he would be. The doubts about the next day's interview still persisted though. He was feeling confident in the manner of how to approach his accuser as it were, but somehow there was a greater feeling of apprehension this time. Almost as if God was to challenge him through this Mr. Wells.

The morning of the interview arrived. Father Connor dressed himself in the full religious uniform; the shirt, trousers and purple cloak were carefully arranged and looking in the mirror he felt a surge of confidence again. He was a well groomed, presentable face of a major religion and would be ready to answer more questions again. The problems of misrepresentation and bad PR that other religions had been troubled with so significantly over the years hadn't really afflicted the Combined Church; though he would never say it himself, it was widely acknowledged that the positive side of the church shown through interviews such as the ones Father Connor delivered truly enabled their faith to be seen as a positive religious brand. They were not seen as patronising, dangerous, insular or corrupt; the Combined Church really had achieved it's objectives. Really it was about continuously achieving objectives; the faith was run as if it were a major business or successful team. Father Connor felt the need to load up the Divine Mechanism for one last question before going off to the interview. He strolled along the familiar corridors and hallways until arriving by the correct room; again his heart felt the same levels of palpitations it always did before entering the Divine Room. He opened the door and went to switch on the device when suddenly there was a flash of light and plume of smoke emanating from the plug; Father Connor felt a wave of panic. Nothing like this had ever happened to the device before. He had no idea whether or not the machine could be fixed or not. His planned questions suddenly became the least of his worries. Despite being a simple machine, any damage to it seemed to Father Connor like a consecration of the holy, as if someone had urinated by an alter or wiped their backside with a bible. He began to wildly panic; would the other priests blame him for what had happened? Would he be seen as wanting to deliberately vandalise a machine that knew more about God than he did? Questions began flowing through his mind, until something dramatically caught his eye; despite the power being switched to off, there remained a message on the computer screen. It simply said, 'I am waiting Father Connor'

Father Bryan Connor began to gather his thoughts, was this some sort of joke? There was no power being sent to the Divine Mechanism so to all intents and purposes there should be no messages on the screen, yet somehow the machine itself seemed to be conversing with him. His thoughts and fears continued to churn through his mind and guts when he noticed that the machine had added to it's previous question;

'You have a question for me, Father Connor'.

He was seriously panicking now, of course he had a question for the machine, he always had questions for the machine that's why he came down to this room to try and get answers for his numerous questions. He decided to ignore thoughts of doubt or feelings that he was hallucinating or dreaming by directly addressing the machine;

'Why must we know of God through questions'

'Because the truth can only be comprehended one step at a time'

The answer made sense, yet somehow infuriated Father Connor. He realised that the truth was complex and unclear, but that still somehow didn't answer his question. Before he could think of another question the machine once again addressed him pre-emptively;

'You wish to know how mankind can be saved'

The machine was correct, that was indeed his intention. He typed in the question, it replied swiftly;

'Only through death'.

There was the crux of the matter; he knew the question and he knew the answer even before the machine started talking to him directly. He understood about the nature of existence and the invariably afflicted a species such as mankind. Whilst it had significantly be questioned over the years that Jesus Christ directly died for our sins, it was well enough established by most faiths come the establishment of the Combined Church that mankind will not be absolved of his sins whilst existing as a sentient being. Even our nominal beings as abstract expressions of a dormant conscious left us as beings of damnation. We could get no closer to God on Earth than we could get close to the wind or to our dreams. Father Connor realised that he even through a malfunctioning device he would probably get closer to God than most other religious beings. Through questioning the machine and processing the answers, Father Connor had gathered a more cynical and hesitant comprehension of God than even his most ardently critical pseudo-atheist political critics. The divine could only be processed by mankind, and now as was evident to him, a true comprehension of perhaps the fully divine of God himself could only be initiated a malfunctioning computer. Father Connor felt the fear of doubt and guilt bubbling through his brain like steam through a valve. He felt terrified simply by the process of typing, by the fears of asking the wrong questions, thinking the wrong thoughts, contemplating the wrong points. Then another message appeared on the screen.

'Why must you ask me questions?'

That took Father Connor aback, he knew precisely what point was being made. He understood how a relationship with God could never be simply a one way process. He got the feeling that this machine was instructing him that God was not in fact a spreadsheet of data and answers. Ironically it seemed as if a machine was telling him not to simply address God in terms of mechanical needs. It felt to him as if perhaps God himself was instructing him through the computer in how to address him. This thought was soon dispatched though; he knew before looking at the plug that it had already been re-switched to the 'on' position. It may have been like this from the very start of engagement with the Divine Mechanism. The questions may have just been a pre-programmed pre-emption of his likely questions. The seemingly proactive approach of the computer could have been because of an unknown system update or brief malfunction. Typically as ever before the questions he asked of God, didn't give answers but instead more questions. He understood however that part of his approach to answering Mr. Wells would be to convey the argument that God and in turn the Combined Church of the True God could never simply be a 'hotline' service or 'customer complaints line', He understood that to truly know and love God it was important to praise the beauty and potential of existence as opposed to simply questioning the operational difficulties of particular human beings. Whatever had just happened regarding the Divine Mechanism, Father Connor felt well prepared for the interview that afternoon.

'Good afternoon viewers and welcome to this edition of Talk Now. We are lucky to have with us today, Justice Minister for the World Government Mr. Graham Wells'

'Good afternoon to you Ted'

'And representing the Combined Church of the True God, our former guest Father Bryan Connor'

'Thank you greatly for the invitation again Ted'.

'So then, to start today's show, as normal we would like to ask our first guest to offer a question to both the audience and in this case Father Connor'

'Yes, good afternoon ladies and gentlemen, citizens of Zone 1. It is an honour to address you and the viewers today. I have a hot seat at the moment that doubtlessly many of you at home and in the audience would love to have. I possess a chair that enables me to question one of the

67

leading figures of the latest corrupt and problematic religion to afflict the rational minds of sane people and conscious minds across the globe. Given the great opportunity that you have presented me here on Talk Now, I would like to ask Father Connor one question'

'Do proceed Mr. Wells, the audience here and at home are already sending in comments for the 'your discussion' phase of today's show'

'Of course, thank you Ted, I would be joining them if I wasn't here. What I would like to ask Father Connor is why do we need God when we already have machines that answer so many of our needs and problems?'

Father Connor felt his heart drop like a stone, damn how did this guy know what had been bothering him about faith and God. The host intervened after a couple of moments silence

'Take your time Father Connor, we have a long show'

'Yes thank you. You say religion as if it were a dirty word Mr. Wells, Well, I guess the answer would have to be that in a sense you are completely right'

'What? Well yes I guess so'

'Please let me continue. Yes you are indeed right in the sense that we don't need God, any more than we need a robotic cleaner or an android lover'

'I don't get your point Father'

'That's fine, let me elaborate; what I am trying to say is that we don't need God to provide us with what he has already given the world'

'So you are saying we should thank God for android lovers then father?'
The audience began to laugh

'Not really Mr. Wells. What I am saying is that the things we create and establish as meaning something are just that, creations of meaning. We do not strictly need God whilst we have so much of his power available to us'

'So are you agreeing with me then father, if we don't need God then he doesn't need to exist'

'This may be a first ladies and gentlemen of the audience, a man of the Combined Church, Father Connor, seems to be truly stumped by the questions of a man and reason and government'

'Well not quite Ted. I'm afraid to tell you Mr. Wells that much in the same way that if you do not eat anything you will die, or if you don't recharge your android lover then it won't have any power...'
The audience quietly laughed knowingly at that point.

'...subsequently then you won't be able to either live or love'
Mr. Wells interjected strongly at that point.

'So what are you saying then, we need food to live, of course we do'

'Please hear me out, Mr. Wells. What I am saying is that there are certain conditions relating to our existence, and one of them I strongly believe is the presence of God'

'But that would be your belief wouldn't it Father Connor, rather than a matter of truth'

'Yes it is a matter of belief, all of God is a matter of belief. I think you fail to appreciate the two way existence of the nature of God. Without him we would not know truth and existence, yet we cannot depend on him simply for those things. Yes we need food to exist, but we need God to truly come into existence'

'I disagree with you Father Connor, if God is required for truth then why have so many religions failed? If God is required for truth then why do we not hear more from him, why does so much scripture apparently from the mouth of God counteract other examples from different faiths?'

'You speak of truth as if it were genuinely an apple, or perhaps a statistic. Truth as a notion isn't something that is there to be consumed, it is there to be strived for and yearned for. Truth simply isn't notional reality, but rather is a point of existential importance'

'So what you are saying is that despite of everything we have found out regarding evolution, cloning, android technology, genetically modified crops and space travel amongst hundreds of other examples of scientific progress, all that is dependent on the truth of your God'

Once again the audience started to laugh. The host began to interject.

'That is indeed the message we are getting through the Sphere from our viewers at home'

'That is understandable. What I would say though is that what good would any of those measures of scientific progression be if there were no life forms out there to enjoy them? Human beings have existed and thrived before science, as have creatures of other planets as we now know. The love of God allows us to progress in whatever way we want to progress. Science need not conflict with God'

'Yet reason instinctively conflicts with faith'

'Not exactly, human reason inherently conflicts with faith. What I am trying to say is that the questioning essential to human reason is what actually conflicts with the nature and truth of God. Truth to use a clumsy metaphor is not simply the result of a hypothetical equation but is in fact the existence of numbers themselves'

'So you believe that God does not block but enables reason- if that is so, then why must so much of scripture and religion be concerned with providing answers that question what scientist would see as reason?'

'Good question Mr. Wells, but again I would give the argument that the answers of science, reason or faith are all as defunct as one another. The truth we construct is eventually nominal. The chemical element of Iron is no more true than the commandment that though shalt not kill'

'But Iron is there, it can be mined and used and studied. The words of the prophets simply offer questions or often even conflicts between religions'

'I don't disagree Mr. Wells, but again you are missing out on the main point. The truth as it were, isn't simply going to be a progressive notion born of science or even as an idea of the divine through prophets; it is simply the existence of questions'.

'So you are arguing that the only truth is the ability to ask questions?'

'Basically yes. Having studied scripture and the Divine Mechanism we have in Winchester I can only offer the answer that I am of the belief that we are bound by certain commandments in the same way that science is bound by chemical comprehension'

'So you are unable to offer me truth then Father Connor'

'I didn't say that, I am able to offer you the truth that I believe, which as I intend to argue is just as important for yourself as for me or any other member of the audience'

'So you are saying that truth is subjective? We all need oxygen though Father Connor'

'No I disagree, we all need what is established as oxygen, or what I would call air. We all need air in the same way that we all need space or depth or matter. The existence of science doesn't offer an answer as to why copper conducts electricity so well, or why potassium is so combustible'

'But you are not a scientist Father Connor, you are a priest and clearly do not understand that Potassium has a composition of elements that make it so susceptible to reaction'

'True, but again the answers of science are just that, answers from science. They are no more the truth than the teachings of Jesus, or the actions of Abraham'

'Again I disagree Father, we can test potassium a thousand times, a million times indeed and get the same result. The truth is earned and established by intellectual veracity'

'Good point Mr. Wells but I would argue that the truth as you see it by potassium, or as other men of religion have seen it as the consequence of temptation, I would argue is just as nominal as one another. We don't know truth as we don't fully know God'

'That is presuming he exists'

'I think it is safe to presume Mr. Wells that there are elements in the deep reaches of outer space not yet codified by man, in the same way I believe that God exists in a manner beyond the comprehension offered by religious understanding so far. I would also argue that you cannot disprove something that exists, thus you cannot disprove God through science'

'So simply because we cannot disprove God exists then he is real?'

'Precisely. You seem to think that as a man of faith I need to conceive of God as if we were a white haired or brown bearded individual. I see God as something incomprehensible and ultimately unknowable, like those elements in deep outer space. There but ultimately unknown until a later date'

'I believe we have discovered all elements Father Connor'

'That is where we differ Mr. Wells'

NEVER TRUST A TIME TRAVELLER

Adam Jensen could not believe what he was seeing in front of him. It had to be impossible; the man standing before him looked and sounded like his close friend and fellow scientist Paul Evans, but was very clearly and without doubt roughly 20 years older than the man he had been speaking to and working with that morning. Paul Evans still had that familiar grin of an utter maniac.

"Paul what the hell is going on here? I saw you this morning looking like you normally do and now this? If you are playing a practical joke on me you better reveal it soon; come on what is going on here?"

He responded in the same tone he did a minute ago,

"Adam, its exactly like I told you; I've travelled through time to from the year 2137 to expressly visit you" same excited voice, same wild eyes.

"I still don't believe you Paul; come on all the latest Vid Screen stories about time travel, from better scientists than either of us I might add, have shown the whole process to be impossible. The laws of physics as we know them just won't allow matter to travel through time"

"I know that Adam!" He was still looking insane, gabbling in a far more frantic and excited manner than he had ever seen from this admittingly strange man.

"The predictions from where I'm from, where I normally exist as it were, you know what mean…"

"Not really Paul"

"Even the scientists from now, 2137; don't have it projected as being possible until 2254. Yet here I am from the future"

"Ok, Paul, if that really and honestly is you, and you truly are from the future, from the year 2137, then what the hell are you doing visiting me now in the boring and time travel less environment of 2117? I'm guessing you should be aware of the hypothetical dangers of seeing your younger self, which would question why you have decided to come back to the lab that you have unquestionably spent years working in. What the hell is going on?"

"You had better sit down Adam" he calmly began.

So the two of them then discussed in detail what had been happening with Paul Evans in the year 2137. Paul made it clear to Adam that his research into time travel had been a very slow and mainly fruitless process for many years. He had been working on the World Government financed project for 20 years before establishing any sort of breakthrough. Any attempts he had made with micro prototypes to increase their speed beyond inter-stellar levels had proved disastrous. People at the lab were probably more concerned if smoke alarms weren't going off than if they were. It was then that his epiphany came;

"What I realised, having previously tried and failed countless times to speed beyond light levels into a hypothetical future, was that it was obvious that this process may indeed be impossible."

"Great, so that's how you didn't invent time travel; come on tell me the scientific details man"

"As I was saying Adam before being rudely interrupted, was that what wasn't actually impossible however was the method of actually slowing down and thus reversing nano gravitational forces to then try and place a being of matter back through the space time continuum and subsequently shoot it into the nominal past"

"I see, guess.", Adam was beginning to understand the potential physics behind the situation.

"So, as a initial experiment, in the lab I mapped out online the potential progress of one of the standard prototype nanotech devices and fed it into the mainframe technical predictor. The design was programmed with the aim of travelling back in time one week. The results of the machine gave a 95% chance!"

"Wow, to be fair Paul that is the highest projected success rate I have ever heard of" Adam was a least impressed by the spiel coming from Paul if maybe not fully convinced by the veracity of his claims.

"Having projected the potential success of such an experiment, and getting 95%, obviously I decided to try and enact the experiment for real. This was about a week ago on your time frame, it seems so much longer than that"

"Come on, give me more details Paul"

"I initiated the experiment with a robo-dog to try and move a large enough object through space to see if it would also at least be hypothetically possible to send a human back by using such a rudimentary nano-tech device"

"Did it work?"

"I thought it was a disaster initially of course. There was a loud bang and the robo-dog did indeed disappear. I really thought that it's mass was probably too great to be transported by the relative reverse nano forces utilized by the machine"

"So that time was a failure then?"

"Oh no far from it Adam. It was after the bang and looking around to see the object that I realised it was actually some point last week that I had moved an oddly placed robo-dog from the lab into storage"

"You, yourself had actually moved the robo-dog into storage right?"

"Yes indeed looking as inactive and faintly ridiculous as ever".

"So then it bloody worked, congratulations!"

Adam was quietly very impressed. Obviously science and technology had progressed in the apparent 20 years that had passed by where this Paul had come from; but still to achieve the seemingly impossible was a commendable move.

"Adam, there is a reason why I've travelled back to see you in particular"

"What, are you going to tell me some lottery numbers to bet on and then share the wealth? Is that why you look a bit smarter than usual?"

"No Adam" he didn't sound like he was joking, and the initial excitement of explaining his success had evidently given way to the more serious business of why he was seeing him and at this time.

"I can't tell you exactly what I want you to do at this very second, because you will then try and convince the Paul you know of to do otherwise and thus alter the path of the future me. Believe me I know. That is just one outcome I am trying to prevent; as I have said this week has been very long"

He did look far more tired than he normal, he looked more tired than he usually did after a full day of micro-examining particles.

"I obviously can't address myself directly as that will pose far too many questions for both my current and future self. Besides the last thing in the world I need right now is for the Paul of 2117 to think any more about cursed time travel"

Adam had a rough idea of these metaphysical implications as well; if the future Paul on the one hand convinced himself against investigating time travel then he would cease to exist, but evidently there was some problem that the future Paul was having with regards to time travel in the future. Adam was beginning to get seriously confused about the intentions of Paul; both now and in the future.

"Adam, you must not see the past me, i.e. the person who you have always known as Paul, for a number of hours"

"What, why is that 'not current' Paul? Come on you've got to fill me on

74

some more basic details. You are really putting me out on a limb here at the moment".

"Your reactions to the Paul from this time, your time line, will indicate you know something suspicious has happened to you. He will know you will be hiding something. Also don't ask me as to how he knows this, but Paul will also certainly be aware that you, Adam, have seen a future version of me".

He always thought that Paul was occasionally absent minded; this encounter gave him some brief idea as to why.

"Adam, it is absolutely vital that you don't see me, the Paul you know of, at any time today"

"Why today? What's so special about this day? Do you want me to try and get a job at another lab, what do you want me to do at the moment Paul? This is all getting very confusing"

"Look just please follow my instructions carefully Adam; like I said I cannot inform you of the full details. Your scientific and personal mind will be far too keen to relay to myself more details about what is happening. Just trust me when I say your task is very important. I can also tell you that it is also important that you stay in this lab as well. You have a very real significance in the future Adam, that is all I can tell you for now"

Adam was still perplexed; it probably wouldn't help him to know that this Paul had tried to contact future versions of Adam to instruct him in the key methods of trying to protect the very existence of Earth.

Adam asked one more question to Paul;

"Do I have an important role in the future of time travel Paul?"

"if everything goes right Adam, hopefully you or I never will".

Adam Jensen paced up and down the lab. His mind was racing with ideas and problems. Why had Paul chosen him to give this information? If the problem was so vast, why hadn't he contacted someone from the World Government or maybe even the CRN? Great he thought, thanks to this guy I now feel reluctant to leave this laboratory. Thanks a bunch stupid future Paul. Why did a friend of his have to be the key man in time travel and give all these cryptic warnings to him? The problem he knew wouldn't simply just go away, and he understood the importance of currently avoiding Paul. He felt a brief flash of jealousy that it was his close associate and not even really technically superior scientist Paul Evans who had seemingly proven to be the key man in the advancement of time travel

75

for humanity. It would obviously be his name known throughout centuries as a watchword for scientific progress; Adam Jensen would prove to be just another fart in the wind. Maybe a biographical footnote for the great Paul Evans. Then a cynical series of thoughts came into Adam's mind. He briefly thought about what would happen if he moved labs and tried to use the basic scientific methods Paul had recently blabbed on to him about. I mean he was able to remember the basic methods; they were simple really: utilise nano-technology in actually decreasing the speed in which the projected matter would then travel through. If he succeeded, it would be his name known forever. The future Paul that visited he thought wouldn't have any need to travel through time again; evidently it was his mistakes in bringing back something or some singular idea back through time that had caused a whole host of problems. Adam knew he wouldn't make the same mistakes given the chance. It was then that Adam felt the strangest sensation of his life and indeed his brief existence; his entire field of vision went pitch black for a nano-second, after which he felt nothing at all and wasn't even certain he existed any longer. Indeed he no longer did.

The young Adam Jensen witnessed it all. He was only 5 years old and was at nursery school. It was 2107 on planet Earth and life seemed good. He had just had a very good morning; having lots of fun with the various toys in the play room. He had shared the red truck with Johnny, and the teacher had given them both gold stars for really good behaviour. He was just starting to enjoy pre-school. He was making friends and the teacher was a very nice lady, Ms. Collins. He walked back with his big sister home. When he got to the door, there was the fresh smell of baking in the air. He hoped that it was hot cross buns or maybe biscuits. The moment before they could enter the back door however there was a flash of bright, brilliant white light that totally covered the skies. When his eyes finally re-opened young Adam Jensen knew that his worries would be over for eternity.

Moments before the Earth was struck by the most devastating atomic attack ever delivered, originating from nano-bombs delivered by the Venetian Armed forces, Earth Ruling Leader Tracey Stevens was given the news. She had been elected in 2104 and was the leader in charge of the World Government in it's most devastating year 2107; she was fully aware of her destiny following instantly given scientific estimations of the impending attack that would eradicate most life on Earth Zones 1-3 in the brief time between intelligence of the attacks was relayed and the time before getting into an escape pod. It became clear from predicted simulations that life on Earth was mainly going to be wiped out following an apparent series of nuclear strikes from the planet Venus. Further predictive intelligence had proved catastrophically awful as well; Earth would not be able to respond or retaliate for many years. Ruling Leader Stevens was informed that it was expected over half of the world's population would be killed following the upcoming attacks. She and her family had been led just in time to the main escape pod situated by the palatial governing headquarters in Earth Sector One. There was only enough time to gather her family and the main members of the World Government defence committee.

The message of the impending attack was received only thirty minutes before the most devastating strike to ever hit planet Earth was recorded. Indeed it was later known that citizens in Earth Zone 5 who had survived the attack were still left blinded simply by witnessing the resulting bright white light following the nano-atomic attack. It became clear that in 2137 the Venetian intelligence forces had intercepted a prototype version of a time travel mechanism from a leading laboratory in Earth Zone 1. The work of the scientists Paul Evans and Adam Johnson had proved instrumental. Spies working from within the lab had followed the early stages of basic laboratory work exploring the potential physics of time travel. The attack was delivered by a worm hole that was created using the time travelling nano-technology and subsequently nano-atomic devices were devastatingly sent through the created rip in the space time continuum to strike against the defenceless Earth forces.

In the thirty minutes between getting the news of the attack and reaching the escape pod, World Leader Stevens knew that attack was 99.7% inevitable. It was painfully clear that there would not be enough time to intercept the nano-atomic devices. The chances of a successful escape for the pod containing Stevens and her family was set at 70 %. She would plan to return in a years time in order to explain to the surviving members of planet Earth her sorrow and guilt about the unexpected attacks from the Venetians and her determination and duty to fully rebuild planet Earth. There was one small problem with the planned mission however; upon returning to the devastated site of Earth exactly one year later, the craft and it's inhabitants immediately experienced a brief almost imperceptible moment of pure visionary blackness; after which they relatively ceased to exist.

… Adam was just considering the point that Paul had made. 'Hopefully you or I never will', it confused the hell out of him. Wasn't Paul desperate to invent time travel and always be known for it? He was so excited relaying the details about how time travel worked, Adam had just thought it was Paul's hopeful destiny to find out more about the revolutionary procedure and to claim great scientific acclaim for inventing the progress. It was then though that Paul spoke to him again;

"Look Adam it is very important that you help me today. You see it was on this day 4th April 2117 that I first successfully tried the prototype design of utilizing nano techniques to harness gravitational energy. It was this very day that I achieved the first successful experiment involving the robo-dog"

"Today, I thought that was later. wow this is getting very serious"

"Please stay focused Adam; yes it does happen today. I have to try and act through you Adam as obviously I couldn't have just interrupted myself and said 'Hello Paul, it's yourself from the year 2137, please don't try and slow down time using nano-technology because if you do you will succeed n destroying half of the Earth and everyone will die"

Adam was stunned by that last part, "What do you mean Paul? Everyone will die how? What the hell are you going on about?"

Paul looked annoyed with himself "Oh damn, talked too much again. Look here is what you have to do…"

Before he could explain what was necessary however Adam heard the sound of familiar bleeps from the lab, they were indicating the fact that he had just received a message on his Vid-Screen.

"Look do you have to get that message now Adam? I don't have a lot of time to give you this information that you urgently you have to hear"

"Give me a minute damn it Paul, this may be an important message from the lab manager". He callously thought, I've still got my own life to lead now, future Paul thank you very much.

The message was stark, simplistic and shocking. It read…

IGNORE EVANS. DESTROY ALL PROTOTYPES IMMEDIATELY. DESTROY ROBO-DOG URGENT. WORLD GOVERNMENT SECURITY ORDER.

He had obviously never seen a message like it in his life; what was Paul going to request he thought to encourage such a message from World

Government security? If it was them he began to think, damn now he had a dilemma over what to do. The message was very strangely marked as being sent from 2254. All of this seemed impossible he thought.

"Look Adam, I need you to get my prototypes and seal them away at your house indefinitely. People from the World Government and I think spies from another planet in the future are looking to get hold of the time travel prototype device I have stored at my work station. I want you to collect them and look after them at your house. Please, Adam this is urgent"

Adam desperately thought of what to do; should he try and distract Paul so that he could go and destroy the devices like that message had stated, or should he follow Paul's instructions to look after the prototypes? He decided to go with the suspicious message rather than his crazy friend this time.

"Ok Paul I understand. I'm going to take you to the coffee lounge on the second floor, where you can watch some TV and calm down. I will get the prototypes and drive them back to my place where this afternoon I will bury them permanently out of sight" it felt strangely hard to lie to Paul, even in this situation.

"Thank you Adam, you won't regret it; the science can be better used by individuals from the future, not by ourselves, it's simply too dangerous"

"I agree, come on; I'll get you a cappuccino"

Adam went back to the lab and proceeded to destroy all of Paul's available prototypes. He also used Paul's login details to destroy any notes or Sphere messages he had sent pertaining to the issue of time travel. It took him about 2 hours in total, but when the job was fully complete he decided to head back to the coffee lounge. By this point Paul had disappeared. Weeks later both he and Paul jointly decided to hide the one lone, inactive robo-dog that was found in storage. They had still not received another visit from anyone from the future by the time there was another moment of perfect blackness.

DOUBLE VISION

There he was again, walking along past the coffee shop on the corner and beyond the fancy delicatessen. It was unclear where exactly in the city he was going, but still Matt Empson followed the gentleman. It wasn't through choice, it was just that their paths seemed to keep following each other. Every time the man turned left, Matt would be going that way. If the stranger began to increase his pace, then for some reason Matt would still be the same distance behind, still following the same path. It was at the moment they passed the bar on East Street corner that the stranger turned around to look at Matt Empson, suddenly revealing an exact doppelgänger of him that he would wake up sweating, very occasionally screaming.

His job was a very boring affair. Unfortunately the 22nd Century had not seen the end to factory work. Matt's role, indeed his intensely important position was to programme the robots that worked on the factory line, and to switch around any faulty mechanisms with temporary replacements. The factory made high grade light bulbs. The machine did 90% of the work so Matt and the few remaining human workers at the site spent most of their time at work incredibly bored. Sometimes there would be small accidents, finished glass bulbs would break, some robots would briefly malfunction when switched to different parts of the assembly line but for the most part the work was seamless. Matt had lived on his own for the last ten years; there were no women who worked in the factory.

Matt returned back to his apartment following a particularly mundane shift. Nothing had gone wrong and the standard delivery targets had been made. He should have been delighted he guessed. Things seemed so empty and lonely in his existence. The guys at work were good to go for the occasional drink with, but he didn't fully fit in. They talked a lot about their partners and other women they slept with. His attempts to join in the conversation always seemed to fall flat and his point was nearly always ignored. Sure, none of them were particularly hostile to him but they weren't friendly either. Matt guessed he wasn't one of the most successful workers to have ever found employment at Eastman's Lighting Company, as often they would seem to be laughing about things he did at work. Ted Pressley, one of the nicer guys of the group told him the truth once.

"It ain't really you, Matt, honest it's not"

"So why do they keep laughing at me during work Ted? I don't do too much wrong, I switch the robots around as effectively as any of those other guys, better than some, I want to know why they find my work so funny"

"I don't really want to tell you, as it might freak you out Matt"

"Come on you can't just say that and not tell me what it means", he was growing impatient.

"Ok, well, to be honest Matt, you look exactly like one guy who used to work here. It's like you're his total double, seriously. This guy, I can't remember his name but he left the company in a big huff about 2 years ago. He said, get this, I can't stand dealing with damn robots any longer. It was just so random"

"So, they remember this guy who left in a strange way. Nothing to do with me?"

"Nah, you just look like him Empson, that's all".

Matt was satisfied by the guy's answers. It was just a coincidence that placed him alongside this strange guy and his unusual exit. He guessed he would find that type of thing funny too. The shift ended without too many incidents.

There was the man again. He was walking along a beach this time. Strolling right by the water, letting the incoming sea gently wash over his shoes and trouser legs like an over friendly dog. Matt was following him again as usual, He was walking by the sea as well but kept trying to avoid the incoming water in case it damaged his shoes. The man had no idea anyone was following him it seemed. Matt wanted to enjoy the view of he sea and the vista out over the ocean beyond it, yet his focus remained on this man as he followed him. Families were enjoying the sun and the sea together. Couples were walking hand in hand, whilst older people were using mobility hover scooters to travel along with comfort by the ocean. The man turned around and actually started walking towards Matt. He wanted with all his physical might to turn the other way and just totally avoid even looking at this man any longer. Yet somehow it wasn't possible and the man kept getting nearer. He then, for the first time Matt had known about vividly, spoke to Matt. He simply said,

"My name is Stephen. You know me". It was when he finished that sentence that Matt leaped out of his bed, in a sweaty stunned state. Just a dream he thought, must get to bed, get some more sleep before the next shift at work. The meeting he had on the beach with Stephen however kept rushing through his brain that night, preventing him getting any additional sleep.

Mike spoke to him during the lunch break at work for the first time in month or maybe it was actually the first ever time since Matt had been there,
"Hey, Matt right? Thought Id just give you the heads up to say you're doing all right don't worry too much. You aren't going to get the sack, more than can be said for some of the others", he started laughing and pointing to some of the other guys on the other side of the room, who were laughing and swearing back to him.
"Ted put you up to this didn't he?" Matt enquired.
"Yeah, sure he did. Just wanted to let you know too that it's not you we're laughing at man. If you had been here when that guy left, you'd find it funny too. He was hopeless I'm telling you; just couldn't handle switching the robots around for some reason. Wasn't their fault, he had hardly any malfunctions to deal with. That guy was just strange"
Matt began thinking about how to ask what was really on his mind. He gave it a go.
"Did this guy do anything really stupid before leaving here? I mean, I just have the feeling that this guy killed himself"
"Whoa, we aren't that heartless Empson. No, the guy didn't shoot himself or anything whilst working here at least. Like I said, he just left in a huff, going on at the robots".
"Sure, good to know. Thanks for telling me Stephen, I mean Mike"
"Whatever man".
The shift ended again with little further incident. Ted nodded over to him a couple of times, and he could definitely hear some of the guys laughing when a couple of the robots he was working on malfunctioned briefly. Matt ignored it and got on with the job of completing another day.

The man was for once sitting down. He was drinking a coffee outside of the little café on the corner. Matt approached him slowly, walking along the other side of the road, his stroll slowing down when he came up to the place. Of course he found his movement controlled by some other force leading him back to the man. He took a seat next to him and sat down for a minute or two. He didn't want to look across and see the disturbing replica of him again. Especially not since he had spoken to Ted at work, had that really happened though? He felt fairly sure that at least that was true, maybe he somehow knew that the guys were laughing because of a guy who looked like him, which explained maybe the mild trauma he was having leading to seeing this direct mirror image of him. Remembering somehow these details he tried to train his sleeping conscious mind into making the visual representation of him speak to this man. It seemed to work to some extent.

"Stephen, who are you?"

"Who are you Matt?"

Somehow that answer seemed predictable. He tried to get his mind to place them both in the factory instead of the café, to try and prompt this man to speak more about what was going on.

"Stephen this is where you used to work, correct?"

"This is where you work Matt"

"Come on Stephen, or whoever you are, you can't just keep invading my dreams and then telling me no answers. I mean who are you?"

"That is now unimportant Mr. Empson".

Trying to control a conversation with a figment of his working imagination whilst in a semi-conscious state was getting frustrating. Then the image of the man spoke again,

"You should hand yourself into the police Matt"

"What, why? I'm not going to do that, I'm an innocent man damn it! You tell me nothing about who you are then ask me that? Are you a relative of mine? A clone? A machine? Come on, you've got to tell me something"

"Matt, I am you"

When he had said that Matt woke up with a sore head and a confused mind. His mouth was dry. Had there been some reason to wipe his memory? Had he seen something terrible at the factory? Was he maybe on some advanced witness protection scheme having been given a whole new mind? None of the possible answers seemed right. It seemed like the guys were actually laughing at him anymore. He wished he didn't look like so much like that last guy; it seemed unfair on him to get a bunch of shit for some other guy.

By the time he got to the factory, he could see a police hover car waiting by the entrance. Oh great what's this, he thought. Probably drug use by some of the guys he thought. They were in a fairly rough part of the city and loads of people were addicted to the designer drug Pulse and it's coarser version P3. Maybe they were here to ask about that last guy he thought. When Matt went through the entrance and clocked in, the police officer was busy chatting to the manager of the factory and indicated for him to come over to speak to them. A stone seemed to drop in Matt's stomach, like a car being dropped from a magnetic crane at a scrap yard. The officer, D.I. Thompson gave the motion for his boss Mr. Anderson to leave them to it.

"What is it officer?"

"You are the man we have been looking for Mr. Empson"

"What is it officer? I've done nothing illegal since working here"

"Nothing since?"

"Damn, you know what I mean"

"I don't think so Mr. Empson"

"It's because I look like that last chap who worked here isn't it? I'm getting blamed for his mistakes again aren't I? Typical"

"Calm down please Mr. Empson. You will not get blamed for his mistakes. The man in question incidentally is Stephen Best. He is wanted for severe damage of commercial property at the factory and for murder"

"What you've got to be kidding me?"

"No, not at all. We want to know from you Mr. Empson about the contact you have had with this man. We know he has rang the number of your apartment 32 times in the last three months and from those calls you have spent over 4 hours speaking to the gentleman in question. So what I want to know Mr. Empson is when are you going to start telling us what we want to hear?"

"Officer please, I have had no phone calls with Stephen Best, whoever he is! Absolutely none. Someone must have framed me, or maybe this Stephen Best has falsified calls with me to create an alibi. It's because I look like him right? This guy has obviously tried to involve me in his life to provide some sort of alibi and to take the blame for his crimes"

"Interesting points Mr. Empson, but all the same we want to know, everything, you know about this wanted criminal. I stress again that you are not under suspicion directly for his crimes, but we know you have some connection. You need to tell us Mr. Empson as we believe that he is actually a terrorist"

"A terrorist? What? You think I'm helping a terrorist"

"No again, we haven't said that. You are keeping something from us and unless you want to spend some time in the cells thinking about Mr. Best in more detail I would talk to me now"

"Ok officer, I'll tell you literally all I know about him. He used to work here at the factory, but apparently left after getting frustrated with the robots. I guess that is where he was guilty of the criminal damage. Anyway, I know I look exactly like him, but I swear to you I've never spoken to this man in my life"

"Go on, Mr. Empson"

"Right, well the other thing about him, this is going to sound insane, but he keeps appearing in my dreams".

"I see Mr. Empson, interesting. Could you elaborate?"

"I'll try officer. This man, I didn't know his name for most of the time I was dreaming, was nearly always walking somewhere and I was following him"

"Where was he walking? This is quite important Mr. Empson"

"I don't know officer I apologise. Where we were varied sometimes, I mean I've seen him walking down the high street, by the beach, at the factory""

"Populated places, I think I see the situation"

"What is it officer?"

"These are likely targets Mr. Empson. I'll get to the point, we have reason to believe that you are being sent information in the form of dreams. We believe he is part of a Venetian terrorist network. We have some spies infiltrated within their ranks, especially within those cells that are located on Earth"

"Right, I don't know which dream is right though? I mean what do they all really mean? I have no clue how this information can help you officer"

"That's ok, Mr. Empson. You can head back to the shop floor now, we will get round to interviewing some of your colleagues after lunch. We will contact you again sometime in the very near future"

"Ok, thanks Officer".

They had gotten to Matt Empson just in time. A bomb disposal unit was sent to the block of flats where Matt lived and thankfully diffused it before any explosion took place. Matt was relieved to know he was safe, but totally horrified when the ordeal was all over. As it had turned out Stephen Best was indeed a terrorist for the Venetian Resistance Movement. He was one of the band of Venetian ex service men who were totally dissatisfied with the terms of peace offered after the Earth-Venus War. He didn't think it right that Venus was banned from having it's own offensive craft force. He felt that the planet had been unjustly neutered and that the people on Earth should pay. Far more Venetians than humans had died and indeed Stephen Best aka Delta-Primus Xenon, wanted revenge. During his career of crime he had tried but failed to sabotage the facilities at Eastman's, which were being used to develop a unique bright light weapons sight that would eventually surpass the rudimentary lasers still being used. He had also assassinated the Venus diplomat in the Second City a week before he had programmed Matt Empson to detonate in the middle of the most popular area of the place, City-Central. As it had turned out Matt Empson was initially an android, programmed and built to work for the Eastman's Lighting Company. He was a very new model, the very latest possible. The others didn't know he was an android, neither did Matt obviously. He was a newer model that was programmed with personalities and in his case dreams. Security forces had found that the cerebral methods of the latest B6 Androids could be conducive for receiving terrorist vid calls. The calls received by Matt were indeed from Stephen Best, the known Venetian terrorist, but they were very much a one way endeavour. Matt Empson had been built to look like Best; it would prove tempting for Best to use a bomb built in his own image on Earth to destroy public areas. Officer Thompson didn't know that Matt Empson was an android; he didn't think there was any need for an android scanner for the visit to the factory. It was Intelligence that gave the word to the bomb disposal unit following the testimony of Matt to D.I. Thompson. Once they had realised his total likeness to Stephen best wasn't a coincidence and that the 'dreams' he was having could be correlated alongside the phone calls received, they were able to deduce that he was probably an android and a likely agent to be manipulated in a terrorist attack.

Ted felt a wave of sadness upon hearing that Matt Empson had been sent away to be deactivated and destroyed. Mike and the other lads still laughed about the situation, not knowing how close they had been to a major terrorist and a major exploding device.

REVENGE OF THE ANDROID

Kenneth Winston felt himself grow hugely tense; his hands were shaking, his feet were tapping out a random rhythm and his heart mechanism was pounding like a pneumatic sonic drill. If he could have cried he would have done. It had taken a few weeks of searching around in the right places for the right answers but eventually Kenneth had found the location of the deposed THX-23I model androids. They were the same make as him. The pile of bodies located on this junk yard floating tanker looked to all intents and purposes like a huge pile of dead human bodies. Kenneth scanned the pile, desperately hoping to see some form of animation, a glimmer of robotic life. He searched painfully and found nothing but silence and mechanical death. He was well into the dangerous, unexplored areas of zone-4, so the only other people to see these android bodies like this would be the robot captain of the ship, and the people originally responsible for killing these androids. The sight was traumatizing even for a mechanized being. He wouldn't be able to forget the sight of hundreds of bodies piled on top of each other like a grotesquely fallen stack of human playing cards. When the container ship returned to the deserted port of Earth Zone 4 Kenneth returned to his hover car and took the quiet route back to his place in the main city of Zone 4, New Brook. He knew how lucky he had been to avoid the mecha-pysche scans that had taken place all throughout the zone. Whilst office buildings and residential blocks were being fully searched for the now illegal THX-23I models, Kenneth had paid very good money to smuggle himself over the border into Zone 5. It had cost him four moths worth of points from his job, but considering he would now be deactivated and dead to the world without paying, it was money well spent. This type of thing had happened before. If anything went wrong with an android, the model guilty would then be deactivated as a collective. Of course the individual found guilty would be publicly shut down and destroyed first; often on television to show that 'justice' was being done. Many crimes had always been blamed on androids. They were a convenient scapegoat to hide man's errors. A faulty machine covered the cracks in the system overall. Androids also had no legal rights themselves either. Despite the efforts of some high profile human rights lawyers, no court in any of the world zones had ratified the treaty denoting that sophisticated conscious loaded androids could have legal representation. If a crime happened involving an android and a human in confrontation i.e. following a minor car crash then the android would always get blamed for the incident and normally shut down for their crimes. Androids had been a huge blessing to factory owners and to cheap bosses. They were more focused than most humans, they were more adaptable than most humans and they certainly had fewer rights than humans. There was no need to offer an android a contract of any kind as most of them would be happy to work for whatever money was offered to them. They possessed humility as well, due to the manufacturers designing them wanted to minimise pride levels and to ensure a high level of work focus. The problem was however that they had to be designed to have a layer of conscious freedom. They couldn't just be programmed to do one job in the same manner as a robot; they cost more than standardized mechanical devices and their real value was in the androids ability to achieve multiple tasks. They were an asset to any company and the latest models were often bought just to stay updated with new technology. They were an advancement of technology, it soon lead to android wives and pets being developed with newer models being integrated with advanced organic ageing methods. Kenneth however was from the earlier design of non-ageing standard android technology; adaptable in programmability and able to socially integrate as a being. His model, the THX-23I was very good at its job, whatever that happened to be at the time it was being programmed. Shut down times weren't required unlike earlier THX models either and the chances of mechanical failure were incredibly low. The only occasional problem that occurred was a brief, literally seconds long momentary loss of eye sight. It wasn't a major flaw but was still sufficient to see billions of points continuing to be invested in android technology. Driving back to his flat, Kenneth couldn't help seeing those lifeless eyes looking out. Dead to the world, they looked to all intents and purposes like embalmed corpses waiting to be put on display. The huge pile of bodies was redolent of cattle pyres or a broken human pyramid. Kenneth had to swerve out of the way of a couple of lorries on his way back, who promptly honked their horns, offering him rude gestures in return for his bad driving. Zone 5 was a real industrial wasteland. The kind of place where nuclear waste or even in this case malfunctioning androids could be sent to be forgotten or ignored. Seeing the pile of bodies engendered an unusual emotion for an android. Kenneth felt a strong and undeniable drive to get revenge on those who did this to his fellow androids.

Work passed by as normal; the humans and newer androids at the factory were oblivious to his plans. His boss was a disinterested man, who left the officious business to those who were above him. The man thankfully didn't even know that there was a zone wide order to get rid of a certain make of android anyway. There was a real lack of professional concern from certain factory bosses. Those companies that got cushy World Government contracts to make things that would be needed by councils like light strips or robot joints. They never needed to look for business, as it was always there through the government contracts. The place Kenneth worked at did indeed make light strips for a governmental contract and as such the work wasn't always punishing. Clocking in was relatively slack, especially by the human workers and there were absolutely no production targets throughout the day. If the main conveyor belt shut down at 09:01 and turned back on at 16:59 none of the workers or floor managers would give a damn. It was unknown by the guys at work that Kenneth was an android, but he still felt some of the people at work viewed him suspiciously. They would smile at him awkwardly occasionally; even if they thought he was an android as they seemed to be honourable guys anyway. He felt really pretty sure that they wouldn't have turned him in to the police scanners even if he had been at the factory during their visit. As a menial worker albeit part robot he was lucky to have a basic bond with some of the more simple minded guys. They didn't have any objections to known android workers anyway, with jobs like this it was just as cheap to hire Zone 4 industrial workers as it was to buy and maintain an android. Zone 4 was a pretty good place to live; there was plenty of work going albeit most of it in factories making products for either the government or for robots and the main cities were interesting enough to pass the time in. Zone 4 didn't really offer any answers to life's great questions however. There wasn't going to be any clues found here as to why his make of android was eliminated wide-scale. Kenneth realised that to get any answers and to get any revenge on the people who ordered this robot pogrom he realised he would have to travel to Zone 1 and more specifically First City.

Kenneth decided the only way he could even enter Zone 1 without suspicion was to travel by public transport. He booked a ticket from the public bus centre in New Brook city centre and began to prepare himself for the journey. Before leaving though Kenneth wanted to get a basic idea of where he could get his answers from. At his flat whilst relaxing with a cold beer he decided to plug into the Sphere from his vid-screen. To begin with he typed in his android model to check for results. <THX-23I generated a massive 1.4million results. He decided to try and narrow down that search for something more productive and helpful. This time he tried the search <THX-23I<DESTROYED. This set of results looked far more promising. Kenneth tried the first news story of this batch which was entitled '30 Deaths on the job: Android model THX-23I blamed'. The story sounded familiar. There had been a large accident at a hover craft plant in Zone 4, 30 human casualties were the result of a very serious malfunction on the manufacturing belt. There had been an error made from the very first stage of production at the factory, which was man-operated and the entire line had been covered in hugely flammable material due to a leak in fluid from the passing body of the vehicle. Most of the line had been covered with the flammable lubricating fluid GS by the time a spark was created from an android worker who was welding parts of the vehicle together at the end of the line. It was totally unfair that he was given the blame due to the accident beginning at the start of the conveyor belt, but still it lead to yet another wide-scale decommissioning. The article obviously took an aggressive, suspicious stance towards the android involved; 'The individual THX-23I model android involved, sometimes known as Phil Jones was deemed responsible for the serious blaze that killed thirty human workers at the hover car plant in District 12. He has since been destroyed. We here at the Daily Report are keen, like so many thousands of our followers to see the more archaic androids banned from working alongside humans. They provide a volatile risk and are prone to making serious mistakes, such as causing the accident here at this plant'. Kenneth looked away from the screen in disgust, "a volatile risk?" Were they kidding? The place he was working at none of the androids he knew of had been responsible for any of the malfunctions at the plant, let alone any accidents. Even the article on the Sphere made it clear that the accident began at the start of the conveyor belt. Typically they didn't say if an android was not involved with a problem as opposed to being the cause of disaster. Kenneth returned back to the search results on the Sphere; he clicked on to another news story, this time entitled 'Androids suspected over shop murders', the story this time focused on the deaths of three people at a supermarket in Zone 2. The victims were found shot precisely in the middle of their foreheads; this time androids were automatically

assumed to be guilty due to the accuracy of the shots. That was sufficient evidence it seemed to begin persecuting androids. The victims were somewhat suspiciously all government workers positioned in a trade division. The motives given for the deaths were the usual insultingly predictable nonsense, 'Android malfunctions lead to the murders of three innocent men'. It infuriated Kenneth, yes perfectly accurate malfunctioning androids. He felt angry at the pre-supposed suspicion of androids, the allowance given to quickly close crimes that were otherwise suspicious. Other than the rare human rights lawyer or even rarer compassionate individuals, the legal damnation and physical destruction of supposedly guilty androids was an accepted procedure. The destruction of a guilty android barely made a news story; it was a presupposed assumption of their guilty verdict. The levels of crimes supposedly related to androids were hugely suspicious. The very design of most androids was to be programmed by the companies or governmental divisions that required them. So unless they were being programmed for murder they shouldn't be able to even know how to kill. Kenneth put that nascent thought to the back of his mind; he didn't believe that the THX-23I androids were involved at all in any of these incidents. He didn't believe that they had been programmed for murder; the THX-23I had been given emotional qualities to ensure working compatibility with humans. They were also a relatively early model for prototype emotional relationship partners. Kenneth didn't want to conceive of himself as literally a potential killing machine. Thankfully the stories he had read so far did not damn the androids involved. He still hadn't found any links though between the THX-23I accidents and the decision to destroy the entire line. Two accidents wouldn't be enough to stop the production of a full batch of androids; more was necessary to precipitate that horrific sight of lifeless dead humanoid machines he witnessed in Zone 4. The next story thankfully shed some life on the situation, "Zone 4 Senator declares war on THX-23I androids, 'no more needless deaths Andrews declares'". Senator Dean Andrews, the name was familiar. The article revealed why, 'Senator Andrews has clearly begun his preparations to run for the role of World President in next years elections. His anti-android stance has proved hugely popular with the Zone 4 farm workers and numerous lower income workers across all zones that are fearful of cheaper wage androids taking over their jobs long-term. Android manufacturers have tried to reassure the general public that androids can never take the long term jobs of the human worker, but Senator Andrew's stance has still resonated. Articles across the Sphere have started to assess the relative qualities of Andrew's compared to his leading rivals, which include the current World President, Phillip De Souza. De Souza has not risen to the bait regarding the android situation and has remained non-committed to the issue, that's possibly due to his bid to have androids recognized as potential democratic voters. Andrew's looks likely to push the issue during next months World President debate". Kenneth had gathered as much evidence as he needed from the news story. He would somehow have to confront and hunt down this powerful man; he needed to get justice for his fellow model androids so recently destroyed under orders.

He felt awkward getting on to the bus; despite the chances of him being apprehended as a vigilante android being next to zero, if that, Kenneth still felt that familiar sensation of shaking limbs and a sweaty back. He took a seat next to the back row and tried to get comfortable in the small cramped space. He had taken his portable vid-screen and decided to keep searching for information on the Sphere whilst took the long journey to Zone 1. He decided to investigate more into the details of Senator Dean Andrews; the first result given after the search was his personal site. It turns out he had studied at Oxford, England in Global Business and Politics and had passed his MBA at Harvard. Brief mention was also made of his extra-curricular pursuits of captaining the rowing team, captaining the debating team and operating somewhat ironically as student president at Harvard. His grades were briefly mentioned as averaging 82%; there was little doubt that Dean Andrews was a brilliant student and one of those frustratingly multi-talented people who are stamped with the mark of success from their early years. Having seen the official version, Kenneth opted to search for more personal accounts of the man who would be World President. Unfortunately Kenneth had to give up after reading about ten pages from fellow alumni; each and every one seemed to offer more glowing praise than the last. "Great guy and committed trainer", "frankly the best student president Harvard has seen for the last fifty years", "If he isn't a millionaire within five years, then I'll eat my degree", "great lover and man". The praise was almost as glittering as his CV; no dirt could be found in connection with his university years at least. This man must have some skeletons Kenneth thought, I want to know why he has suddenly become so committed to destroying androids. He decided to search more directly, opting to search the terms, Dean Andrews Android. The first site proved to be the most interesting by a long-way. It at least offered a basic explanation to what was happening, "Senator jilted by wife for a non-human lover!" The story proved to be spurious, yet it had clearly generated a lot of responses. It questioned his personal credentials as a lover, questioned the motives of his wife and questioned, would you sleep with an android? Kenneth couldn't help but laugh; androids were just replications of humans who were better at working he thought. Many women will have probably unwittingly slept with an android, and as the article seemed to conclude many women would willingly do so anyway. Surely a Senator wouldn't issue the destruction of hundreds of androids due to one affair? The explanation didn't seem enough on it's own. He went back to the list of results. One story interested him on the second page; it ran 'Android Politician plans eventual run for World President'. Kenneth checked over his shoulder to check no one was looking over his shoulder from the back row as they chugged along. He opened the story, 'Gavin McKenzie, a THX-20 android, who has been stationed within the council offices of New Brook city has shocked the world of city politics and possibly beyond New Brook by deciding to publicly run for Senator in the next election. McKenzie didn't stop there however. In an explosive statement he pledged this move to be Senator was simply a stepping stone on the way to eventually becoming the first ever android to hold the office of World President'. Kenneth couldn't believe what he had just read, there was an android in his zone, zone 4 that was open with his identity and had huge plans within politics? It seemed so crazy, but the story gave him a real burst of optimism briefly. Maybe true integration will be possible in the future, where androids no longer have to hide themselves or be treated just as extensions of an assembly line. Kenneth then paused suddenly struck by a depressing point; it was hugely likely that without politics Gavin McKenzie would just be another mechanical body on the scrapheap. Hundreds at least like him would have been discontinued and destroyed without ever being known. Senator Andrews must have intervened he thought following the public prominence of an android. He must have reacted angrily to a mecha-human like Gavin McKenzie planning to enter politics so soon after his wife had an intimate affair with one. His male pride must have been hurt leading to such an over-reaction. Kenneth had at least established a potential motive for the destruction of his line of androids and he certainly had a suspect. It would be enough for him to try and confront the senator at the hotel where he was due to be giving a conference later in the week. Senator Andrew's site probably gave more away of himself than he intended to.

Kenneth checked into the hotel himself. He scanned the corridors and the bar to try and catch a glimpse of Andrews. His vision was bought back to the receptionist following a polite cough. The lady at the desk undoubtedly had some attractive qualities to her. She clearly made an effort to keep her hair well dyed and looked to have a fabulous physique under her staff shirt.
"Do you have any specific requirements Mr. Winston?"
Kenneth felt mildly distracted thinking briefly about her body.
"None at all thank you" he tried to regain a semblance of composure.
"Would you perhaps like a wake up call" the lady politely inquired.
"Yes, that would be nice actually. 7.00am please"
"Certainly. Enjoy your stay at The Grosvenor Mr. Winston"
"Thank you, I hope to".
He picked up his bag and began to head for the lift. Just as the doors were shutting, Kenneth managed to catch a glimpse of a man who distinctly seemed to match the profile photo of Senator Andrews on his Sphere site. Damn! It probably was him; then would have been a good time to speak to him before he became surrounded by press and doubtlessly his political team. Kenneth knew that the process of speaking to someone famous and in power would require either a great deal of luck or some very serious jumping through hoops. He got the feeling that a lucky occasion had just walked by him and past the lift he was now stuck in. The room he was staying in looked impressively compact somehow. Everything was there; TV, shower, toilet, coffee machine, even a spare Vid-Screen on hand. He decided not to leave sensitive searches so coarsely on show however. He certainly didn't need any random hotel worker knowing that he was interested in the personal details of a fellow guest, let alone a famous one. This was going to be very difficult he thought. He had to be sure that Senator Andrews was guilty of the android killing order before assassinating the man himself. He wanted to be sure before engaging in such drastic action. Getting to talk to the man evidently seemed an impossible task, so Kenneth decided to consult his portable Vid-Screen in order find out some more details. Business interests seemed a good place to continue researching into the Senator. He typed in SENATOR

ANDREWS<BUSINESS<OWNERSHIP into the Sphere but got no matching results. He decided to try again with more vague search requirements to increase the matching field results. He tried this time SENATOR<DEAN ANDREWS<OWNERSHIP and received three results. The first immediately perked his interest; the story read 'Prime-Tech industries seeks new World Government contract'; the story from the business section made for very damning reading. As it transpired the company that Senator Andrews has a 10% share in was looking to develop a brand new variant of android with the intention of replacing the currently active models, which meant of course the THX-23I. Kenneth read on, "Prime-Tech are looking to revolutionise the automated workers sector, by introducing a new model to the market. The planned ST-40 model, thought to be named after the current Senator and his age, is apparently ready to roll off the production line. Indeed as the Senator himself claims, 'This new model which I am proud to name is going to be the forerunner in terms of android technology. Who knows this model may actually eventually be President!" Indeed the model is already being hailed by leading android scientists as the future. Frank Bennett from Harvard Tech has already hailed the new design as "seamless, perfect design. Human intuition could actually be advanced with the intellectual capabilities of this new ST-40 model. It offers seamless and advanced mechanical operation. Previous models like the THX and earlier designs obviously worked brilliantly when being shown how to use various machinery and have been programmed with social interaction skills, but these newer models are even more organic and responsive. They have been designed by the top minds to replace the top minds. I guess the success of androids like Gavin McKenzie has removed that previous fear that existed' Yeah right Kenneth thought, the destruction of the THX-23I was a deliberate move to show the dominance that organic human beings like Senator Andrews still presumably had. This article did change things somewhat though; Senator Andrews obviously had a vested interest in promoting the ST-40, and obviously the severe malfunction of a fellow modern android would help to depict literally his line of androids as the premier model. Kenneth wouldn't have been surprised if Andrews had ordered the entire range to look like him. That provided one explanation as to why his range had been destroyed, but somehow 10% of a technology firm and a spurious rumour about an android affair didn't seem to be sufficient. Kenneth decided to cut to the chase when searching on the Vid-Screen, he

tried SENATOR DEAN ANDREWS<THX-23I. There was only one search result; Kenneth opened it. It read 'Senator Andrews blames THX-23I models for economic problems'. There was no need to read the story from then on; Andrews had multiple motives and infinite potential to order the destruction. Kenneth would have to try and confront him about it. He wanted to hear it from the man himself moments before Kenneth would assassinate the man who killed so many of his fellow models. He would get his revenge for the destruction and long-term oppression of androids.

Following a night of recharging, Kenneth went down and sat in the hotel lobby, reading a newspaper in a suspicious manner; involuntarily lowering the large pages from time to time, whilst searching for any member of Senator Andrew's team. There had been no luck all morning and when he was just about to ask for his fourth refill of coffee a man came scrambling out of the lift. He was talking franticly on his mobile; Kenneth tried to tune in using his hearing mode, all he could catch where snippets of the conversation like 'later this morning…sure he's ready', 'forget about the other domestic rival, that guy has got some serious skeletons… Andrew's knows about 'em all', '…sure that android guy could be a problem, being treated very seriously'. This guy was at least delivering the goods; Senator Andrew's was definitely concerned about the potential android politician Gavin McKenzie. The other details seemed pretty standard, no major clues as to why his line of fellow androids had been so ruthlessly destroyed. Kenneth then decided to make a reckless decision; he would confront this aide of the Andrews team by posing initially as a journalist. Dumping the paper and glugging the coffee he decided to confront this guy about Senator Dean Andrews and his previous decisions on androids and the smearing of his fellow THX-23I models with regards to the assembly line fire and the head shot murders. Again Kenneth felt his mechanical heart offering it's familiarly tense palpitations, like some sort of manically hopping creature was living in there. He quickly went over in his pre-active mind about what to say, how to put across his key points regarding the senator. Should he be direct, telling this man that people were beginning to get on his case regarding the THX-23I destruction- not that many individuals other than fellow androids would share his determined concern. He thought about asking directly, 'do you know that your boss, the senator is responsible for killing hundreds of individuals?' He composed himself and began to head towards the guy who was still on his mobile. By the time he crossed the lobby to meet him however the man was greeted by a group of about five others; presumably more people involved in the Senator Andrew's team. His confrontation with the Andrew's team would have to wait. Kenneth decided to abandon the more direct approach and decided to see what change he could get out of the hotel receptionist. He went to the bored looking girl sitting at the desk and tried to remember any way he could be charming;

'Hi, could you tell me anything about the Senator Andrew's party?'

'No.'

The more direct approach had obviously proved flawed. Kenneth tried plan B.

'Hey you do know who Senator Andrew's is don't you?'

'Sure, he's some famous guy who wants to be the World President, and isn't too far away from it from what I hear'

'So you do know then. What can you tell me about his stay here miss?'

'Look, sir, I'm going to have to call security if you keep continuing with these strange questions. We noticed you with your newspaper waiting round the lobby all morning. We guessed it was about Senator Andrews'

'So you've got me rumbled'

'Looks like it Mr. Winston'

'Could you tell me anything for 100 points?'

'Right for that amount sir I guess I could tell you he and his party are on the third floor'. Kenneth began to get excited

'And for another hundred points miss?'

'Well for another hundred I guess I could tell you... come close over the desk Mr. Winston' He shamelessly felt himself get excited.

'Room 237'.

'That is very good of you, thanks I'll leave you to your day' she had delivered the jackpot! Kenneth decided he would have to be direct about the whole situation and wait outside Room 237 and then try and attack Senator Andrews with his electric pistol. He knew the plan wasn't flawless but Kenneth knew that decisive action was going to be necessary.

Kenneth was half awake when the loud bang physically shook him out of his partly disconnected state. Instantly he knew it had to be something with happening on the third floor. There was a loud knock on his door, and the lady from the downstairs desk was telling him to get outside immediately with the other guests of the hotel. There was a lot of debris and thick heavy smoke filled the air as if the oxygen within had been painted black. Despite his servers ensuring panic was the dominant mode of thought, Kenneth was still able to access other cerebral areas. He knew that Senator Andrews had to be the target; the big question would be as to whether the protagonists were successful. Eventually all of the available hotel guests were ushered into the registry position designed for such emergencies. Kenneth glanced at a list held by one of the receptionists from the ground floor. None of the names from level 3 had been ticked and it was evident that a couple of early morning cleaning androids had not yet been discovered. It wasn't their deaths or disappearances that would make the news however. The possible death of leading World President candidate and currently successful Senator would prove huge news around the world. Before he knew it, journalists and TV crews began to arrive in their hover vans and hover cars to follow up on leads that were posted on the Sphere. The local rumour that there had been a terrorist attack on The Grosvenor soon spread as well; the area outside the now clearly damaged and still aflame hotel was generating serious interest. People knew that something big was happening, as did Kenneth. He immediately knew somehow, whether through programmed intuition or not, that his intention to confront Senator Andrew's in the First City in Zone 1 was going to prove a sad failure. Sure the end result had happened; Senator Dean Andrews was well and truly dead, literally blown apart whist he slept, but still his death felt unsatisfactory. As if he had committed suicide prior to being sent on to death row. Kenneth had seen his intentions change, yet somehow be fulfilled. He sadly composed himself, spoke to the police who he should have feared seeing and then received his compensation from the people at the hotel. The receptionist he had spoken to was looking teary-eyed, she looked like she was feeling some real guilt. He wanted to go across to her and inform her that her disclosures to him were not the reason behind this attack on the hotel and on Senator Andrews. But he didn't. He didn't really feel compelled to do so despite the brief emotional reminder from his programmed conscious. Indeed the only dominant emotion really was disappointment. He wanted an android, he wanted himself to punish the man who was guilty of mindlessly killing so many fellow individuals. Kenneth resigned himself again to the trip back to Zone 4. He took the subway to the main bus depot and waited for the 10:15 service back to his zone. Glancing through the main newspaper of First City, Kenneth came upon an article that immediately made him leap up from his seat to return back to the city centre.

'Andrews in proposed THX-23I android apology sensation! Senator Andrews planned to give sensational pledge allowing all models of conscious androids voting rights'- the story seemed totally unbelievable to him. How could it be the case that the man who had ordered the destruction of his species of androids now developed his own android conscious as it were? Kenneth read on, 'it was with great regret that I recently ordered the destruction of the THX-23I individual responsible for the New Brook assembly fire. The subsequent order of the destruction of the line has saddened me. It was not an easy decision to terminate a conscious beings believe me. It was a decision made under certain political pressure. I want to offer a brand of progressive politics, and I do not intend for just the line of most up to date androids, indeed launched by Prime-Tech, to have voting rights. I have learnt humility with regards to the intelligence potential of even the most humble android. I intend for Zone 4 to be the pioneering zone with regards to android rights. I intend for this to be the key area for my push for the World President position'. The article was upsetting for many reasons. Kenneth felt his emotional chip fully whirring actively recognising the potential brilliance of the now dead Senator. The man clearly wasn't the main driving force behind the destruction of the THX-23I. Even worse he was actually an activist regarding android rights! He wanted to liberate rather than destroy most of the androids out there; he wanted to be a hero to them as opposed to a leading force of their destruction. There must have been another figure responsible for the termination of his line of android. The point made about 'political pressure' was now the focus of Kenneth's mind. Evidently the senator had managed to convey before dying that he wasn't the main force behind the destruction of the THX-23I line. The matter must have been viewed by some as having a potentially politically explosive impact. Someone was behind the destruction of the THX-23I and didn't want the world to know. Someone or some group perhaps were evidently anti-android and wanted to minimise the awareness of themselves. Maybe it really was someone within the Senator's camp who wanted Zone 4 to remain a fully human zone? Perhaps it was his leading rival and actual android Gavin McKenzie who ordered the attack to remain the leading representative of android rights in the long-term run up to the World President elections? There was the chance it was a decision made from the

World President's office who may have had different private views as opposed to personal ones. There was always the chance of course that it was national terrorists, who focused on representatives of the six world zones. Political representatives of the less wealthy zones were always more vulnerable to these types of terrorist attacks. It actually began to sadden Kenneth to think that this man he was intending to assassinate in person has since turned out to be a representative of android rights and has been cruelly killed by others. The thought of Senator Andrews death moved very quickly in Kenneth's mechanical conscious from being an operational necessity to an incidental tragedy. Whatever had caused the attack and death of Senator Andrews, Kenneth knew that he had to stay within the First City until he found out who was responsible for his death. This time it was to get revenge for the Senator himself.

Someone out there was against the interests of androids Kenneth thought from his new hotel room in a down town area of the city. Somebody or some group out there obviously reacted badly to the plans of Senator Dean Andrews to give androids voting rights. But obviously that story only came out after the violent attack at the hotel, so surely it must have been an insider from within the Senators camp? Focus he thought, national terrorists would be unconcerned with android plans if they were behind the attack. Kenneth racked his brain and fully focused on his analytical capabilities; other individuals and groups may have wanted Andrews dead before this pro-android approach but still the announcement of full android rights especially after the evidently reluctant wide decommissioning of the THX-23I series proved potentially explosive political material. If Andrews didn't want the THX destruction, then who did? Someone in his operational team maybe, or another future rival like Gavin McKenzie? Who knows it may have been another android who blamed the Senator for the mass destruction of the THX-23I series prior to the announcement after the attack. That eventuality seemed unlikely considering Kenneth had to smuggle himself off to Zone 5 in order to prevent being detected and subsequently destroyed. A THX android will have needed to be as lucky and ingenious as Kenneth was. So who was to blame then for killing the Senator of Zone 4 and future World President contender Mr. Dean Andrews? Kenneth assembled his thoughts and began to consider some conclusions; the person or people involved probably had some objections to his android stance. He decided to look again on his Vid-Screen to try and scan the Sphere for particular information regarding the potential assassins of Senator Andrews. To begin with he tried SENATOR ANDREWS< DEATH< SUSPECTS which generated twenty five clear results; Kenneth scanned down the list, most unfortunately were just repeating the same story from a set press release, indeed most of them used exactly the same words apparently. There was one potentially interesting story from a citizen journalist, but his story was just another basic regurgitation of events. None of these stories offered any potential insight at all. The general conclusion offered by the leading stories was that Senator Andrews death was probably the result of terrorists from Zone 4, looking to strike again at leading officials who were compromising 'national identities'. That idea seemed too simple for Kenneth; despite having the brain of a relative simple android even he was suspicious of the extent that 'national terrorists' were blamed. They were automatically blamed basically in the cases where androids couldn't be. Kenneth tried another search, SENATOR ANDREWS< HOTEL< ANDROID; this time he was given just three complete results. The first one was definitely the most interesting, 'Exclusive: opposition existed within the Andrews camp with regards to android rights'. Kenneth read on; 'After the initial shock and emotion following the unfortunate and violent death of Senator Andrews reports are now coming to us here at Zonal News that individual backers and groups within the Zone 4 operational committee were against the android rights plans. The verdict has been established as 'terrorist attack' but we here are hearing some questions regarding the real definition of what happened. There is some suggestion that a powerful anti-android group based here in Zone 2 have been focusing their opposition against pro-android groups. There were rumours floating about that Senator candidate and of course leading android Gavin McKenzie was to be targeted and killed. We here at Zonal News do not consider the case regarding Senator Andrews to be closed and will continue to ask certain questions'. Kenneth was intrigued by the article; was the death of the Senator really down to a powerful anti-android group? He felt embarrassed for underestimating the levels of opposition that existed regarding androids and there rights. He decided to search the Sphere himself for information on these anti-android people. He tried the search ANDROID< OPPOSITION< SENATOR ANDREWS which yielded just one result that was a perfunctory account of how Andrews initially had some opposition to androids dating back to the assembly line fire and the rumours of an android affair. Kenneth tried again, with more specific requirements HOTEL< TERRORISM< SENATOR ANDREWS this time leading to twenty results. Kenneth scanned the list and opted for an article entitled 'Terrorist attack on Andrews; motives questioned'; the piece was from a source that regularly questioned the verdicts given against 'national terrorists'. It began 'The recent death of Senator Andrews in the First City has been blamed conventionally on a national terrorist source despite no evidence to indicate this. Indeed we here at the Daily Update have uncovered some shocking information; a leading member of the Andrews team has been uncovered as an anti-android protester who was captured by scanners seven years ago waving placards in Zone 4 against the influx of android workers. The Andrews team have disagreed with our source and claim that all of their members are vetted regarding attitudes to conscious beings and asked for their team to be given privacy following the death of their political and personal representative. We here at The Update however remain sceptical. We feel that the individual concerned, a Mr. Tim Graves, is a real suspect in the death of Senator Andrews. We suspect and smell corruption in the air, and Tim Graves truly stinks at the moment'. Kenneth didn't know what to make of the report; he tried to use his full analytical capability which unfortunately kept drawing a blank. He couldn't process effectively whether or not this Tim Graves was involved or indeed capable of ordering the death of one of the most powerful men in the world. One way or another he had to know why the THX-23I series was really destroyed, and now also why the recently android compassionate Senator Andrews had been killed.

When he woke up, Kenneth noticed a news story that was on going. Gavin McKenzie was now due to give a statement and a series of media interviews regarding the sad death of Senator Andrews. Despite being half asleep Kenneth quickly poured himself a strong coffee and switched on his attentive mental capabilities. Something told him this was going to be an important announcement. He listened to the news presenters going on about the planned events;

'Later on today hopeful Senator and indeed now leading candidate Gavin McKenzie is due to give a speech showing his regret for the violent death of the last ruling Senator of Zone 4, Dean Andrews'.

'Indeed Janet, this is a personal as well as professional occasion for hopeful Senator McKenzie, We are just hearing that the death has been officially blamed by the Zone 4 governmental office on national terrorists.

This is an exclusive, Mike'

'Indeed, thanks for the update, Janet. It is clear then that national terrorists have been on unnamed national terrorists, again attacking the established structure of World Government. Back to the potential new Senator though Janet; it's clear that Mr. McKenzie will have shared a common interest with the eventual latter day interests of Senator Andrews regarding the future voting rights of operational androids'

'True Mike, as most residents of Zone 4 and the more aware political followers know here, Gavin McKenzie is actually the first full android to actually run for political office'

'Yes indeed, it seems clear from the reporters we have heard from in Zone 4 that Mr. McKenzie is indeed shocked following the sudden death of a fellow politician that shared his interests'

'We'll be back after these brief messages'.

After seeing the news something struck Kenneth like a speeding train. Mentally he pieced together what had happened recently he knew the real reason behind the ordered destruction of the THX-231 models of androids, and almost certainly the death of Senator Dean Andrews. Deciding upon a quick course of action, Kenneth utilised his interface abilities to gain a journalist pass from the Daily Update, it would be needed in order to infiltrate the upcoming McKenzie conference and to get some real answers. There was something suspicious about the connections of events; the only detail that didn't seem to make sense was the anti-android member of McKenzie's team. Was he the man responsible for the attack on the Andrews team at The Grosvenor Hotel? Having printed off his pass from the Vid-Screen Kenneth went out of his hotel and hauled down a cab.

'Where to friend?'

'The Civic Conference Centre please, quickly'

'Sure thing, you there to see that android guy?'

'Yeah something like that'

Kenneth then realised there was another detail he urgently had to check.

'Do you get a Vid-Screen reception in here at all?'

'Yeah sure, it's automatic. Will just add a few points to your bill, ok?'

'No problem, put it on the bill that's fine'

He went immediately online to the Sphere, and tried the terms GAVIN MCKENZIE< HISTORY< RUMOUR; instinct somehow was guiding his search and the first result delivered what he hoped. The first result was a story from a local newspaper in Zone the story was simply entitled 'Gavin

McKenzie: Man or Machine?', The article went on to question the presumed assumption that Gavin McKenzie was a THX-20 model android. This article would be explosive stuff to McKenzie if he saw it. Not all news from the Sphere made it to the major television stations for lots of reasons. Not all of them about the validity of the story. There were more than a few accounts on the Sphere from smaller print and online news outlets that would never make it onto the major papers or the leading news stations. A reporter from this local Zone 4 paper though had even managed to pysche-scan McKenzie during an interview he was giving. Indeed the results had shown him to be all human. If voters knew McKenzie had lied about his identity it would be very hard to regain the trust of potential android voters and harder still to get human support back on side. The story though clearly hadn't made it yet to the larger papers for some reason. Since getting to the First City he hadn't had time to check back on the news from Zone 4; this piece was only found due to his search for rumours rather than news stories. Sure it may be false and the reported pysche-scan could just be standard over exaggeration from certain journalists, but still somehow the details were highly suspicious. Having seen this article though in the context of recent well known news events it all started to make sense for Kenneth. Gavin McKenzie never was an android; he was just a politician who had elaborated a plan to be seen as the leading candidate for future android voters. He was obviously mentally set on being the only android representative, hence the assassination of the briefly pro-android Senator of Zone 4 Dean Andrews. He had obviously given the order to destroy the THX-23I models in order to reassure certain humans still suspicious of androids that the renegade models were being discontinued and destroyed. Kenneth knew then that McKenzie intended to manage the android voters of all of the zones; the 23I models were clearly deemed a necessary sacrifice to create and maintain the good democratic name of potential android voters. With the numbers of androids in Zone 4, McKenzie was almost certain to be elected the next Senator, without them he was just another liar in politics. He would get the android votes provided of course that all of the androids in the zone plus a few sympathising humans were on his side. He didn't want to chance an already popular Senator increasing his support to include franchised androids. Obviously the news story doubting his android heritage that had been released locally in Zone 4 needed to be hidden and silenced by a larger story. Kenneth was keen to check and recheck the details; indeed the rumour story actually dated from before the ordered destruction of the THX-23I models. Evidently McKenzie didn't want any questions regarding his android heritage so engineered the destruction of the newer THX-23I models. He then must have arranged for the pro-android Senator Andrews to be assassinated. He allowed the 23I models to take the fall for the previously common hatred of androids. Androids had to be seen as literally a new breed of voter; not a group of malfunctioning machines. This guy Tim Graves was obviously a fall guy to redirect any lingering android mistrust; they wanted to show anti-android sentiment as being irrational. McKenzie obviously wanted to carefully manage the android voters out there; he wanted them to feel respected and understood. Kenneth was going to make sure however that Gavin McKenzie regretted not destroying every individual android within his particular entire range. He would make McKenzie regret sacrificing so many conscious minds for his own sense of mecha-moral worth.

The taxi eventually pulled up outside the Civic Conference Centre. The driver charged the usual exorbitant fee before flying off to rip off more individuals. Kenneth went through his plan using his analytical mental capacities. He already had a pass to enter in to the press conference, but the real difficulty was going to be how to confront the prospective Senator. Obviously McKenzie would have a security team to manage the crowd and to prevent anyone from getting too close. Kenneth had managed to smuggle in his electronic pistol from detectors so far. He had used his brief time in Zone 5 wisely; amongst the waste tankers and hidden bodies lay a complex black market for guns and drugs. Whatever was hard to get in Zone 4, was cheap and easy to find in Zone 5. No-one would really want to live in Zone 5, but a hell of a lot of individuals would pay it a quick visit to get a supply of pulse; or in Kenneth's case an electronic pistol that was carbon-coated in a plastic poly-fibre preventing it from being detected by any conventional scanners. In the more cosmopolitan and up to date Zone 1, Androids were no longer allowed to be immediately stopped if scanned ; so frankly even if he had been carrying a normal electric pistol the Police would have needed to find it before searching him. No scanners outside the Civic Conference Centre had seen anything suspicious about Kenneth so he was allowed through to the main hall. The guys maintaining the scanners almost certainly assumed, if they even noticed, that this individual was just another supporter of that android politician. Gavin

McKenzie was starting to get some real press coverage even in Zone 1; the death of Senator Andrew's had given his campaign to takeover as Zone 4 as Senator a sense of real poignancy. A real false sense of poignancy, Kenneth thought. Somehow he was experiencing a synthetic sense of injustice; since finding out about the case regarding the destruction of the THX-23I models, he had experienced a real emotional attachment to finding out who did it and why. He was really engaged with his full mental capacity with regards to finding those responsible. It wasn't just a passing electric instruction; it was almost a compulsion. Kenneth ignored the reasons behind his motivations and redirected his mental energy to the act of publicly showing up Gavin McKenzie. He wanted the watching world to know that Mr. McKenzie was as human as they come and was the real reason behind the removal of the THX-23I series and the murder of Senator Andrews.

'I stand before you today, saddened and humbled. The death of such a fine human individual has emotionally affected me in ways I'm sure the designer of my model would be surprised at. Senator Dean Andrews was more than just a great man; he was a decent man, a kind man and a man who wanted to stand for the rights of every conscious being. Senator Andrews was a man who was committed to expanding the electorate beyond it's known bounds; no longer would it just be human beings that would determine the course of so many conscious beings, indeed such as myself. Following on from his bold course of action proposed on the eve of the Senator's tragic death; I would like to just reassure the general public, which now includes both humans and all conscious androids and say that his work will never be forgotten'. At this point the audience went crazy; there was manic clapping and whooping from the audience. People were clearly charmed by this chap as well, he knew what to say and when. Kenneth knew he would have to be patient even after McKenzie had finished speaking; there would be a lot of other questions from the huddled mass of journalists. Everyone there seemed desperate to know Gavin McKenzie's emotional account regarding the death of Senator Andrews. 'I plan to run straight away for Senator of Zone 4, to continue on with the great vision and work of Senator Andrews and to ensure his momentum is not lost. His tragic death will not simply be treated as another terrorist atrocity; indeed it will be used to lay a foundation ensuring the enduring rights of humans and androids alike'.

The crowd increased their volume of applause from before; there seemed to be a real emotional attachment engendered between McKenzie and the audience.

'Now I ask the assembled journalists if they have any questions?' Kenneth immediately raised his hand and enquired loudly 'Mr McKenzie over here' unfortunately though the first question went to a journalist on the front row who was probably planted.

'Mr. McKenzie, should another accident happen along the lines of the New Brook assembly line fire, will you order the destruction of the android involved?'

'Good question Graham; well this is one area I differ with the previous Senator. Androids involved in work place accidents will be given the same tribunal rights as any human workers involved in similar events. No longer will lines of androids be destroyed on a whim to get revenge or to sway public sentiment'

Kenneth silently seethed whilst the crowd started clapping loudly at his response, some of those present were even calling out; he heard things like 'about time' and 'damn right' ring out from around the hall.

'Any other questions?' the murdering liar enquired.

Kenneth saw his chance,

'Just one Mr. McKenzie'

'Right, what is that sir?'

'It's about the destruction of the THX-23I line of androids'

'Indeed, a terrible decision made from a past era I might add. It was decided by a prior Senator in a different era'

'Only it wasn't ordered by Senator Andrews was it Mr. McKenzie. He had already considered pro-android options following a meeting with the World President hadn't he?'

'Could we leave any more questions with this chap for outside?' McKenzie sounded and looked desperate; his goons were now beginning to close in and around on Kenneth.

'No, you can answer my questions here and now. It wasn't Senator Andrews who ordered the destruction of the THX-23I line was it, it was you'

'And what's that to you then'

'I'm the last THX android left pal', with that Kenneth pulled out his hidden electric pistol and shot the evidently human stomach of Gavin McKenzie. There was a sudden spray of blood from the exit wounds and a brief cry of agony. Having seen McKenzie fall to the ground shot and in agony, Kenneth used his electric pistol as a warning to force his way through the crowd to finally confront McKenzie.

'You, you're a THX-23I model aren't you? I ordered you all dead, no-one should have known about that'

'Guess what pal, your good friend, prior to blowing him up at least, Senator Andrews programmed me with the instructions to be safe from the mecha-pysche scans and gave me some clues regarding your guilt'

'What, that's impossible!'

'No it's not, McKenzie. I found out about you when the word 'rumour' was activated in my cerebral cortex when searching your name on the Sphere. Senator Andrews had programmed in the appropriate prompts into my operational mechanism when I was in Zone 5 getting the electric pistol that will kill you Mr. McKenzie'

'What, so Andrews knew about me?'

'Yes. He didn't expect or plan for such a violent attack on where he was staying, but he knew he needed contingency plans regarding you.'

'He knew I was planning to go for the android votes?'

'Yes of course. He didn't want to do anything prior to suspicious activity from you. Unfortunately for Senator Andrews, the suspicious events that prompted me hunting you down began with the good Senators death'

'I wanted to kill him before he could announce his pro-android plans'

'Indeed, unfortunately for you Mr. McKenzie your planning days are over'. Kenneth levelled the pistol at McKenzie's forehead, slap bang in the middle but then stopped. The goons supposedly protecting McKenzie hadn't intervened whilst Kenneth was hunched over him. They were waiting for him to finish to then grab him.

'I'm not going to kill you McKenzie. Death is going to be the making of Senator Dean Andrews, for you it will be the conclusion of failure'

Before the goons came in to grab Kenneth the Zone 1 First City down town police division intervened. They burst in, calling out to the few remaining crowd members to get the hell out of the way.

'Mr, Winston you are under arrest for the attempted murder of Mr. Gavin McKenzie'

McKenzie interjected, 'Good stuff, throw away the key; damn android'

'You are under arrest too Mr. McKenzie for the murder of Senator Dean Andrews. We have found out about your human origins through the portable Vid-Screen of Mr. Winston. We started scanning from it following the highly suspicious search results that began following the attack at The Grosvenor Hotel by one Kenneth Winston. Gentlemen you are both required to enter the police hover van parked outside. You both have the right to remain silent and to see an attorney; after that your rights with us end'

The two of them were bundled outside and placed in separate sections of the police hover van. Kenneth knew he had done the right thing by Senator Andrews; his devotion to androids had been very real. He wanted to give conscious beings genuine rights. McKenzie was a profiteer looking to exploit the good work of Senator Andrews with the blood of the THX-23I android line. The world soon found out via the flood of news crews resulting from the shots fired by Kenneth that Gavin McKenzie wasn't really an android and was just an opportunistic human looking to gain popularity from a newly franchised group. Thanks to the work of Senator Andrews before his death and the android intuition of Kenneth, the crimes of Gavin McKenzie would duly be punished.

HOME SWEET VENUS

At 5.30pm Andrew Lomas went out of the main exit at Thompson-Henderson Estate Agents and headed back to his flat. It had been a long day of answering calls, guiding people around medium priced city apartments and updating the Sphere site for the company. Work had felt stressful despite Andrew Lomas switching his mental capacities onto fast play from standard. Andrew had a large secret that was hard for him to keep; he was actually a Venetian ex-spy who was left to rot on Earth following the end of the Earth-Venus War in which millions of lives had been lost. As a result of Earth winning the war, treaties with the V-government had seen the Venetians pledge not to engage in any other communication with Earth. The deal was made at diplomatic gunpoint; Andrew Lomas was still working as a spy in the Second City of Earth Zone 1 by the time the treaty was signed. If he had come out as a spy for the Venetian Government there is a very high chance he would have been executed. He knew that the V-Government would have made no efforts to get him back to Venus if it would have compromised the fragile basis of an agreement with Earth. So here he was stuck on Earth, trying to blend in like a normal human citizen whilst using his hybrid brain to gain some advantages in what remained of his life. Lomas was a spy without orders or objectives; since being abandoned by the Venetian government he had also begun to find himself contemptible towards the beings from is own planet. He felt aggrieved that his home planet reacted fairly quickly to the probes that were sent from Earth to Venus. Yes the probes were armed but that didn't necessarily infer that Earth would be a hostile force. Unfortunately Earth did of course turn out to be a greedy, hostile force. Lomas felt contempt for both Earth and Venus really. Bitterness had began to course through his veins like an angry stream of vitriolic bile. The beings on Venus were disloyal, pliable and contemptuous whilst the humans he had dealt with on Earth were all brain-dead half wits who could scarcely live their own pathetically dismal lives let alone try and control the more challenging environment of Venus. He guessed though that he hated humans more; it was after all this tediously primitive and stupid species that had initiated a war with the advanced intellects of the Venetians. In 200 years time he felt Venus would win any wars between them, but for now their technology simply did not match the advances of Earth. Humans were a lucky species because of the advanced treatment

111

God had given them ; not to mention the focus given to that base species of imbeciles by the fallen angel Lucifer. That guy had proven to be a blessing and a curse for Earth. Due to his presence more advanced species had taken it on themselves to offer methods for countering the now disgraced adversary of God. His presence however had almost meant that any lingering disagreements with God now had a head figure to turn to. By the time of the Venetian War though Lucifer was just a secret memory really; known by those who foolishly turned to him, basically forgotten however by those that didn't. Venetians had watched the ongoings regarding Lucifer, but decided not to intervene. They could have however. Despite not having the military technology to succeed against Earth, they could have used their advanced telepathic minds to try and counter the direction of the fallen angel upon his arrival in the chaos that exists outside of the realm of God. The Venetians however decided to leave Earth to it's own devices, something Andrew Lomas had bet they were regretting now. Venus had intelligent life you see well before God had given Adam the chance to advance humanity in an Earthly paradise. There was some tension as to whether he could succeed on his own, which of course he didn't. His and Eve's failure to obey the laws of God probably set the wheels of Earth's destruction into gear. It just wouldn't be the Venetians and certainly not Andrew Lomas that achieved this ultimate destruction.

Andrew Lomas was particularly contemptible of the people he worked with. They just seemed to represent the desperate, almost yearning idiocy of humanity. The people he worked with seemed keen to be more stupid and trivial by the day. Simple instructions he often gave, just for a few photocopies or for a couple of calls to set up some details with a client, almost always resulted in an abject failure to achieve the task. Alongside being lazy the people he worked with were clearly desperately dissatisfied for some reason. Not one single person he worked with seemed to have any sense of being complete as an individual. The people despite being blessed with families, over cars, luxury holidays, expensive clothes and so on, just could not exist as satisfied beings. It was clear that they didn't possess a want for things; a want for knowledge, a want for family, a want of a new car. No indeed these people subsumed on need; they needed a husband, they needed a family, they needed a new hover car, they needed a new dress. Frankly he was disgusted, the people living on Earth in 2094 needed nothing. None of these things that the people he worked with were obsessed by were needed. There was no need for food for anyone in Zone 1, there was no real need for a hover car in zone 1 and there was no need for luxury holidays on zone 1. No, these people were just trying desperately to find any sort of brief solace in their lives to displace the continued emptiness that came from ultimately being a species tarred with damnation. They had never really gotten over the problems of Adam, Andrew thought. Everyone still wanted forbidden fruit to feast upon. Everybody still ignored the bounty of the Earth, to be tempted by a low life fallen deity. The morals of most human beings were very weak. Paradise had been an option but the ease in which the species were tempted was embarrassing. The Venetian species had a far closer understanding of God. Religion wasn't something that was desperately contorted by rival interests more interested in power than redemption; no religion on Venus meant the understanding of profound meaning. It meant the holistic comprehension of the limits of animal identity as it were. The Venetians, for the most part, gave themselves to God. There had been ancient tests and laws given to the earliest Venetians of course, they however had passed these tests. Andrew Lomas however was still stuck on a planet damned with existential failure. Everywhere he turned he felt disgust towards a species that had rejected God for the wares of a nobody. Lucifer would have been laughed off Venus frankly.

Andrew Lomas found integration and success on Earth relatively easy however. His contempt for the species was often curtailed by fellow workers or other people massaging his ego. Sure he had the latest social technique module given him prior to his now defunct mission and he was also fortunate to have high end charm uploaded to him. As a result dealing with people for the most part was easy. He obviously hid his frustration at the failure to manage simple tasks. His thought patterns were also premium downloads which meant there was absolutely no way for the thought scanners to read his mind and note he was actually a Venetian. Nobody he had met gave any clue that they doubted his veracity as a human. The charm certainly helped; most of the time he just told people what they wanted to hear. It had certainly heed him sell a hell of a lot of homes in the Second City generating some more than sizeable commissions. Thankfully though it was now only one more week before the Nexus ran Interspace Transporters actually began to send regular routes to Astera on Venus. He would actually be able to go home! He would be back with people who were concerned beyond the boundaries of himself; back with minds that looked beyond animal limitations, back on a planet that hadn't rejected God. He was even looking forward to dealing again with the elders who were in charge of his mission. Despite their disdain for his younger mind and their disregard for his differing views on subjects like interplanetary travel, they would still provide more interesting conversations than those offered by the monkey-brained selfish cretins that were so popular on Earth. That was all true, until Andrew Lomas met Zera.

Just one week before he had planned to leave Earth for Astera, Andrew met the most beautiful creature he had ever seen. She delayed, temporarily at least, his urge to return back to Venus. She had totally stunned and silenced him for once by telling him directly that she knew his secret. She was fully aware that he was a Venetian but still wanted to be with him. The measures given to have him integrate on Earth had obviously worked! He had known he wanted to spend time with this woman when their eyes met at the District 10 Nexus Store. There was just something different and captivating about her. It didn't take long to find out what that was; she was actually a more advanced human replica sent from Venus than he was. Andrew was absolutely certain about that. His anatomy was functionally human and for a brief while he enjoyed the pretence of just being an average man having sexual relations with a woman, albeit one who was really an advanced Venetian spy. Oh he was absolutely certain she was a Venetian, probably an android, but despite this he decided he would spend the week with her before offering her the chance to join him on the journey back to Venus

The week they spent together had meant long walks holding hands in the park, fine meals enjoyed together at top restaurants like the Vitoria and late night talks about life and the stars. Both of them had good jobs and he had decided to fully wine and dine this beautiful woman before at least one of them went back to Venus. He thanked God that he had least bought his own ticket already. Whilst she had refused to join him in travelling back to Venus, she still wanted to be with him. She begged for him to cancel the booking and to live with her at her apartment. Evidently she was totally besotted by the more advanced love and attention offered by a fully functioning Venetian man. Ultimately though Andrew wasn't remotely interested by the idea of staying on Earth. He wanted to get back to life on

Venus and hopefully a decent job in domestic intelligence with the Venetian Army. He wasn't remotely interested in staying at all; until Zera told him that she was pregnant.

"But that's impossible!" he cried out
"What do you mean? The test was decisive Andrew, they are 100% accurate you know
"Yes I do know that babe. Oh wow, wow this just seems so unlikely."
"You don't always turn on the anti-fertility scanners by the bed Andy"
She was right of course, and he was an idiot.
"Ok Zee for the sake of you and the baby I'll stay here on Earth".
The damn designers from the Venetian army had obviously made him too damn human he thought. As well as being an incredibly charming guy, he was now evidently a fully functioning baby making machine.

Watching the news stories of people travelling to Venus for the first time made him hugely depressed. All of these people had far less right than him to go to Venus. Hopefully though at least some of these primates should learn about culture and compassion he thought. It didn't seem a hugely likely occurrence frankly. He settled himself down on the sofa and finished off his latest beer. His mind had become foggy with thoughts about how he would have to be an adult human father now. He would have responsibilities and tasks; he would have to learn how to love humans and actually raise one to be loved and successful. All of these points began to depress him.

It was later that afternoon however that Zera revealed the full truth to him.
"Sit down Andrew please, there is something you need to know"
He began to feel quite distressed; was it an abortion she wanted? Was she leaving him? Did she want him to quit his job for the sake of the baby?
"Look I'm not pregnant"
"Ha! I knew you were too perfect to actually be a human woman" he blurted out.
"Yes about that" she replied
"What is it?"
"I really am a human, and I know you're not"
"Sure I know you know that. Hang on, what do you mean you're human you just seemed so…"

"Be quiet please Andrew. I work for the Network, for the Infiltration Division"

Andrew Lomas felt like someone had dropped an anvil on the top of his very being.

"I'm sorry Mr. Lomas but there is no way you can be allowed to return back to Venus" she calmly stated

"What so you mean I'm stuck on Earth?"

"I'm sorry Andrew".

Those were the last words she said to him before calmly shooting him in the stomach with an electric pistol. He died instantly.

Zera packed her bags and called the Network to assemble a clear up team. She thought that Andrew Lomas was the last of the remaining Venetian spies left alive on Earth. There was going to be a lot more thought scans made by the check out desk of individuals heading to Astera though. If any more were found she would be called on again.

WORD TO THE WISE

"And though his life had become but a dream, Conrad knew that from then on he would finally know Happiness". 'The Life and Times of an Interplanetary Man' 2153 © Epsilon Nano-Publishing Inc. Jack O'Neill had finally put words of his latest, and undoubtedly greatest, novel into the personal MC Vid-Screen. It was a sprawling romantic epic, chronicling the life of an intergalactic land owner in the year 2085. The protagonist, Conrad, and his attempts to find the ideal wife whist being called up for World War Four was almost certain to gain keen literary praise. He was satisfied with the work and overjoyed by the impeding 500,000points into his account. He knew his work was popular and despite his latest departure in terms of literary tone he felt it would still sell. Jack O'Neill was a fairly handsome and successful man. He stood at 5"11, and had light brown hair, that stood full and resplendent on the top of his angular, intelligent looking head. He had large blue eyes, and more than a certain way with the ladies. He was able to show this charm both in his personality and sometimes through his writing. People who met him, remembered him. Indeed, every Low and Mid School pupil knew about Jack O'Neill and his popular series of teen-horror books. Ha, more is the pity he briefly thought. He aspired to write more, to stretch beyond the boundaries that damn series of pseudo-horror books offered. The money had been great, it gave him a fine house and it almost certainly contributed to the more than reasonably attractive girl and subsequent wife he married. Life felt good, especially since he had switched publishers. They actually wanted him to write more expansive work! Even though the market they were after was almost certainly smaller, they still felt it was sufficient to pay him up to 500,000points. 'If the market was there great, if not I'm buying boat' he absently thought. Jack had got into writing early. Almost before graduation from his Primary University Course, at London Harvard publishers were bidding thousands for his proposed novels. He had a great upbringing with an encouraging set of well off parents and a very early desire to read from the vast library of centuries old books they had available at his mansion home. He had engulfed many great works, Dickens he devoured, Hemingway he hard-lined, Jackson (probably the pre-eminent post millennium writer) he loved more than the others combined. Jackson was probably the main reason he came to believe in the Prime Lord and attend worship with the Central Religious Network. The Network as it was mainly known, had come to represent the definitive, unified organization for the worship, study and comprehension of what people pre the CRN would know as God, but what had since came to seen as the Prime Lord. The leaders of the CRN had proved quite brilliant at re-integrating aspects of different religions and their seemingly incompatible comprehensions of God. In other words the Network had become the site of all religions. There were to be no more crusades, no more fundamentalist terrorists, definitely no more religion inspired blocks of nations warring with one another. The history of the Network was undoubtedly complex, but as a general scholar in life Jack had understood that one of the basic aims of the CRN was to really unify those religions that had different comprehensions of God, who of course came to be known as the Prime Lord. The Prime Lord they asserted was Allah, he was Buddha, he was Jesus, briefly they even ascertained that John Paul II was God. All religions were appealed to, even those faiths deemed to be non-Holy. The Mormons were praised for their attempts to see God in the strangest of places. The Scientologists were given praise by seeing God as a pseudo-Alien presence on Earth, that is indeed what the Prime Lord had came to be seen as on Earth. Yes they were a fantastic organization and he was happily paid member. Enough History Lessons! He thought. It was a morning for celebrations, first things first time to get one of those ice cold cans of Premium Lager to enjoy at leisure. The drinks went down beautifully alongside one of those news vid updates that were essentially about minor news, and the football obviously. Quick and simple, how the bloody news should always be thought! He went into the kitchen and asked the Robo-Staff on duty to please make a large cup of coffee with a bacon sandwich, "Immediately Sir it will done", 'many thanks Robo' he replied. That machine knew perfectly his tastes down to a frankly supernatural degree. Having sat back down after going quickly to urinate off some of lager, he settled down for a cup of strong coffee, with the perfect splash of milk as usual. That briefly settled moment would prove to be the start of a series of events that would totally and utterly change everything about his life.

His TM Vid-Screen was registering a CALL from a totally unknown number…

"Hello, Jack O'Neill speaking" he replied.
"Yes, we knew it would be you" the calm voice came back. On his vid screen, Jack could faintly make out the figure of a bald, middle aged

gentleman. He was wearing smart wire frame glasses and looked to be serious. He tried to think who on Earth would be calling- someone wanting to speak to his wife? He composed his thoughts and considered how this man knew he would pick up.

"You knew? Hello, who is speaking please"

"Do not worry Mr. O'Neill, please at least not yet" the voice was sounding firmer.

Who the hell was this he thought, bothering me after a long tiring damn day of scan typing the book,

"I am pleased to say we request your assistance Mr. O'Neill. This is the Central Religious Network contacting you"

"Yeah right!" He scoffed and hung up immediately. The Network wasn't involved with people on a personal basis, they talked and you listened. That was the quiet and centuries old agreement. The Network was distant, authoritative and incontestable. They had no presence on the Sphere System, they certainly offered no numbers that you could call them on. You paid if you wanted to join the Network, indeed most people did. Thoughts of the afterlife had become a more serious concern following the last intergalactic war. He felt relaxed briefly, stupid prank callers were still unfortunately going he guessed. He sort of wished that his wife was in so they could laugh about it; she may have taken it seriously though he guessed. No, actually she wouldn't either. It was a very unlikely call, like the Pope or President calling or something.

Then the voice came directly through the speaker, totally startling Jack. He thanked his lucky stars that he switched off the monitor, so they couldn't see him leap about two feet from his chair.

"Look Mr. O'Neill, this isn't a prank call, and we are certainly not accustomed to wasting our time so I shall get to the point. You are the only man we want to have assist us. There is no contract, and the terms of any agreement are silent"

He stood silent himself for a minute, ignoring how they knew his thoughts. He knew anything that followed would be bad. Instinct told him the Central Religious Network wouldn't contact him with requests and then let said person blab to all and sundry about it. Shit! What did they want? What was this all about? He collected his thoughts for a moment, and quietly replied…

"Okay, what can you tell me this is about"

"Your love for Jackson was a factor. We may have an urgent and evidently top secret World Government situation"

Before he could reply they continued

"You are to help us to write the hidden gospels of Kuthalu"

"I don't understand, the what of Ku…Kuthalu?" his thoughts were distant, his mind was still stunned.

"These documents Mr. O'Neill suffice it to say will show ancient contact being made between the hitherto unknown Kuthalu people of Earth Sector 6 and the Prime Lord"

"You want me to write about the human contact between the… Kuthalu… and the Prime Lord?…The God of All…are you serious? Is this some stupid trick by my publishers/" He couldn't believe what he was hearing.

"Not at all".

He suddenly gained mental clarity and quickly his doubts about the veracity of this strange call hit.

"Look if you really are from the Central Religious Network, why haven't you past scanned this supposedly miraculous event. You don't need me to write anything". He knew if something this amazing had been discovered they would want to show it in it's full glory. Make people now the full power of the Prime Lord, and subsequently the CRN of course.

"If we could past scan this event" the voice impatiently interjected "then the Earth Government would certainly not be involved. We shall be direct, we are willing to pay your writing fees for life- let us just say your brother would also be well covered as well for example".

He felt nervous but more intrigued by the call. They didn't want to kill him, well at least not yet.

"The project will not be easy"

Ah.

"You were chosen somewhat ironically for your overall lack of beliefs in the true meaning of the Prime Lord.

"What?" he spluttered, feeling somehow that his honour or honesty had been questioned.

"I'll have you know that I am a fully paid member" he felt like blaspheming but decided against under the circumstances

"Look you of all people should know this, I am a believer of course I am a believer for goodness sake!"

"I think we shouldn't need to explain at this point that we at least know your constant thoughts Mr. O'Neill. Unfortunately for your pride anyway, you are not a full believer in the meaning of the Prime Lord. Evidently nor are certain others"

"You mean Sector 6 don't you" he almost muttered

"Yes, unfortunately we do. A receiving station was burnt down last week, and we have received plans for many other similar or even more dangerous attacks".

He felt shocked "Ah, I wasn't aware of these attacks".

"Of course you were not"

That wasn't really an insult, a nano-atomic bomb on Earth Zone 6 would scarcely require a vid-screen news report. The Zone was God-forsaken, literally really, until now.

"We can scarce afford the seeds of rebellion anywhere Mr. O'Neill. People can and certainly do leave Earth Zone 6. We would not wish for word of these strikes against the CRN to be known. Dissension has been shown to be a very negative force against organized religions Mr. O'Neill"

He understood, even after this odd and intrusive call he still felt vaguely protective of the CRN, despite their questioning of his faith!

We question everybody's faith, came the thought suddenly into his mind.

"You will know and understand more when I meet you at the Heli-port. Also Mr. O'Neill, I am sorry to report your wife is dead. No-one can know any of this".

"My wife is what?" He felt a sudden surge of total fear and alarm sweep over him like a radioactive injection. The injection had seized and paralysed his body and mind. It took a moment for the grim shock to subside before he replied.

"Look this is over I refuse, how dare you contact me with this! The Central Government and the Pillars of Justice will immediately hear of this"

"You should calm down Mr. O'Neill. I should explain, let us just say your wife is legally dead. Here on Earth Zone 1 at least. Your feelings for her and the ramifications for us of murder did not go unconsidered. But you shall never see or speak to her again. We shall discuss more at the Heli-port",

"What, legally?", he kept wondering why they had chosen him and what on Earth was going on.

"I think you know why we have chosen you Mr. O'Neill, we can only say again that we have partially chosen you for your lack of faith"

He knew there was not a great deal of choice with the situation. He went upstairs to pack his bag and nervously prepare for the upcoming job.

Relieved on the one hand is wife was still alive, totally despondent on the other knowing he would never sample any of her joys again. His emotions were being kept in check by means other the Anger Management daily sessions. There something deep inside him, thinking this is what needed to happen, and I am ready. That feeling was more than matched though by his hitherto unknown to him doubts about the general meaning of the CRN. Why did they need him? Lack of belief! He was still feeling aggrieved, and was getting more than a little scared by the scale of the task at hand.

The roads were thankfully quiet on journey to the Central Heli-port. Any traffic would have probably lead him to start screaming out loud, crying out loudly again and again. Another huge pressure on his life was starting to really get to this mental stability, He began to panic thinking about whether they would have the right cure and treatment for him- could they really cure him? Was his insanity going to hinder such an important job? Surely they must be mad to go for such a clumsy hack like myself. They can't have damn well read my last book, "The Life and Times of an Interplanetary Mind". Hell in that he implied with heavy metaphor that an intergalactic war between two distant planets was simply designed to keep people living in fear about threats to security that went beyond nationhood. He wanted to really awaken people to the fact that the Fourth World War and Venetian Wars were set up by the Government and maybe even the CRN to show the need for the literally mind controlling World Government. The World Government needed such wars. He stopped thinking briefly, hell they know all of these damn points especially now. Attempts to counteract the values of the CRN and World Government had been outlawed in the Beijing Treaty in 2099 following World War Four. He felt fear and another huge metaphorical wave of guilt sweeping over him. They know everything I've said against them, they know all my doubts about the Prime Lord- I should be closer to being labelled a heretic! Never mind they still seem to have picked me, there are no messages saying 'hey look sorry, your wife is fine go back relax, and try to copulate whilst she ovulates!'. They would know about his, or more accurately his wife's, attempts to get pregnant as well. Hey, I'm only 29 he thought, I'll eventually be some form of Dad. The realisation though that his wife was now fully gone depressed him deeply and quickly. For the first and probably last time, he really hoped that she wasn't pregnant. The horrifying thought of his child being brought up in a lesser zone snobbishly came into his mind. He wanted his progeny to be as rich and successful as had been. He wanted to spread out his advantages to others. He felt it sort of as a religious duty, even though he wasn't a full believer apparently! He was beginning to seriously worry and question his mind, his future and his faith. Why did they really choose me? Never mind, the process had began and he would go along with it. A few more million points would buy another wife he cynically mused. Damn, I really am a callous ass-hole he thought. His wife would obviously not be just replaceable- she really did drive him wild in so many ways, He couldn't understand why she hadn't got pregnant yet, they were having sex way more than he had with his previous partners combined even when not married- he wasn't a perfect member of the CRN admittedly! She was a nice person, a good person - he was starting to get worried about his lack of concern for her going though. His emotions were complex and stirring around in his mind. There was just something, a quietly calm presence within him, the hushed nagging thought that this was what he was meant to do all along and that his wife was just really an existential detour. It suddenly dawned on him as well, it was almost certainly them, the CRN, or heck even maybe the Central Government that was preventing his wife from getting pregnant. They didn't want to get involved evidently in moving a child as well from Earth Zone 1. They obviously didn't want his emotions getting too complicated. There was still evidently a conscience somewhere at the top thank God. He knew his belief was with God, and not the Prime Lord as commonly espoused. He began to seriously worry whether he was honestly the man for such a monumental job. Simple thoughts began to pick at his conscious. Would he write well enough? Could he write well enough? If he didn't would they end up killing him? No mistakes would be possible, no hidden draft copies of words that would somehow show up the Prime Lord. Then it hit him- he would be the voice of the Prime Lord! Someday the words that may be transmogrified into vid-screen broadcasts, would at least initially use his words! He felt simultaneous pangs of guilt and elation, he felt like he had just won the lottery, but the prize had been altered into certain death. He felt strangely like he did in one of his dreams, the most recurrent one. It always involved this kid he had never met, or so he thought, (after the fiftieth time or so he realized the kid was actually him) - the kid wearing a stupid baseball cap, saying "Hey, Mr. O'Neill, I'm your number one fan". To which I would always go "Hey thanks to you, can I sign anything?". To which he would then always go, "You misunderstand me Mr. O'Neill - I am your number one fan. As in the number one, first and only. We all ultimately hate you. Rip-off merchant. I know all of the lines you copy and from which editions, you total fraud. You write like you've just scanned in paragraphs from other better writers. Keep thinking of the future Jack".

It was always that last part that shook him awake from these brief and confusing bouts of R.E.M. It always had him waking lightly drizzled in sweat, shocking him into morning consciousness. That shock was especially present when the young boy- he kept forgetting it was himself- said out 'Jack'. Being talked to by your younger self, it always disturbed him. He told his wife and she just shrugged (as was a common response to any of his emotional difficulties) "I've had worse, honey".

Sometimes he didn't really like her lack of compassion, even though she was well read and bought up. Gone now forever he lamented again. Even her damn flaws would never return. Hey, hang on a minute he thought. She's probably glad and on another damn space cruise with some guy or group of girls. More suspicion like that and she may have left anyway, if he wasn't a famous author. Sometimes he really thought they would take him away after he'd occasionally loudly reply to her in a rude manner. The brain scanners did a good job of patrolling and monitoring all citizens emotions. He was always legally right though- he never overstepped the mark, with help of course from the extensive Anger Manager vids. Sometimes though it felt, just surely felt, that the Anger Management broadcast he would watch- every day- like all proles and dukes too, would be a bit longer than his wife's. More suspicion, which he guessed was another more unusual occurrence these days too. He knew he wasn't a normal citizen, a reliable norm like so many other billions. He felt a quick wave of shame followed by an undeniable blush covering his face like forest fire. A red rash marking his face physically indicating his mental state was not as collected and functional as the majority. This will make up for that though, he optimistically thought- I'll show them all that my Faith and Mind are pure. I will enable such a great moment to be retold with perfect clarity to the billions that would read, and eventually see the events. He had to be the best, it was finally his time.

It had been over a century since the last recorded contact between Man and God was made. Indeed, the last true moment that shook the world. Order was well and truly established after that point. The separation of the Earth into zones had become the logical conclusion to the destruction imposed by national identities. A World Government informing the actions of each zones had become an undeniably sane solution to the Fourth World War, which destroyed so many populated sites. The rapid shift between wars of alliances following the earlier Third World War had forced another one on the world. Eventually though people and governments had truly tired of international deaths from warfare. After the Wars Globalisation had seemingly reached it's peak. Nations were, for the most part, very happy with their economic, social and political integration. This enabled a very reasonable expansion of peace and prosperity for most of the globe. The dramatic and destructive inter galactic wars however, initially involving the small planet Valix from Persia-Galaxy 8 and subsequently the Venetian War which had destructively exploded this century, decimating so many parts of the World ended that prosperity, for a time at least. Both intergalactic wars had fully justified the need for an overall Government determining World, or rather Earth actions. The succession of domestic and inter galactic wars made people yearn for peace and stability again. After, during and even really before the Third and Fourth World Wars people had become placid for so many reasons- sedative drugs were knowingly included in all sources of milk, Anger Management was a daily broadcast, laws were immediately enforced and thought scanners patrolled the streets. Evidently the CRN could scan minds even without patrols he thought. The World had unified behind certain ideas encased both in the World Government and in the Central Religious Network. The duopoly offered had satisfied most people's concerns, both in terms of purpose and meaning. The human psyche was truly well mapped, and after a destructive and successful putsch (managed by the CRN/ World Government dynamic of course) this had lead to the stabilizing of human minds and human desires. The conditions were set for a perfect, harmonised world order. Except of course for the reluctance of the CRN to accept Homo-sexual individuals into the Network and the neglect of Earth Zone 6 by mainly the World Government. The problems remained as small painful ancient scars in a World seemingly perfectly ordered. Dissatisfaction was seriously beginning to collect amongst both the well read poor of Earth Zone 6 but also with some of the influential dilettantes of Earth 1. The up to date Sphere watchers in some of the other zones were also beginning to feel emotionally compromised too with regards to the dying in Earth Zone 6. Questions about fairness and justice could still prove devastating to the World Government and the CRN. Any chance that the zones could be compromised or even the horrific possibility that all zones questioned their meaning would be disastrous- new identities from individuals would be sought, new thoughts and dear God more ideologies would form. "Free Thought" was still a blessing as people believed thankfully what the World Government and CRN felt they should believe. Rival established ideologies could pose so many problems- there would be more attempts to return to domestic governments, attempts to return to the overt barbarism of international relations and the horrific situation of humans killing humans again. It would be another insurmountable problem leading to disenfranchised or dead citizens. In other words a Earth sized Petri-dish over flowing with deadly thought formed bacteria. In the years after the World Wars Three and Four, CRN and the World Government really did minimise so many different potential sources of dissidence. After these latest, unreported attacks, it was felt though to be finally necessary to integrate the poorer areas of Earth 6, all of it really, with more prosperous regions. The planned message that Mr. O'Neill would script would provide Earth Zone 6 with hope meaning, and eventually citizens offer economic growth. Mr. O'Neill would also provide in the message appeal to the disenfranchised homo-sexual individuals in all the main sectors (Earth Zone 2 especially for some reason). These were people who had also been abandoned and isolated religiously. Their rejection and inferred damnation was up until now clear by known scripture and also from Vid Screen messages showing the immorality of the practice.

Jack however was going to help solve these two major dilemmas with one big event. He understood the purpose of the mission, it was simple overall: on the one hand rewrite versions of ancient scripture to show citizens the sacred values and duties of living with Wild Animals and people of early tribes, I.e. the Kuthalu. The other hand was the one he would struggle with more though. It was the section they required him to write showing how homosexual acts were not an "Abomination" in the eyes of the Prime Lord. He had to somehow write about the compassionate understanding shown by the Prime Lord to many diverged practices, much in the same way he himself had believed that the Hangaard findings in the earl 22nd Century highlighted the acceptability of sex before marriage. The new form of faith, the CRN, really comprehended the way religious values had to be incorporated with modern means and not vice versa. Pre Scanning had made the interjection and clear insights shown within new sources of scripture and engagements with the Prime Lord as big news stories. All the major Vid Screen Channels were of course owned by the CRN. It's fair to say that religion had changed it's brand spectacularly in the 21st and 22nd Centuries and had since offered via the CRN a personalized, constant and brilliantly effective personal and spiritual assessment. The Network, despite the claims of the World Government was almost certainly the most effective factor in the overall management of citizen behaviour amongst other aspects of course. The World Government still had it's influence and it's events such as Buy-Day were unavoidable obviously. Both worked in a effective dual manner- the World Government would order an execution subsequently the CRN would then powerfully lobby on the importance of the fundamental human rights I.e. the rights to life, to liberty and to joy. The response from the World Government was always similar however. "We, as citizens, have a right to peace, a right to have support and the right to protection of police". The World Government was beginning to win more cases and a higher moral standing with convictions particularly in regard to gay individuals getting attacked. The top people of the CRN felt a very serious and influential event would re-swing the balance back into their power even if only on a temporary basis. The chiefs at the CRN still felt there was an element within the World Government that was still yearning to bring back national identities. It was felt by many at the CRN that the World Government was too keen to give state centric type arguments for the statistics that were showing far greater levels of overall Earth level crimes, particularly post the introduction of the Zonal System as compared to the relatively similar data stream derived from pre Zone days. That was when the CRN deemed it essential to establish another monumental event, to cement their place in power as the group that truly has made mankind closer than ever to it's actual God, The Prime Lord. The argument of no life being possible without the Prime Lord was also persuasive. The power and application of religion was something the Elders of the Network were constantly and desperately assessing. Indeed they made sure the Youngsters keenly monitored Sphere activity to note and hopefully disclaim any false accusations against CRN beliefs. Most of the typed pieces that were noticed when scanning for dissidence were often fairly trivial slides, saying out messages like "The Prime Lord only loves the Rich" and more cynical pieces like "So Zone 3 deserves 4billion points per year, whilst Zone 4 gets 1billion points for a place with more people!- The CRN is unjustly spending the Prime Lord's bounty". The messages often had good points but frankly the majority of them were easy to deal with standard replied responses, "The Prime Lord remains with us all in all zones. Forget not that God helps redirect you to your glory. In despair the Prime Lord is there. The Prime Lord is there for all of us, Youngsters were passing on their concerns to the Elders at only a small rate, but nevertheless a real sense of concern about the application of the CRN was getting through to the top. After the attacks on stations in Zone 6 it was deemed imperative to create a message that would simultaneously placate some of the worst off individuals in 6 but that would also become a larger message bemoaning economic injustice which would hopefully spread and lead to full zonal appeal for the Network. The CRN had to be seen to feel all people's pain. Individuals from the very top of CRN were also desperate to include a Prime Lord account that would show the religious and spiritual acceptability of the practice of same sex couples. If this could happen, and that chap O'Neill could actually deliver a fantastic written account in Z6, then greater stability could be returned and the CRN would re-establish itself as the pre-eminent form of moral knowledge. Frank Adams was well set to meet the bright young writer. After rearranging his wire frame glasses on his sharp bald head, he felt prepared in himself. He knew all he needed for understanding Mr. O'Neill's mind. His knowledge of him was set well beyond the psycho-scans that had already taken place, and their earlier conversation of course. The man was probably genius (or a sub norm), but Frank Adams still felt Jack would do the correct thing for the Central Religious Network.

He looked out of his heli-pod as the ground flashed past him at high speed. The ground flashed past as a blur of crimson red. Jack thought about how barren and raw the ground looked especially as it was after flying past the high rise mega blocks of the rich zones. It looked to all intents and purposes like a red, acrid version of hell on Earth. No wonder so many of the damn people were unhappy- there was nothing there! He only occasionally glimpsed metal objects, even they only looked like large sheds as they cruised along continuing at high speed and higher altitude. Already he was feeling guilty about having his mood pills and his high taste meal. Half of these people must have died of starvation he thought, mood pills would be as much good to them here as a frying pan is to a chicken. The craft felt like it was slowing down, so John prepared for the heavy landing. It didn't feel as bad strangely as when they had taken off, maybe he was just used to these things now. He kept thinking about the task ahead. What was it that bald guy had said to him? "I think you know why we have chosen you Mr. O'Neill, we can only say we have partially chosen you for your lack of faith", that last point kept puzzling him. Like so many others he felt closely defined by his faith, and those words "we have chosen you for your lack of faith" continued to sting his soul and ring in his ears. He kept trying to physically scan his brain for instances when he had not fully accepted and worshipped the Prime Lord. Surely they can't be bothered that he still referred to the Prime Lord as God, much in the same way as his ancient predecessors had? God just seemed a more natural way to address such a higher being. The Prime Lord still sounded like some sort of parliamentary position- an integration of the divine into the norm. The thought depressed him- he fully believed that the name of God was the last thing needed to love and worship him. This insistence on a single name of God for centralized worship also occasionally worried him. Some days at worship he loved the sight of so many divergent individuals sitting, praying and singing together. Other days strangely he longed for the more solitary form of worship, a holy and personal communion with his God, the Prime Lord. He had heard about some Jewish Prime Lord sect buildings, but that wasn't right for him really. He just didn't fully fit in with the congregation- but he was always there, he thought. I pray, I sing, I kneel! It bothered him that they wanted someone like him to write the Kathulu gospel. If they were right that he wasn't the most faithful man, which he guessed was true, then why would the Central Religious Network need a man like him to write for and about the Prime Lord? Walking across the exceptionally low grade heli-port, Jack bought an exorbitantly expensive bottle of water and geared himself mentally for the challenges that would face him. Frank Adams motioned for him to get into the land cruiser by the taxi bay - he looked like he meant business.

As they sped along in the land cruiser, Frank turned from the front passenger seat and began talking to Jack.
"I am pleased your flight went without incident Mr. O'Neill"
"Yes, I am too"
"We need you to be fully focused on your work, much as you were during the writing of that last book"
Indeed, my written record of heresy he thought. Full proof that he was at least in mind, a modern druid or worse a modern atheist.

"Belief in any form is not something we take lightly Mr. O'Neill. If you insist on thinking of yourself as a heretic then continue, but it is of no concern to us"

"Good, that's good" he replied, still quietly adjusting to the fact that his thoughts were being monitored even without any visible thought scanner.

"I feel now is the time for us to expand upon our intentions. Obviously you have discerned that I am a high figure from the CRN"

Jack nodded.

"And I would presume you understand our intentions are not to misrepresent what you know of as God"

He felt that within him, despite their wife stealing behaviour.

"Unfortunately Mr. O'Neill further action was needed to have you focused on creating this event. It was a painful decision. The first part of the message is currently, in political terms at least the most important"

He looked absently out of the window, seeing the landscape shift along as a predominant sea of red, he thought he saw the outlines of one of the Z6 cities, possibly Cazid, but he couldn't be sure.

"As I was saying, the most important task is to show how the Prime Lord is still concerned with the worst off in society and the world at large"

God as a Marxist, he found that very ironic.

"Certainly not Mr. O'Neill. You will show the Prime Lord's spirit of concern for the worst off. We know of course that you are well versed in the book of Exodus. You are required to show how God, as you would have it, intervening to aid the Kuthulu people when they are at their most oppressed. We toyed with the idea of having a Z1 company being the villains of your story, and showing how they exploited the tribe's people whilst they were digging by simple tools for valuable and volatile Helium-3 deposits…"

But you didn't want to upset any rich members he thought

"No because we don't want to evoke class problems Mr. O'Neill. I think we can safely say that the re-emergence of class centric ideologies may lead to pseudo national identities being re-established which could lead to another set of catastrophic wars. The price would be far too high, even for the rich".

He fully agreed with the point. Ideologies were dangerous, his long personal history of reading had certainly indicated that.

"So, how should I show the Prime Lord intervening. Is this another burning bush situation- or a direct sight of the true form of God, I mean the

Prime Lord. You know another floating, gaseous cloud telepathically informing and directing people like with the book of Hangaard?".
"The latter Mr. O'Neill".
He thought so.
"We need you to show, the Prime Lord informing the chief of the Kuthulu tribe about the economic potential of the canlas plant"
"You mean the canlas plant... as in the basis for all of the major calming mood pills? That must be invaluable"
"Yes of course. We aim via this message to eventually reimburse the Kuthulu people and their common ancestors spread across Z6 with hundreds of billions of points. Per the major families as well."
"What?" He was totally stunned. "The CRN are going to pay thousands of billions of points to individual families within Z6?"
"It is the only way they will be able to rebuild their zone Mr. O'Neill. The Network has felt emotionally compromised too by such a zone. Whilst this is classified Mr. O'Neill we can also inform you that people are feeling and thinking themselves falsely virtuous after making 10 and 100 point donations to charities representing Z6. We certainly do not intend to falsely lead people morally. A soul lost to misunderstood virtue would be a tragedy for us"
Is charity not a virtue he thought, was it not holy?
"No it is not. I think we need not remind you of all people Mr. O'Neill that pride is a sin"
He was certainly aware of that.
The robo-driver quietly spoke to Frank Adams. They had reached their destination.

Jack looked around his room in the hostel he was stationed in. Sheesh, he thought, he had never seen a room this bad before. Heck even following his gap year travels around some of the more obscure cities in Z4 he had stayed in vastly better places. It was the smell here more than anything. Putrid and repellent, the non-shifting stink of recent animal death was clinging to the air. It was like nothing he dreamed he would ever smell, like smelling your own rotting corpse. They were near a farm on the outskirts of some God forsaken city. He had no idea where exactly in the zone they were, and he didn't want to know. He just wanted to scan type his words into his laptop and get out of this place. Back to "normality", he thought. Mr. Adams had shown him to his room and subsequently disappeared. He could have sworn he heard the land cruiser shoot off again, but when he squinted out of the window he could still see it sitting their lazily in the dirt like some sort of dead dog. He was certain that the stranger would revisit, especially when and if his thoughts about God got into trouble. Where to start, where to start? He kept thinking. How on Earth am I going to accurately rewrite something of the magnitude of Hangaard or Exodus he thought? Two years ago I was writing about amorous vampires and about ghosts that lived in schools, and now I need to write about and for the Prime Lord. He started laughing, he just couldn't help it. Loudly and in a long fashion he blurted out laughter. Oh my goodness, a halfwit of faith, a doubter of the veracity of the Prime Lord filling in his words like some sort of teleprompter! The type his publishing company always made him read from when doing Vid-Screen interviews. It wouldn't be so simple this time. He couldn't any longer say "I think that adolescents are often more in tune with emotions and in turn with horror than adults are". He couldn't just say "well I think we all know by now about the analogous properties of vampires- the letting of blood, the baring of teeth, the changes in appearance". He wrote about these things because they had paid him enough to do so, and really what was really the difference now? Would he be writing for Satan if the dark lord had guaranteed him a one million points, three book deal? Yes of course he would. Faith was something interchangeable with life he always believed. Another alien thought came into his mind, 'That is why you were chosen'.

The first line was nearly always the hardest. Ten variants at least raced through his mind, all competing to be put on the page. There were probably at least two hundred although half of them would be utter gibberish. Maybe that is a good point he thought, if God were able to speak direct to us would our semi-monkey brains hear the same nonsense as the caged animals do when living at zoos when we speak to them? Probably. Despite our land cruisers and heli-ports he still mainly conceived of humans as animals. Advanced ones mind, the type that smokes pipes and push buttons with pictures of food on them. The preposterous notion that man was built in the Prime Lord's image had been absolutely shattered by both Hangaard and the late 21st Century new edition of The Bible. It had saddened him that so much of what the ancients believed had been incorrect, yet past scans had seemingly indicated that at least Exodus was true. At least Moses was real. Now he would have to write, to totally make up, a new story of Moses. The idea still felt insane, yet something in his mind registered- does a story or event have to be real to have a seismic impact? Does it have to be true? Is art itself real? Since the devastation of the real as exemplified by World War Three and Four, surely greater solace and meaning could be found in the unreal, the made up? He kept thinking about what is and was truly unreal. Most ideas about Jesus had been questioned, yet he was told by the Network that he remained in billions of prayers. Did that then lessen his impact to mankind? Mankind, now there was a contradiction in terms. Kind when blitzed by drugs and monitored by floating mind scanners he thought. Before then man-unkind may have been more apt. Or man-waste perhaps. Jack realized that his basic task was simply to update, or remake in other words, the central story of Exodus. The people of Kuthulu would be freed as well. He could just see now a computer scanned Charlton Heston being animated into a gaseous cloud form, "Let my people go! And give them billions of points". He laughed quietly this time to himself. Films had taken on a somewhat holier form in the time since past scanning had been advanced. Entertainment films still existed, thankfully, since he had received probably millions off the back of them. This would be a bit different from vampires he thought, or even satirically conceived land owners. The last book which even whilst he was writing it felt like a moral departure, had somehow triggered this fantastic opportunity to conceive the words of the Prime Lord. He mused, my doubts are true whilst my faith is false. Another thought came into his mind, 'God is true'.

"People of Kuthulu your hardship on Earth will not go unknown in the afterlife. What has been denied to you now will not be in heaven. Keep faith, love one another as you love your God, and know that, I, the Prime Lord will indeed return to guide and liberate you." and with that Jack O'Neill put down his Vid-Scan laptop. It had taken a while and especially after scanning the Sphere for full references of Exodus, both the pre Hangaard and post versions. Following the notes he had made in turn meant the process of writing came surprisingly easily. He felt guilty about the ease of the writing in fact. The thought came to his head that, 'Hey, shouldn't providing the words of the Prime Lord be harder than that?;, when another alien thought arrived, 'Not if you truly believe'. He felt reasonably satisfied thought strangely exhausted. The task, despite being simple, had somehow drained him. It felt like part of his essence was being left on the screen. He thought briefly about when that bald guy, Mr. Adams, would return. He felt a strange urge to show him the work. Stupid monkey-brain need for approval! he mused. Despite all the mind scanning and drugs the World Government hadn't yet worked out how to remove that innate need for approval and reassurance. It certainly hadn't worked out how to remove the need for hunger. Despite the stench, which his nostrils had now adapted to in the same way that you get used to the smell of a sweaty traveller on public transport, Jack yearned for something, really anything, to eat. He kept envisaging various types of food, both fast and other, and decided to head out of his room to the initially unpromising looking canteen. There was no queue, surprisingly, for the metal trays of brown or grey looking slop. The tray that he guessed contained rice, looked at least three days old, whilst the fruit on display at the end of the line appeared to be some sort of strange insult. The orange sitting there was distinctly not orange, and the feeble attempt at a banana made a mockery of it's more delicious cousins. Still he asked the lady to fill his plate with rice and brown, and decided upon the one edible looking piece of fruit, the apple. Here comes knowledge he thought, when eventually eating the apple. His little amusing reference seemed less funny when he saw that Frank Adams was sitting in the corner of the canteen, busily reading from his own Vid-Screen laptop. So he hadn't left this place yet he thought. Jack hoped that he would go unnoticed, so he could quickly eat this stuff in peace. His fears were confirmed when Adams motioned for him to come over.

"Your text is acceptable" he finally said, when looking up from the screen.
"Oh, thanks" Jack instinctively replied.
"You have captured that essence of what we intended to convey through the Kuthulu".
Relief came over him quickly and soothingly, like frozen peas on a bruised head.
" I thought you had travelled back to the heli-port" Jack found himself saying.
"No. There is certainly more work to be done Mr. O'Neill"
He remembered about the other hand. The need to integrate same sex couples into the accepted kingdom of God.
"The Prime Lord still, if you would Mr. O'Neill"
He put his thoughts back into order, right indeed, the Prime Lord.

"The last challenge, the Kuthulu was relatively easy, you know just another re-telling of Exodus but this next challenge, it goes against what so much has been written. Even the New Bible doesn't contain any passages at all, that I've seen at least, justifying or even allowing same sex relationships". Jack was panicking, the thought came again to him that he wasn't up for this challenge.

"Mr. O'Neill what do you conceive of the Prime Lord's love?" Frank Adams asked the question carefully and quietly.

"I don't know. Erm that he loves all of his creation", he remained confused and anxious.

"Precisely correct"

"But surely other known passages of scripture show that his, the Prime Lord's, love means he wants creation to perpetuate itself" he quoted "What God hath joined together let man not separate".

"You are forgetting the gift of liberty Mr. O'Neill" Adams calmly stated.

"Yes, to an extent, we are free to do as we please. But as Hangaard implicated, "Man is not advised to travel across a road blindfolded" There are some things God allows us to do, that he does not fully approve of".

"Do you believe that God approved of your relationships before marriage Mr. O'Neill?"

He knew where the bald guy was coming from.

"No, I suppose not. I understand what you are saying"

"I feel you do not Mr. O'Neill".

"Let me try to understand" He interrupted, somewhat impatiently. "I think you are saying there isn't a great hierarchy of sins, and that my sexual pre-marriage activities are comparable to homosexual acts", Jack felt offended again, hey they did pick me for a reason he thought, despite his not full beliefs.

"Perhaps I underestimated you Mr. O'Neill, you let on more than your mind indicates".

This man thinks beyond the monkey-brain Jack thought. Still it was going to be far harder to convey the message about the Prime Lord's relative acceptance of sins, than his intervention to help the worst members of the global society.

"Mr. O'Neill, this isn't about the acceptance of sins, but the acceptance of choice. The decision to engage in sexual intercourse before pledging your relationship to God is not a modern one. The choice of intimate relationships between consenting adults is one we believe the Prime Lord

135

is accepting of"
Jack was confused, "So you are saying that it's ok to be gay?"
"That is the correct message".
Meeting this man, first on the Vid-Screen and alarmingly in person, Jack d
that the bald gentlemen from the Network had totally changed his beliefs
and conception of the Prime Lord.

Despite his initial reservations about the second part of the job, Jack had
found that the words began to flow easily.
"Let it be known that the almighty judgement of I, the Prime Lord, is not
based on mankind's created morality, but on the infinite existence of law.
Those who love one another, shall not be judged if this love is true".
When the final word was placed on screen, Jack felt a comparable surge of
relief to the last encounter with the Prime Lord he had written. Questions
of course still remained. Surely there must be comparable events to past
scan? Surely I am blaspheming and guilty of sin to provide the words of
the Prime Lord? What if they at the Network are wrong about homosexual
relationships? What if Frank Adams isn't part of the Network and is part of
a conspiracy to discredit the one true global religion left and to ensure the
moral high ground remains with the World Government? He took a deep
breath and calmed himself down. He believed that this work was genuine.
He thought that indeed overall, the true meaning and values of the Prime
Lord may not be accurately conveyed by past scans. True meaning from
the Prime Lord may not have fully filtered down to Earth and he have been
instructed by the Network to find it. He heard a knocking on his door and
got up from his rickety, hard bed to see who was there

Unsurprisingly it was Adams.
"Right Mr. O'Neill we know you have finished and we know that the work
is of a sufficient standard".
Sufficient, he thought bitterly, that's all you require for the word's of the
Prime Lord.
"Please follow me out to the land cruiser. We greatly hope that if you ever
have to return to this part of Earth, there will far more superior facilities to
stay in. Resources have been already began to be allocated for the
distribution of the billions of points".
"So it is actually happening" Jack said, still somewhat surprised that Z6
would actually be getting some investment and more importantly, fair

treatment. Whilst walking towards the land cruiser he thought, hell, even Las Vegas must have looked a bit like this place at some time. London briefly did following World War Four.

They approached the cruiser.

"You're assistance has been invaluable Mr. O'Neill", Adams warmly stated.

"No problem, just put the points in my account"- the money obviously still mattered to Jack, but he couldn't shake the other feeling of exaltation that his words would be used to represent the Prime Lord despite the loss of his wife to him.

Frank Adam's continued his special trick of interrupting his thoughts accurately,

"I hope you know Jack, your words represent more than just what the Network would like the Prime Lord to say

"In what way?" Jack quietly asked, feeling a very strange sensation of his guts dropping down to his feet.

"Do I have to spell it out Jack?" Frank Adams asked.

No he didn't. Jack knew then, possibly he had known from the first moment he saw Frank Adam's angular, intelligent head and wire frame glasses. He understood that all along he had actually been talking to God. The alien thought interjected again- You know that the Prime Lord was a necessary creation to prevent further international war don't you Jack?

"Yes" he said out loud. The reading of his thoughts without a visible scanner at any point had always been suspicious. Frank Adams settled himself into the front of the land cruiser and instructed the robo-driver to take them back to the heli-port. At that point that point Jack realized he had known all along. He had been chosen to provide the words of God and not the Prime Lord, whatever that was. Whilst cruising off through the currently barren, empty and until then presumably God-less Zone 6, Jack sat back and thought to himself that the greatest act of God he had known was to sacrifice himself to the World. Neither Frank Adams nor any alien voice interrupted this time to disagree with him.

THE THOUGHTS OF PHELOX

Priest Patrick Klein examined the collection of files that was staring up at him. The old records office of the Atkins Robot Plant had been unexamined for years. He was here simply on a hunch; he had been given a classified, very hush-hush piece of information from a former worker at the plant who was also a current congregation member. Tim had told him in utmost secrecy that one of the individuals that worked at Atkins 30 years ago was actually one of the first, if not possibly even the first, Venusian to actively collect information about Earth. Patrick was very much an amateur historian so the chance to see primary material regarding what a peacetime Venusian thought about Earth was too tempting not to examine. The man who gave him the lead, Tim Smithson, was sketchy about the details regarding possible findings. Patrick got the feeling this fellow was trying to avoid disappointing his priest. Little did he know really that Father Klein was the type of man who would give his left foot to examine any potentially significant primary material first hand. He was a man who loved the mystery and intrigue of personal collection; it wasn't a crime, but he refrained from telling members of his congregation about his personal letter collection that dated from various stages throughout the 21st Century. His love of history was not born from collecting dates and figures that were important; his real interest wasn't simply based on the numbers killed, or numbers born. It came from what really drove people to begin the first intergalactic war, what really caused World War Four, why did so few people have religious beliefs in the late 20th Century and so on. Seeing facts and figures only raised questions in his mind. It was quite an ironic situation that his strong personal faith in the unknown actually prompted a great desire to know things. His belief in God was of course born of a study of scripture and a knowledge of divine intervention, but Patrick somehow felt that his role as a Priest or indeed as a being of Earth would not be complete if he just accepted prior scripture. He knew enough about God to realise that his interventions would never simply be limited to one people, one person or one faith. All were as important as the other in his view; God was a complete holy and holistic force of existence. Patrick believed that he wasn't simply a priest, he was a vessel of God, allowing the holy force apparent through tenants and scriptures to be directed through him to his congregation. He wanted this role to be active and not simply passive. His desperation to know about the real reasons for the Venusian War had certainly prompted his searching intellect to find out more. He didn't just want to be a malleable tool for presumed knowledge. He wanted to be an active instigator in establishing an updated notion of divinity. Whilst God was never changing and always perfect, we as human beings or indeed as Venusians, as he hoped would be the case with these findings, could use history to stretch their knowledge to new limits. Looking around the dark, shut off room, Father Klein spotted a bunch of plastic bound documents stacked in the corner. He examined the first one; it was sales records of robotic parts from 2060-2070. He kept looking through the pile, most were official looking documents that just contained reams and reams of computer processed figures. It was then that he noticed a folder written in pen that was simply entitled 'Earth- 2069 to unknown'. That last part intrigued him. He opened up the folder and began reading the first page....

Friday 8th October 2069

It has been made clear to me on Earth the nature of difference. As a telepathic creature of Venus some of these attitudes have appeared to me as at best quaint and at worst destructive. The nature of humility intrigued me. Humans allow forgiveness for retracted misjudgements I hope they know the beauty of their compassion, as the mental creatures of the planet Venus have more of a definitive intellectual approach to the understanding our fellow creatures. We see others on the basis of what they have done. Forgiveness has been mentioned as a virtue by the elders, but most Venusians judge as we see. It seems so fascinating that despite the dominant notions of immediate judgements, the potential for forgiveness and compassion are there. Perhaps it is a remnant of the man known as Jesus, but I feel it is actually a display of the more progressive design that humans are blessed with. Of course the animal aspects of humanity, I will always refrain from using the term mankind, are often prominent in war, or in desire but overall the latent capabilities of emotional intelligence displayed by these creatures is really quite remarkable. There is so much from my brief time on Earth that I want to relay. I should say that my arrival and existence here came before the much prophesied Earth and Venus war. Of course I cannot be certain that there hasn't been intervention to prevent such a destructive conflict, but I have unfortunately come to the conclusion that the most base and disruptive elements on Earth will precipitate a long war between our two species. I learnt much about the nature of humans from being on Earth. The nature and notion of possession has proved to be a massively persuasive force. They identify themselves not as a species but as a series of nations, which are divisions of land into smaller places all with their own identities. Some reasons are apparent but frankly after the progression of conflict from the very beginning of 'nationhood' , I feel it should have been re-examined. Frankly a study of nations reveals the rudimentary conclusion that this approach to identity of human individuals is inherently conflictual and destructive. We have seen briefly in future scans however certain plans for a World Government that is imminent. It will divide the world not into hundreds of different nations and identities but actually into six zones. I am hopeful that this measure will ensure peace between us and their predominately primitive species, but the chances are not high. I remain hesitant to use our basic psyche scan techniques here and now as it may disrupt the operational capabilities of the human mind.

Tuesday 22nd November 2069

I have found many individuals here on Earth to be quite fine specimens. Many of them are indeed intelligent and kind in their approach to life. Despite the conditions for conflict and difficulty that are really quite prevalent on Earth many have greater aspirations. The ability of quite a few individuals to strive above their standings, which are very often reinforced and permanently established. The strange situation of those who have been worst affected by their given circumstances actually showing greater levels of existential comprehension is impressive. There is an awareness from a surprising amount of individuals that the wares of Earth are not infinitely satisfying. I need not inform you of the Venusians experience of the being that they on Earth call Lucifer. Suffice it to say the conditions of temptation have remained quite prevalent on Earth despite the obvious downfall and removal of Lucifer elsewhere. Many humans have remained almost cocooned in the primitive and simplistic version of 'evil' that has been apparent on Earth since the fall of the first man. Indeed my original intention, albeit one obviously not approved by the elders of Venus was to show how the beings of Earth could strive for greater intellectual and spiritual existence. I wanted to show the people of Earth however briefly that they have actually been conned and connived by a dormant intergalactic presence. Lucifer is barely a memory on Venus as you will know. He as forgotten on Venus as a figure such as Elijah is here on Earth. That they are being bound simply by the memory and notion of evil, let alone it's actual existence is quite depressing for a being of intellect. Over the course of my time here on Earth however, thankfully not all events transpired to agree with the supposedly dominant notion of evil. This collection of thoughts itself was began to help try and maintain some sort of record of my findings whilst stationed here. I wanted to keep my status as a pioneering figure in trying to comprehend humans to try and implement any measures that may help to prevent the severity of the war between our species. My time is short here, people are severely suspecting my intentions on Earth already. Work at the factory is fine, as I just basically replicate the actions of the most average individuals, but when speaking to fellow workers I am suspected. I have even heard some of them refer to me as a potential android. I am running out of excuses, but I do not want to return yet to Venus. I am intent on remaining here for as long as possible to get any potentially vital information. People in the town I have been staying in have started to be suspicious of my motives. I am looked at as a criminal when entering the public house or main shop. People do not know who I am exactly, which is on the one hand a good thing as the may be hostile to a physical alien, but on the other hand them not knowing my real identity allows questions and gossip to develop. I do not help by enquiring personally to individuals. I do not hide from wanting to know their motives, desires and fears. If they knew the truth I don't think they would object, unfortunately they do not and really cannot.

Tuesday 3rd January 2070...

I have found somewhere safe to stay and upload my accounts. The cities here are vast and large. I am often confused by the flashing lights, masses of people and blaring music that often emanates from the high rise buildings. I have been more settled since arriving in Second Global City. The people are too busy to be rude, unlike most of the inhabitants of the small towns I was staying in. I have found basic employment here, working as a cleaner at a robot factory. The pay is appalling but I am not at the job for the money. The time spent with factory workers has been very insightful. There is obviously a selection of but it is safe to say the more likeable and agreeable types were on the 'shop floor' working alongside myself on the conveyor belt of passing robot parts. The operation managers were a varied crew but they all had an element of sourness to them. They seemed somehow dissatisfied with their jobs, despite over seeing people who were literally beneath them. The human dynamic could be well studied at work; people did just enough to maintain their jobs. Nobody strived to do an excellent job, or to somehow find identity through their work. The job was simply somewhere to be during the day. They did not seem infused by the prospect of making something; it wasn't a work of art as we would see it. The conveyor belt and procedural nature of production at the factory I was working at could be seen as a larger metaphor for the nature of humanity as I experienced it. They as a species seem happy to experience life as a series of predicted or even pre-determined events. They do not yearn for individual enlightenment or identity; rather the autonomous nature of the supra-individual elements such as government or businesses seem to offer sufficient levels of identification to prevent yearning for any more. I would definitely like to know more about this strange phenomena.

Monday 16th March 2070

I have not learnt much more since the last entry. I remain here in the city. I have developed an understanding at least of the temporal but still pleasurable influences that humans like to utilise. Alcohol as a drug remains very prominent in their levels of consumption, as does often consumption of a drug called 'pulse'. Individuals remain sated by the identities they are given seemingly on the basis that drugs they consume answer any greater questions they have. Alcohol as a drug is very commonly used to minimise feelings of dissatisfaction, indeed it is a very persuasive substance I must report. People in the city seem to have greater access to calming and reassuring influences; they are different from the townsfolk in the sense that there is at least a diversification of thoughts on offer, even if they still cannot access the truth fully. Levels of religiously aspirant thoughts are also strangely more persuasive in the city than in the town. People are more questioning of their identity when presented with diversified influence. I found most, definitely not all I should report, of the townsfolk to be relatively more malleable by the nascent and problematic influences on offer. Perhaps that was just the one town I was staying in; I have gathered from human writings that in fact certain towns and rural areas are actually very active in assuming a strong personal identity different from that of nationhood. That was not my experience however.

Friday 22nd June 2070

I had my first encounter with the police forces today. I was very nervous that the people of Earth had developed psyche scan technology and had become aware that I was an unregistered Venusian living here temporarily. I feel my explanation would not be easily accepted. The officer was an unhappy gentleman who was strangely probing me about a man who worked in the factory I have been working at. I knew nothing much of the man, other than his name and photo. He revealed that the man was a potential terrorist for Venus and was under suspicion. Needless to say I became very nervous, physically exerting my fear through sweat and hands that shook took vigorously. The officer eyed me suspiciously but did not proceed with measures such as going to the Police HQ or giving a DNA sample thank God. I would have been either imprisoned or deported if this officer had any suspicion that I too was from Venus. I am nervous that the armed forces of Venus are priming an attack on Earth on the basis of psyche scans of the future. They have already experienced a sense of hostility from Earth that will in all likelihood lead to war. Personally I still feel it is wrong to damn humanity and Earth on the basis of things they have not done yet. I retain a hope that my findings and evidence acquired here will be sufficient to prevent a devastating intergalactic war. Besides the Venusian forces should know that their technology will not be sufficient to defeat the more military minded figures of Earth. I want findings to prevent war for both philosophical and practical reasons. Despite our advanced intelligence it is very clear to me the combined forces of Earth, which have but recently been fighting one another in another world war, as they call it, have been active and devastating. We would be foolish to provoke measures of fire and force. A day will come when our telepathic measures could easily defeat the leaders of Earth I am certain, and indeed despite great political opposition, the realisation on Venus that we too will need fire-power will greatly help in the future defence of our way of life. At present we remain hugely vulnerable; I fear the egos of the current elders however will force a conflict with the admittingly destructive probing forces of Earth. I feel they should await more of my findings and the discoveries of other spies which I hope will be sent. I am not an idealist or a dreamer like Humis or Braxus, however I still feel the influence of our intellect can prevent a fully violent conflict. I am still of the belief that our resources one day can be shared. The people of Earth seem to have very little interest in the progression of intelligence in the manner that we do. They appear a destructive and complacent race, but more work is needed to find grounds for co-operative as opposed to conflictual relations. My findings are still preliminary due to the suspicious nature of those I have dealt with thus far, but I shall continue to probe and report back whilst it is possible. Mankind really is an incorrect term I feel due to their innately fearful constitutions and their propensity for war.

Tuesday 3rd July 2070

I have seen many problems with the social ordering of Earth. There is a great reverence to what was once known as money and is now referred to as 'points', Individuals are just as obsessed by this concept as companies and governments. Life is actually designed around obtaining more and more numbers of these points. Points are seen to judge how successful you are; they are gained through work or through inheritance or through chance. Evidently the notion of personal progression and enlightenment as we are fully aware of on Venus are not so present here. There is not the same idea of interconnected joy as we know it; obviously the species on Earth do not share our telepathic abilities however they nominally share an idea of mistrust. Not knowing the thoughts of their fellow man is actually leads to more confusion. There is not a great deal of co-operation between divergent groups; isolation of ideas and identities is a frequent problem. The identities of males starkly differ depending on location, age and background whilst despite being slightly more integrated, the massed identities of women also remain innately hostile. In spite of various religious and philosophical teachings widely available to many I have not yet witnessed any kenosis or emotional elevation to indicate potentially latent spiritual knowledge. The needs and knowledge of the current time prove sufficient for most individuals. I would advise our cultural ambassadors to be ready for a long and difficult process should we decide to peaceful engage with the governments on Earth. My hopes remain low for any successful cultural engagements. Warfare should be expected unfortunately. Day by day my feelings that an intergalactic conflict can be prevented or even postponed are dissipating. The probes sent to Venus from Earth were armed and programmed to be conflictual. They sent probes that were heavily loaded with weaponry and designed to fire on any crafts that looked to have weaponry capability. They seem to immediately be designed for conflict and warfare. I very much fear or my safety if any humans and especially if any human figures within the military discover my true identity.

Father Klein stopped reading momentarily at that point. He realised what this individual was aiming at; he identified with the concern about humans being somehow naturally militaristic or conflictual almost by default. His fear of being identified as a spy or renegade also for some reason resonated with the Priest. He understood the feeling of being treated as an outsider. The inevitability of conflict this figure from Venus believed in was troubling; somehow he thought that there would be sufficient men of reason on Earth to help prevent an intergalactic war. There had been one smaller scale skirmish with forces from a star from a distant nebular prior to the Venusian War. Father Klein, like some others, held the view that the conflict with Nebula 4 was a precursor to a large scale intergalactic conflict. There was some evidence in this account that some Venusians were actively trying to prevent war! Far be it from it just being an account of war as destiny, this individual here had given an account of war as a potential occurrence in the future simply predicted by their telepathic brains. Father Klein also found it fascinating to consider the possibility that the elders on Venus had proved to be a comparable problem to the governments of Earth. This individual here seemed to share Klein's inherent mistrust in aggressive military behaviour; he actively seemed to regret the hostile reaction to probes that were sent from Earth. Father Klein decided he had read enough for the time being. It was evident that the war between Earth and Venus was in fact probably the fault of the governments on Earth and possibly even the conflictual mentality of humans as a species. Father Klein decided he would spend some of his sermons from now trying to communicate some of the higher and more peaceful virtues of the Venusians as he had experienced from the document he had been reading.

WORKING FROM THE MAINFRAME

Alex Spalding was one of the most important people in the world despite the fact that absolutely nobody from the general public would know his name or recognise his appearance, He was a man who was absolutely vital in the process of keeping people fed with the right knowledge, with the right beliefs and with the right desires. He worked for TV stations, advertising firms, corporations, governments, radio stations, newspapers, alien races and powerful individuals. He had a million different superiors all of them as demanding as the last; the work was a never ending shift of maintaining a central morality. The work was both thanklessly exhausting and cruel. He knew that his boss was about the most sinister being in the entire universe and that all of the stooges or superiors that gave him such a damn hard time were bad people. The work he was doing was all about control. Controlling what people think, controlling what people believing and controlling what people want to desire or indeed want to think. He was basically there to totally forge the human sub conscious and to ensure people thought was necessary and did what the people he worked for wanted. He was there to maintain a singularity of message for his employer; the main brief was to ensure that God was not to be the most dominant force on Earth. He was a silent operator, never to be shown. His work was constant, tireless and thankless. He had been appointed following a more complex interview process than any pope or president had to complete; the first interview was conducting by the secret services of Zone 3, the zone he was born in. They asked him at least two hundred questions regarding his past; it felt as if they literally wanted to know everything he had ever done or thought of doing that was even remotely unusual. They asked about his shopping habits, his eating habits and his leisure habits. They had known everything anyway; they told him how old he was when he first drank alcohol, the day and time of his first cigarette, the precise minute of his first experience of marijuana. Whenever he either inadvertently or deliberately tried to give a wrong answer, they were onto him immediately. When he tried to claim he had never tried ecstasy or LSD they pulled out a mini Vid-Screen and actually played him the footage of him taking the drugs. He was totally and utterly unravelled in the first interview; they practically examined his subconscious to try and assess whether he would instinctively make a correct or incorrect decision. Alex Spalding, social security no. 45565, age 29, right handed, 13 stone and 5"11, was a man truly known by the authorities. Months passed following the interview, which of course he was not able to tell anyone about, until he finally received a letter through the post. It simply stated a time and destination for him to attend; it was of course for a second interview that made the first one seem like an encounter with a stranger at a ticket booth. They played him clips of his life and asked him to explain in precise perfect detail what happened next. Each progressive clip seemed to be more obscure than the last; it was a real high pressure interview this time. They were saying things like 'if you don't deliver the perfect detail innocent people will die Alex. You are going to be responsible for the deaths of many innocent people if you get a single detail wrong". Strangely he managed to meet the pressure of the burly interviewer; the more he seemed to press for the right answer the more Alex felt like h was able to find the right answers. Things seemed to come to his recollection instantly. He knew the moment he went 30mph above the speed limit; he knew what he said to the attractive girl waiting in the café and he knew what he said to some of the security cams when very drunk a few years ago. He practically felt like asking them some questions about what happened later; judging by the stern and humourless demeanour of everyone he had dealt with so far with these guys it didn't feel like the move would go down too well. When the main man finally gave Alex an envelope and asked him to leave the premises he knew that he had got the job.

After the hugely strenuous interview process and a lengthy induction session, which introduced all of the machines and the techniques required to ensure that the right stream of information was broadcast, the job felt easy enough. The hard part for his employers was getting to know the character of the people being hired; that much became hugely clear to Alex after watching over potential other Alex's getting given the same trial induction periods. One time one of the people being given the full low-down actually burst into tears and practically cried out, 'I can't do this, I just can't handle all of this'. Some of the people really couldn't handle all that was required which was no real surprise to Alex; the needs of the job were incredibly complex. You had to be working every moment of the time at the building; it would be impossible to give anything less than 100%. The people that were in charge, who the fellow low level employees dealt with, probably had about ten bosses themselves, and they let you get away with absolutely nothing. Every single one of us working at the place knew the intense importance of delivering the right message, keeping the newspapers, TV stations and even people in the bars and pubs on track. The mission to deliver the truth was relentless; we had to make sure that the right information was always being passed on. Alex knew the basics of the message; that was all he was qualified to be able to handle. The core of what he delivered to editors, journalists and the occasional random other was to ensure (in this order of relevance) that people found answers to their questions in buying products, the World Government had everyone's interest at heart and that God was to be only addressed if religions became a problem to the other objectives. The work was clear enough and he knew his role. Life was totally and utterly job orientated. He didn't have time for pursuits outside of work and his work and mentality didn't exactly match up with great potential for mating partners. It was a long-term difficult job that melded with his daily life. Alex couldn't remember the reason why he decided to rebel against the orders of his bosses, but he felt compelled to.

His rebellion started small; the very first example was when he made a tiny alteration to subtly change the wording of an order given to a small scale newspaper editor. The story was about a mental health patient guilty of murder (which was a fabricated lie obviously set from the team working for both a powerful individual and a leading government) and was to have the headline, 'Escaped patient kills on rampage'. Alex however in his first minuscule act of professional alteration subtly changed the proposed headline to 'Escape patient killed on rampage'. The wording was only very minimally altered yet still from most employees would have been changed and treated as a slight mistake in grammar or a small alteration from the newspaper itself. The truth was however that he had developed enough of a reputation to deliver headlines to regional newspapers himself. The superiors at the building had seen his unbelievable productivity and had clearly deemed Alex as a responsible worker, which to the main extent was true. He was indeed very, very good at his job and was able to juggle different deadlines with confident aplomb. To be in this sanctified company people were seen as totally reliable. Sometimes he thought that most of his colleagues must have been robots; hell, some of the time he felt little more than a functioning robot himself. The tests that were required to work at this place were more demanding that any Olympic requirements, or any nano technological processes in his opinion. He was required to deliver the answers himself to the problems; there were no unquestionable formulas, indeed it was to be the job of his immediate superiors to ensure that he was able to be fluent and flexible in delivering those three core objectives. They were projected onto a huge screen set up at the front of the office; where there were other desks all pointing towards the giant monitor. The office wasn't crammed with desks; he had plenty of space in which to do his work as did the others. All workers had sufficient room to ensure that their conversations didn't overlap with those of other employees. There was almost a serenity to the task; he had his list of contact points and it was simply a case of sending Vid-Screen messages to the required contacts and to post reminder messages on the Sphere to ensure that the key individuals he was entrusted with dealing with knew about the central importance of the three main principles. That part of the job was easy enough; as always getting to this job was far harder than anything the work required. The job was definitely on the wrong side of mundane most of the time; repetition of the message and the monotony of being so single sided in dealing with everything was the hardest part. He was indeed a small cog in a very big machine; still he was a cog, ever spinning really. He couldn't ignore a single duty, they all had to be done. It was that which really offered Alex the potential to rebel really; the scale and scope of the duty really allowed a bit of freedom in the application of their needs. It was a small flaw in an otherwise perfect system, but still the powers that be should have incorporated more of an intensely scrutinising routine of the people that worked from within. So much effort was dedicated to controlling what the general public thought that there wasn't really any time focused on the internal machinations of the key workers. The induction process and interview process was perfect for the most part; they did indeed root out any free thinkers at all, they totally removed anyone with a history of dissension literally dating back to whether the individual answered back to teachers or parents. The interview process featured at least ten psychometric tests examining the personality profile of literally every possible candidate and interviewee. Ironically it was Alex who had scored the most perfect match of all time with his individual profile. He was seen as diligent, unquestioning, subservient and productive. Nobody had come close frankly to his levels of compatibility. He was the ideal candidate for one of the most important jobs in the world and whilst the scrutiny still remained over his job the people above him were deep down only concerned with their targets pertaining to people like

Alex, and frankly people like Alex were people like Alex. You could map out the DNA of their intellectual profile in the same manner as if he were a sponge or single celled creature. Alex would be the first and the last of the rebel cogs for various reasons.

The headline in the local newspaper may have gone seemingly undetected by his superiors and his bosses, however the impact of the news story was instantly felt. Alex found himself faced with a batch of four 'mental health patient' stories. The people at the top had clearly felt and covered a clear reaction from the general public. Indeed it was true; in the district where the paper was printed the powers that be had noticed that general levels of mistrust related to mental health problems, which was gauged through a manner of monitoring techniques, some of which were legal such as following any Sphere searches and other illegal approaches such as scanning subconscious reactions to people walking past the main district mental hospital in the area. It was a key concern of his employers that there was a them and us attitude maintained between 'normal people' and 'mental health patients'. If anyone in his office had known it was his subtle change to the headline had led to such a drop in patient suspicion he would have doubtlessly been fired and possibly worse even for such a relatively minor act of subterfuge. There was no chance anyone fired from his type of job could put it on their CV and those who were forced to leave for various reasons were normally never heard from again. Alex was aware of this and never clearly stuck his head above the parapet; no one did really in his position. He was simply a cog in the machine and the constant perpetual nature of the work meant that there wasn't time to do anything too stupid. The machine like nature of the operation was precisely the reason however that he was able to show his small act of distension.

Alex couldn't stop feeling like Winston Smith. Here he was in the year 2025 and he was actually doing the work of more than Big Brother. 1984 may have been nearly 50 years ago, yet here he was working away like an agent of the party, another cog in the information machine. He was living his compact life, unknown to basically anyone, being used to metaphorically generate the daily hate. That was probably the main reason he began to rebel. He was inspired by the hidden written letters of Smith; he wanted to offer more of a rebellion however. Something deep within him, hidden from the most glaring eye in the world, reached out and wanted to subtly infiltrate the barriers of meaning. Alex wanted to silently liberate people from the generated notions of fear and control that he was ironically and painfully so closely aligned with. It was only due to his phenomenal profile match that the bosses weren't scrutinising him; he was having his brief but blissful honeymoon period. The second attempt was slightly more daring than the first. He was asked by a leading corporation to spread the story that nutritional needs had changed in the last ten years and that to cover the effects of less vitamin D due to the increase in bad weather (which was indeed a five year trend, started by another employer) the 'required' number of fruit and vegetable portions increased from '5- a day' to '6- a day'. The truth was of course that following the increased spread of globalisation from China to prosperous African nations the levels of disposable income had notably increased whilst production costs had remained relatively the same. It also helped another employer to maintain the central and essential image of nutritional maintenance; man clearly could not live by bread alone or indeed with simply four of five pieces of fruit. Alex went to work; both for the company and as the slight continuation of his tiny rebellion. The sub headline sent to a major daily newspaper was changed from 'Leading nutritional expert Dr. Anders (a made up doctor of course) has recommended that adults and growing children should eat at least six pieces of fruit to ensure that the digestive system is able to break down complex sugars found in processed foods' to 'Leading expert Dr. Anders has released a new report showing the newly recommended daily allowance of six portions of fruit due to nutritional requirements". The summary was easy enough to follow; he was trying to slowly and careful integrate questions regarding perceptions of these reports. Even changes like this if discovered would have definitely seen him sacked and much more would have probably seen him killed. This early on however in the process gave him time and potential to begin to try and influence the national conscious. He couldn't remove the feeling that he had to differ from the line given to him by his employers. The need to rebel had been there the first day in the job. Something within him, something deep inside told him that the information being given had to be changed somehow, no matter how subtly. His mind was still theoretically perfect for the job; there were absolutely no indicators that he would cause any problems or make any mistakes. They had been tracing him for years and had great confidence in his ability to implement ideas. The job began as soon as the induction time had finished it was that comprehensive. They taught him literally everything he would need to know regarding the scale of the work. Or so he thought.

There was one exception. His task briefing for once was faintly vague. The instructions in the message simply read 'convince people of the need for insurance- newspaper, deadline Tues'. It didn't make any sense to him; it was the first time that had done anything remotely vague since he had began working for them. The job was so meticulous, they told him when he needed to go to the toilet. Yet here was a briefing from on high giving him leeway to decide how best to supply the case for insurance. Evidently the wording of the question was such that they trusted him to a far greater degree than he had thought. He was feeling nervous, a guilty energy had been coursing through his veins ever since he began his tiny rebellion. It felt strange to him that having initiated an approach that was critical of the instructions suddenly he was being given free reign to disagree as much as he wanted practically. The decision was swiftly made to give the headline 'insurance always pays out'. The work at the office had become autonomous; he didn't have to think for the last three months unless he actively told himself to. The truth was for 99.9% of the time, he was simply regurgitating press releases from any number of his bosses. The rebellious stories had seemed somehow necessary at the time; it felt to him that he needed to question the basics of authority no matter how small his counteractions were. Yet suddenly it seemed as though his employers were unconcerned with minor deviation. Having gone through the trauma basically of such an induction trial here he was working as basically a minor unimportant cog. The joke that a trained animal could do his job wasn't a joke; he knew in his heart of hearts that spending the same amount of time training an octopus or maybe a mechanical spider would produce someone at least as effective as him. Plus the mecha-spider or trained octopus would not go off message every three months to try a feeble unseen rebellion. The job had got to him frankly. He had joined the organisation a well trained, hugely achieving MBA graduate with a wealth of global experience and following placements a working knowledge of much of the expanding financial sectors globally. He was well trained for basically any job; M15 had tried to hire him as had the Foreign Office and an unnamed American firm. All had expressed close interest in utilising his skills; he was set to have a fantastically successful career in whatever field he chose. That was of course when he received the message that he was being head-hunted by the organisation he currently worked for and still didn't have the name of The leading organisations all knew about his talents which meant that all of the major shadow organisations knew about him too. Frankly he had suspicions that a firm such as the one he now worked for existed. There obviously didn't advertise the position he was eventually hired for. They simply called him out of nowhere one weekend. They informed him heavily about his potential skills and the importance of the job. All of this build up, all of the promise and potential he had and now he was used as nothing more than a speaking fax machine. A body that just about type faster than a robot spider or an octopus. Suddenly he felt annoyed at himself for the small scale rebellion; he felt angry for tweaking the edges of his work which was mundane enough as it was. The tiny rebellion basically was a mirror for his tiny life. Used by the powers that be; manipulated as much as any one of the normal people who hadn't had conversations with the top brass of any group. He suddenly felt cheated; he was more of a cog than any guy working a long shift at a factory. They both shared the limits on taking a piss though. It all seemed ridiculous; the five years at top university, the efforts of schooling, the work and business placements and for what? To retype the orders of the people who gave all of the orders as they always had done. He had the delusion and the sense that his life would be more. He was the top of the list in almost literally every single class he had ever been in. People from government agencies were always giving him tests after school and he was being given briefings from the age of 13 about the types of jobs that were being lined up for him. Something though still nagged in the back of his head; just get them to think about insurance. Just get people to change their mind from getting it out of fear to getting it as a positive measure to protect their home or business. Still work from the inside Alex; use the position of privilege you have to very subtly alter the more oppressive nature of the orders given to him. It was then that he thought perhaps the rebellious moves were not so small after all. Any measures whatsoever that questioned the unseen hierarchy of high command was a forward step. He had only met the people who had trained him through the grotesque induction. He had no clue whatsoever which people, come to think of it which nations or which companies or whoever that were given the orders. His orders were simply that, orders. It was probably a slight rebellious streak he had inherited from his Father that encouraged him to consider going against his orders. It wasn't as if he was instigating a mutiny; he was simply looking to smooth the edges of the instructions. From the story about insurance to the fruit story and the mental health dilemmas, Alex was very slowly (or so he thought) beginning to initiate a real campaign of change from his lowly position. That was partially the case, until the day he was called to the top floor office.

"Greetings, Mr. Spalding correct?"

"Yes sir" Alex felt his heart beat faster than an interplanetary jet craft; a surge of guilt was also coursing through his veins like some sort of radioactive lava.

"We have a new assignment for you"

"Really? I mean of course yes that's fine; I'm only trained for news and information consumption at the moment"

"We are aware of that, and also that the job may not be the best way to utilise a man of your talents"

Alex was feeling very strange and light headed. He had been one million per cent certain that this meeting with a chief from the company would result in his sacking and a comprehensive debriefing at best. At worst it would have been a short meeting with the chief followed by a shorter meeting with one of the more violent members of the firm.

"You're ability to present information effectively and clearly has not gone unnoticed Mr. Spalding"

Alex was feeling totally sick at this point; he knew in his heart of hearts that they must have spotted his rebellious stories. Sure for the most part he was disciplined but those acts, they stuck out so clearly in his mind.

"We need you to meet someone Alex"

"Right, yes I could do that of course sir"

"We need you to meet the key representative of the Asian branch of our firm. He will be in London for literally four hours this Friday and we need someone relatively uninformed in our private practices to meet him".

"This job sounds too big for me, sir"

"No, it's ideal for you Mr. Spalding. You see we know that the Asian branch of our organisation shares the same mind scanning technology that we have recently acquired. I could not do the job as too much would be revealed regarding our more covert aspects of business. They are doubtlessly sending someone similar to yourself Mr. Spalding. The problem of industrial espionage is one we take incredibly seriously"

The doubt and fear that had gripped Alex at the start of the meeting returned, seemingly grabbing hold of his mind and body, leaving him totally helpless and scared. [1]

"Allow my colleague to take you back to your desk. Good luck Mr. Spalding"

On his way back down to his floor office further questions and doubts flawed through his mind like an ever churning whirlpool. All he could see in the bottom of the whirlpool was an octopus typing away. Then a thought struck him, in a bad way. If they had mind reading technology against the Asian representatives surely they would be able to read and understand his thoughts regarding a potential rebellion.

Alex didn't get the chance to introduce himself to his Asian counterpart; indeed it was they who introduced themselves to him by loading him into the back of an unnamed hover van.

"Who do you work for Mr. Spalding?"

He felt terrified beyond all belief.

"What, the same organisation as you guys. What the hell is going on? Why have you captured me?"

"Stop asking questions Mr. Spalding, we know about your acts of sabotage. We know about your changes made to the mental health stories, the changes relating to the 6- a day plan and the changes made about insurance. Did you really expect us not to follow up on these acts of sabotage Mr. Spalding?"

"Shit, shit, shit. No I didn't expect a follow up, it's my fault"

"We know; all we now require is for you to tell us who exactly it was who gave you the orders to change the stories and we will release you and allow to go back to your normal life"

"That's the thing", Alex could hear his heart pound like an automated press, "Nobody gave the orders. It was me, I made the changes".

"Alex, the one thing that bothers us more than espionage from fellow professionals at the firm, is someone who then doesn't give us what we need to know. You've been caught Spalding, so give us some names"

"Names? There are no names; listen to me, please I'm telling you it was me, I initiated the measures, no-one else, please believe me"

"We cannot, so perhaps you need some more convincing". At this point one of the burly assistants to his apparent Asian counterpart pulled out

---

1

both a small laser pistol and a pair of pliers.

"In five minutes Mr. Spalding if we don't have an answer, you won't have any thumbs. In ten minutes you won't have any toes and any longer than that and you will no longer be with us. So, I ask you again, and there shall not be many more opportunities to address this question, tell me who gave you the orders to change the stories"

Blind panic was still rushing through him at an uncontrollable rate; the fear he was feeling was more intense than any other experience in his whole life. He kept searching for how to begin, he decided to bluff.

"Look I'll tell you, but you have to at put away that fucking pistol"

"Tell us a name Spalding, or you'll know everything you need to know about this particular weapon"

Names kept surging through his mind; people who he could blame. They must have known that he didn't know the names of any other employees there, from what he was told no one did. He tried the only person he could think of

"It's the top floor boss; I don't know his name I tell you. He gave me the instructions. I'll tell you everything you need to know. He wanted to start counteracting your Asian operation". The bluff was in full flow now.

"He… he wanted to begin offering a different message. However slight; he told me he wanted to start making inroads with your firm. He wanted a kinder message to be delivered, at a cost. He wanted to begin a rebellion"

"A rebellion?" The guy was fuming. "A rebellion? Damn it!"

"If you are lying Mr. Spalding we will find you and this incident will feel like a honeymoon with Miss fucking Universe. Understand us? You'll live alright, but on my terms. So you're finally telling us it's the top floor branch at the London sector?"

"Yes, God yes, just let me go, I won't tell them a thing, I'll just get back to work as normal, I'll forget all about this"

"Damn correct Mr. Spalding. We find out you give any indication whatsoever to your boss, then we will kill you on sight. Any message to a worker on your floor, we will kill all of the employees on your floor to keep things clean. You should not have worked for such an employer, but for the name we will let you live, for now"

Alex felt drained of existence upon getting back to his flat. He felt both ashamed and scared that people high up within his organisation had known about what he was doing. The fact that people had been monitoring him for the minuscule deviations got terrified thinking about what else they may have sensed during his time at work. Was this just a way of setting him up for his permanent removal from the company; I mean he legally couldn't tell anyone, ever, about his time working for such a firm and they actively discouraged emotional relationships during the time of working for such a firm. He felt that unmoveable fear; these Asian representatives were going to kill him he felt certain of that. The guy who he met was bad enough, but the people he had working alongside him could probably snap him in two with their hands. The rebellion had been a terrible idea and he knew it. The compressed guilt kept asking him to define why he had rebelled, why he had compromised such a lucrative and important job, and the worst thing was, was that he couldn't think of a clear answer. He had no boss to hate, he had no difficult colleagues to deal with, he had a flawless childhood and providing nothing went wrong with the firm, which was already too late of course, then he could have absolutely had his pick of any job due to the elaborately faked references that would have set him up for any work. He couldn't ignore the idea that maybe he was rebelling for his Dad rather than the usual against; he didn't worry too much about the psychological stuff though frankly, he had the personality profile that was perfect for high achievement within large organisations. He was adaptive, resourceful, disciplined and communicative. Well for the most part. The job felt like it was totally getting the better of him, and it was only because he would have to either be debriefed, or frankly much worse, after working for such an organisation that he wasn't dead. He felt like that time inside the hover van, with the Asian boss and his heavies, all from Japan seemingly, that he thought it was all over. No more 21 hour shifts, no more setting out the plans for the days news, no more politely threatening phone calls. It still felt to Alex like the end; he had his shift by the gears of power and somewhat surprisingly to himself he had failed. His mind had made him rebel and now as a result of his rebellion he had probably both damned himself and his newly met boss on the top floor to execution. Getting ready the next day for work seemed to take an eternity. The mundane of his final day alive, and of work, seemed far too much like another procedural event. If his mind wasn't already calibrated with drugs, he probably would have felt depressed.

Having entered his code, faced the retina scan, given the password to the door guard and finally given a thumb scan he entered his first floor office and slinked to his desk. No-one was about at this time as usual due to the different shift patterns of the people in his position. For all of the repetitive boredom of the work and his position permanently as a lackey for others he still possessed a certain amount of power, which the huge empty office in front of him attested to. He was the main individual there to 'cross the Ta and dot the Is'. He was a human franking machine basically giving that finally seal of approval like a modern form of waxy monk. In spite of all this he still felt dehumanised; it was the oppressive nature of the orders. Obviously as he was still in a job he had sufficiently learnt to follow those orders given, bar the spectacularly punished exceptions, and he was more focused than ever on being that functional cog again. Five minutes into his last working day on the first floor and for only the second time in his relatively short career, Alex was summoned to see the top floor boss. He duly shut down and his monitor and promptly followed the bespectacled higher level employee to the elevator heading to the top floor.

Then the shots were fired; at first Alex felt sure he had been hit and was dead. The air was filled with the smoke of a laser pistol and the still echoing shatter of the glass doors in front of him. After what seemed like an eternity, Alex heard the familiar voice of his Japanese captor who simply said, 'come in Alex'. Next to him, smiling in an eerie manner was the top floor boss who he had suspected had been the first target of such a dramatic assassination attempt. He spoke quietly to Alex in a direct manner
'Please excuse the fireworks Mr. Spalding but we had no choice'
'What, we? What is going on sir, are you going to kill you'
'We already have Mr. Spalding' came the reply from the Asian boss.
'What I'm dead? I feel about as alive as I did this morning'
'You are still literally alive Spalding, but to the employees of this organisation in both Asian and UK branches you are now legally dead'
Alex was beginning to understand the significance; if they wanted him killed the shots from the laser pistol would have been between his eyes rather than at the glass office doors.
'You passed our test Mr. Spalding' came the boss.
'What test sir?'
'The ambition test Mr. Spalding!' laughed the Japanese boss.
'You would not believe the amount of employees in your position who don't give a name for their misdeeds. You had the guts to give the on name

in the firm you had;

'But… but I was lying'

'Not exactly actually Alex'

'What do you refer to sir?'

'Well we at this branch and the Asian branch had to check to see the extent of your loyalty'

'The insurance question was set by us in the Asian department; we knew about your deviations of course Mr. Spalding. What you may be unaware of however is the simple fact that everyone the organisation has ever hired and doubtlessly will ever hire have in some way deviated'

'If that's true' began Alex, 'then why fake the capture? Why trap me and threaten me with a fucking laser pistol?'

'We had to make sure that you would be capable enough to improvise during more testing conditions. Needless to say we will debrief you on what you can and can't do, in your new position, but what I can assure you now is that it will be you pointing the laser pistol at others from now on'

'Right, why me though? What about the others who had similarly deviated, some must have indicated the top floor workers?'

'They are indeed with us in other positions. The entire first floor operation you have been with so far is a front. It is simply a test of mental ability, flexibility and adaptability. You were not chosen like the others as one of the best in order to simply cover press releases. Yet we needed to know if that was what was required of you for months as cover, that you would do it'

'So none of the work was sent out?'

'None Mr. Spalding we have more than enough other employees in order to cover such duties. You were selected as one of the best and haven't let us down'

'But I pointed out the guy in the first floor, you sir, as the person who was guilty despite knowing you had nothing to do with it'

'We are not totally inflexible ourselves, Mr Spalding. Simply know that you passed enough of the tests to eventually start field work'.

With that Alex was handed his issued laser pistol and immediately given a briefing for work in the Asian market. There was an employee who had began a small scale alterations to the orders given at a Chinese newspaper; the irony was not lost on him. Still he gathered his composure, left the office and headed to the airport. The top brass of the organisation would find out too late about his partnership with the worker and their inroads into the Chinese news market. Alex Spalding lived to fight and rebel another day, aiming to slowly but surely bring down the organisation in China first, Asia second and then the UK market. His life as a professional rebel had just begun.

EARTH 2030

It all happened when no one was paying attention; everything came when we thought we had nothing to fear and could control everything. They knew that; they had always known that about us. I think if it wasn't them, the Apolites, we would have faced another invasion from the Martians or some giant plants or something else. We were least prepared for the Apolites because they were so much like us; they had humanoid shapes and evidently human ideas about conquest and Empire. Earth had become just an outpost where our resources were mined and we were treated like second class citizens. They came with their giant ships and they had taken command of every continent within a week. They just waited whilst the military bombarded the giant crafts with almost literally everything we had. Everyone in the US at least was sent miles underground to avoid nuclear fallout and risk of death. In the poorer countries it was mainly just the dignitaries and ambassadors that were sent to security underground; too many innocent people lost their lives. Communication had been returned in the last year, and it was clear most of Earth was a bomb site. It felt ironic that without the food from the Apolites, seeking to keep an Earthbound work force alive we would all be dead. The strange thing about the whole invasion was that any damage done to the surface of the Earth, to those not able to make it to safety in the secluded parts of the world away from the potential reprieve of modern life, was done by us. The innocent lives of literally millions were taken by the effects of our weapons against their ships, they themselves fired no shots. They killed no individuals upon landing either; I wasn't the first person to think they were more human than we ever were. Those that survived on the scorched Earth were sent to makeshift towns built by the Apolites; they gave the people shelter, food and work. They seemed interested in providing and supplying our needs rather than denying them. They didn't just think in terms of killing or attacking either, they waited for any surface attacks before moving in. I don't doubt that those giant ships could have blown up half of the world if they wanted to do so, but they didn't. After the week of attacks, smaller crafts were sent down to move the survivors into the zones being prepared for human life. The Apolites did more for the poor and defenceless than any government had done; nobody talked about that much though. No, the word from the underground was always of hate towards the Apolites. Word was always being spread about the terrible things they were planning or had done; you name it and I guarantee a rumour was spread about it. I always thought it was the government officials down here starting them, but they were always spread by the rest of the people, it was hard to know or care about the difference. Attacks, killings, blood sucking, scalping, probing, mind control, death rays all came up regularly. Occasionally I'd hear a rumour that they were experimenting with our DNA, I always thought though why would they need our DNA I have no idea, still though the rumours persisted. They would always be seen as the enemy. The life underground was tense; there was more room than you'd think in these subterranean homes, but still it was arguments were always persistent. It was probably the lack of natural light that was making everyone a bit tense. Life suddenly felt truly unnatural, even though it was hardly different though from working 9 to 5 in a cramped office desk. It took aliens to make us think about what humanity truly was. I still didn't really know after 6 months of being down here; fear and doubt were always pertinent. People just kept spreading the rumours, which I always felt were lies. We were never shown the surface, we were just shown daily updates from the remains of the World Government telling us about what the Apolites had done and what was being attempted to deal with them. They were always being described as invaders, as aliens, as heartless individuals harvesting the riches of the world at the expense of us. It all seemed a bit ridiculous, the attempts to demonise creatures so akin to humans it was almost comical. The endless criticisms of the Apolites would have been pertinent if they weren't just repeating the actions of humanity in a vastly more effective, and frankly humane manner. Humanity was never questioned underground; we were always right they were always wrong. People would cheer the announcements of the World Government; 'weapons are being designed to paralyse the minds of the Apolites', 'we have captured an Apolite worker and are interrogating him now', 'any day now a surface assault will be launched'. All of these planned actions against a few aliens that had actually taught us a thing or two about dealing with the truly destitute. When it came to the delivery of food parcels to us down below, sadly there were always arguments and problems; people were unhappy with their lot, always asking more for themselves or their children. Food had become a scarce commodity with the World Government still at war with the Apolites. That was the official story anyway. I didn't mind the packages, I was a single guy so was almost at the bottom of the list but they provided fruit, vegetables and bread. Meat was pretty scarce unfortunately, but living in an underground communal prison with cramped individual rooms suddenly haute cuisine seemed less than pertinent. We were given the basics and nothing more, so as you could imagine some of the complaints got pretty heated. I never bothered with the arguments myself; the people providing the food had guns, and I had a normal human body, which still hadn't developed any form of natural resistance to bullets funnily enough, so I took my deliveries quietly and with perfunctory thanks. Some people were like me to an extent, they just were thankful to get some food whilst we were being ruled by aliens, but some of the other complaints were raucous. People would demand the strangest things; 'I want some proper fucking cereal damn it!', 'Why the hell can't we have veal?' 'I want some proper fruit, like mangoes'. People seemed to use the food deliveries as an excuse to vent their frustration at the general levels of denial. We all had space to live, families got larger quarters than single people, but still I guess the lack of privacy got some people more down than others. It was ironic that suspicion of one another grew almost as much as our suspicion of the Apolites. There were always rumours about who had chocolate, who was negotiating to get back to the surface and who was having an affair with who. The place had a crazy atmosphere, and everyone seemed to be negotiating to get back to the surface to try and regain their normal lives. The guards though were practically Nazis; any discussions they heard about planning an escape to the surface lead to a meeting with the Commander. The Commander was the man who introduced the television broadcasts to us; he was a huge, broad, greying man who seethed with rage whenever he had to mention the Apolites. He kept us informed of military engagements and always offered us information about when we were due to get back to Earth. Sometimes the date was sooner than last week, sometimes it was later, but basically the date for returning to the surface was always some nominal time in the near future. I never paid much attention to the dates of the Commander; he just seemed a bit too crazy. His influence was felt though; some people would have the same expression as the Commander when discussing the Apolites, it was kind of crazy really. Thankfully not everyone down here was crazy. There was this one guy, Alan, who used to be a Catholic priest on the old Earth. He would talk to us about how some of The Bible prophesied such an out coming involving 'other' beings. It was through Alan that I came to find out about the close link between the God that we once knew, and the Apolites. Ted was not the first person to see the arrival

163

of such a powerful force as being representative of judgement day; although wildly different from what was predicted in Revelations, as a man of faith and scripture, Alan genuinely believed these aliens, these Apolites, were a divine force sent by God to punish the Earth for it's misdeeds. Not too many of the fellow believers in the underground disagreed with him.

Ted didn't tell this story to everyone; he was more than wary about being highlighted as an outsider, or maybe some sort of nut job that would need processing, but to those that he probably thought were on a similar wave length to him, which included me and a few others, he would give a sermon to. He said to us,
'Look this story is going to sound crazy, but I can tell you guys that some of this information came from a very high grade priest I had contacted in Rome, who I trust much more than I do any of you guys so you can take most of what follows as being fairly true".
The man looked a bit unhinged when speaking to us; he had a mad glint in his eye as if he'd seen something strange a policeman or someone else had constantly ignored him about. I took it to be a reasonable sign that he knew what he was talking about. He began, as always, with context;
'When the first alien came to see us, the world was young and knowledge was scarce. God was just the man that brought the winds and the grain. Sometimes he wasn't even that. The idea of God was as a man in the sky, keeping watch over the world. People still worshipped, but it was more in a reactionary fashion. People would celebrate great feasts, abundant rains or the birth of a child. God was someone to thank in the good times, and pray to in the bad times. He remained an unknown force really; the ancient man who witnessed the first alien visit didn't even have scripture to follow, there were no knowledgeable priests or even those pretending to be knowledgeable priests (that line would always raise a small laugh with the crowd). It was a monumental occasion for those that witnessed the event. The only recorded witness was a man in Egypt, he was a tribesman who recorded the major events on a papyrus scroll. His information was very brief but it was enough to pass on eventually to Rome. The event began when this tribesman, Ahmet, recorded going outside his tent with his wife to examine a 'loud noise'. An object described as a giant wingless bird flew over the head of the pair, this man, Ahmet, is then described as going alone to follow the sound of the craft. He went over to examine the craft

and described how there was a 'large creature that looked like a very white man' was lying there injured. He is described as speaking to the creature, who is recorded as saying I swear to you, and don't forget this incident is well over 2500 years ago people may I remind you, 'Thank you Ahmet, I am Phelox of the Apolites, you're kindness will be rewarded'.

A youngster interrupted Alan, 'wow so you mean, the Egyptians they knew about these guys, and they didn't do anything to help or to warn the rest of us'.

'That isn't strictly true my inquisitive friend, it is documented on that papyrus, and I swear to you now that this is the genuine truth from my friend of the cloth, 'you shall be saved when my people return'.

'But, none of us we're saved sir, we were all made to live underground, they didn't save any of us we all have to wait here until they are ready for us to work'.

'To an extent that is true young man, but consider the fact that there have been no reported deaths from the actions of the Apolites at all. More people have died choking on food than have been killed by the aliens; they kept to their word by killing none of us. I'm of the belief that that one guy, Phelox will eventually return and rescue us all as thanks for the efforts of the prophet Ahmet'. When he'd finished the sentence, the main sceptic, Geoff chipped in.

'I can't believe you keep telling people that Alan. Your attempts to generate hope especially to the youngsters here who are vulnerable enough is going to do more harm than good. We've been down here for more than five years, eating the same crap and doing the same things. There ain't gonna be an alien saviour who rescues us. These guys came and saw all of the cool stuff we had on Earth and took it. Shit, they probably got the idea from the way we treated those Indian tribes or the way that black people were made to be slaves and all. They saw us come and pay nothing for the stuff the guys made in the poorer countries and they thought, 'hell if these humans can exploit the resources so quickly we'll exploit them. It's a case of chickens coming home to roost; we as humans were never gonna be the only one's out there looking for oil or coal or food. God weren't there for the Indians or the black man when they were being used and killed, he sure as heck ain't gonna be there for us ordinary white folk when someone comes to exploit you'.

One of the old farmers, John, intervened,

'Hey not everyone supported slavery Frank, some of us try and treat

165

people as being the same whatever colour, ain't that right Alan?'.

'Yes of course, but I hear what brother Frank is trying to say; it could well be that the Apolites are here to bring about Judgement Day, to remove evil from the face of the Earth and begin the process of separating the damned from the saved'.

One of the most cynical members of the group, Graham, then intervened, 'When are you going to get it Alan? Don't you realise that the day has passed. We've been judged and this place sure as hell isn't heaven; it's over, none of us passed, not you, not the youngster and not Mr. Frank Willis either. We all fucked up the whole planet, it ain't right you bringing up the possibility of some saviour from the aliens, it just ain't going to happen. We had one and it went, story over. He came all them years ago and look what happened, he was killed by the people he was trying to save. The same ones, Alan! We're being punished for all of that shit killing innocent people and for starting all them wars'.

Alan tried to give his case as usual, 'Look I understand that view but come off it Graham, you know the whole world wasn't just exploiting people and starting wars. There were good people, people of faith living their lives according to God and The Bible and Jesus, you know that'.

'So cos a few people in the south pray a bit we ain't guilty of ruining the Earth? You really believe that Alan, three years after being here with no proper food and living on each others toes?'

'For forty days and forty nights Jesus was tested by the devil, I believe this is the same'

'Sure and look how that turned out! He was killed cos there weren't enough good people out there to defend him; heck you know I'm religious, that's why I'm here but you bringing up Jesus and how he died for us, well it isn't a sign to me that things are going to get better'.

'You do believe in the resurrection though don't you Graham?' Alan felt a bit aghast, internally aware perhaps for one of those occasions in his life about the destination of his faith.

'I don't know anymore. Maybe, but if he came back how come we don't know what he did afterwards, it's only the stuff he did before he died and then his death, that's all we know about'.

'But that's the important bit, the key to the message; he died for our sins Graham, I hope you still believe that'.

'I don't know any more; he died because of our sins Alan, that's what I think. It isn't as if he really just came down from heaven and just

166

magically took away our sins is it? If he did, why did these aliens come and put us all under the ground like damned sardines?'

'Look I understand your emotions I really do, but this whole picture is complicated, faith in God means….'

Graham interrupted, 'It's always faith though isn't it? Why do we have to rely on just faith that things are going to work out right? Things isn't too right at the moment are they? We ain't blessed by God and Jesus, I'm sure as anything he hasn't saved us from our sins. This is the end Alan. I mean if these aliens, sure there nice enough now, but if they use up all our oil or coal or diamonds whatever the hell these people want, if they use it all up there ain't no need to keep us alive'.

'There is one possible way though we can all be saved Graham',

'What's that Alan, try and give them a Bible or something, pretend to be dead so they leave us alone?'

'I want to talk to them, and to try and find out if there ever was or still is a Phelox amongst them'.

'What and you think just cos one of them met up years ago with some guy in Asia or wherever all that time ago, just one of em, that they are just gonna go, "well, hey you're right that old guy did come here and heck he was treated real nice so lets just move all of our machines and let all them people back on to the Earth. In case I need to remind you Alan, there ain't an Earth to return to; you know as well as I do that our military did more damage to the resources than them aliens. We were the first ones to fuck up this planet and we'll be the last, you know it'

'Maybe though, if I can get to them, to teach them then we may just somehow convince them that we ourselves can rebuild the Earth'

'So what, just remain their pets but working on the land instead of operating some machines? No thanks, I ain't being a slave'

'Maybe we've got no choice Graham'.

'We've always got a choice Alan, shouldn't you be trying to work out an escape route rather than just trying to negotiate with these guys? We own this planet we should be fighting these guys not just living like damn ants on an ant farm'.

'Do we own this planet Graham? Why do we own it more than the Apolites? They've got better machines and weapons so they took us over; it should be a familiar story'

'Not this again; look I'm fed up about apologising for all the wars, Hitler, Saddam Hussein, these were bad people and you know it'.

'I know I hear you, but what about the First World War? There wasn't always a clear enemy to fight, so much of warfare was devastating and unnecessary'.

'You make it sound like we're innocent, Alan; you know it ain't the case. You know as well as I do that Judgement Day has come, God has spoken and, well, heck we've all been damned. Sorry kids but that's how I feel'.

'We aren't dead though yet, we have the chance for redemption and I believe I can reason with these guys'

'Look I've had enough of this sermon and so forth for tonight gentlemen, so I'm off to recline elsewhere. Good night good sirs. Good sirs, shit'

Frank intervened 'I'm sorry about all that, the guy can get emotional dealing with this claustrophobia and all'

'That's fine thank you Frank. Wearing these religious garments in public can lead to some of the most insulting things you can imagine. Graham was very much a gentlemen in comparison'

'Do you think we've been damned then Alan?'

'Well, honestly; to an extent yes I think we've been judged but I believe there is a lot more to God than just scripture, far more than just Revelations in the New Testament too'

'That's why you're going to talk to them isn't it?'

'Yes. I believe we can all be saved Graham'

'I agree with some of the stuff he said. I guess it's true, you may be too late Alan, you know that don't you?'.

'Despite that, to be honest sir I have more faith in these Apolites than in any of the humans I've met, my contact in Rome included Graham'.

'Sure thing, night Alan; come on kid, let's get some sleep'

The rest of the group soon left after that and Alan was left to think. He couldn't shift the image of Ahmet, being promised freedom. Perhaps those people in Egypt had already been freed though he began to think. Maybe the other guys, Frank and Graham were right. There was a likely chance that the prophesied Judgement Day and come and gone in the shape of these aliens, the Apolites. No, that can't be, he assured himself. I will escape from these confines, convince the humans running the facility to take me to see the leaders of the Apolites and I will see us all freed on the promise of Ahmet. Unbeknownst to Alan however, there was already opposition to his plan.

Franklin hated Alan. Deep down it burnt into what was left of his sorry soul; the worst part was that he agreed with so much of what was being said. That was what killed him inside, he knew that what with the world as it was there just wasn't the time or room to complain. Every weekend would be the same; hearing the same damn sermons, getting the same moralising from the one official priest. Franklin never let on to anyone that he was Jewish. It seemed difficult to bring up what with all the talk of saviours. That wasn't it though; he just felt isolated by the tone of Alan. He always knew better than the others, always bringing up that stuff about the guy in Egypt, he hated it. He hated the fact that he always seemed to know more about the ancient world than a devout Semite such as himself. He never told anyone in the compound about his true faith, truth is no one asked him about it. There was just the same old sermons, telling us about Jesus and how he died and how the sacrifices of this guy Ahmet (if he was so damn important how come nobody had heard of him other than Alan?) would save us again. The days were long at this place. Franklin felt the cabin fever worse than most of the others. Obviously the first lot of guys sent down here by them who were a real problem, the type that would cause huge arguments about resources and such were dealt with effectively by the Apolites. They had obviously learnt from us about the powerful influence of solitary confinement. The guys who spent any time in those places came back totally changed; I guess it was a bit scary at first. It seemed ironic that we were being treated like animals, penned in like pigs waiting to be gutted. Hell they treated us better than that; thank God they didn't get a taste for human flesh. Franklin never really had a problem with the Apolites, they treated us well enough. People here weren't judged on colour, race or faith. We were all treated equally and were told everything that was going on. The compound wasn't tiny thankfully, there was space to stretch your legs occasionally. These aliens had come and would release us when the Earth was ready on time; it just felt like Alan was trying to take some sort of divine glory from the intervention of the Apolites. Something bothered Franklin about the way Alan had reacted to the situation. He had really taken a religious zeal to discussing the eventual 'salvation' of us in the end. Humanity was once again being depicted as a species always unclean and requiring rescuing through a sacrificial saviour. I mean Alan didn't even really pay lip service to the idea that the Apolites were here to punish those humans who failed; he didn't even consider that they were as a form of holy punishment to damn mankind for all of the wars, slaughter, starvation, fascists and terrorists. He just kept on

169

with the idea that we would all eventually be saved. Well maybe some of us didn't deserve to be saved; salvation seemed like such an act of magic and just somehow felt out of step with Franklin's belief in God. Salvation came to those who sought it, it wasn't merely a present. Alan doled out the hope of salvation to everyone like it was a cup of coffee or something. Something troubled him and he knew it about Alan; hell it was probably just the way he always owned the room whenever he was speaking. He had that way with words which captured the attention, and looks of some of the ladies in particular. It was the tightness of the confines more than anything; the inability of escape and to just go somewhere new; to just take a walk somewhere new and be free of all the chatter and all the talk of destiny and God and such like. Sure he found refuge with some of the non-religious guys in the places they frequented but truth was too many of them seemed depressed and didn't want to talk about the current situation at all.

John was one of the guys who had no interest in worshipping God; for all he cared God left as soon as those aliens in their massive space ships came and started making us all live together underground. He had been bought up a Christian in a small town in America; he went to the local church every week for Sunday School and was made by this parents to read The Bible. He knew about religion and about what a bastard God was described as being. Sunday School didn't help; as far as he was concerned sending his only son to die for our sins wasn't exactly the actions of a compassionate being if that was the truth. John was disturbed by the sheer pace that a religious coalition formed around Alan. He had this power to convince people and his rhetoric had proved spectacularly convincing. Everyone wanted to hear about his stories and his views, especially that bullshit stuff about that Arab guy Ahmet. Something about Alan reminded him of his old preacher; sure Alan was better at hiding the fire and brimstone stuff than Father Prendegast but still he seemed to contain that dangerous element of righteous verbal power. John was no idiot; he knew that whilst guys like Prendegast and Alan were good people overall. They really believed in being decent to your fellow man and preparing for the afterlife, they just unfortunately seemed to have that aura of being able to convince anyone of anything. These people, maybe not the really religious ones, these were the people who got black guys hung. They were the people in olden times that would force out Jewish communities; they would be the groups who would kill abortionists and who would

170

eventually start religious wars. John knew they were far from being terrible people and it was that which made them even more dangerous. Despite knowing this something still sat inside his mind; he feared greatly for the direction of the people under the Apolites. Hell, sometimes he felt that Alan probably was one of those damn aliens and he was just there to keep these people imprisoned with lies about hope and messages of peace. Probably sent here by the same people who had damn well locked us all up underground and away from the Earth we were supposed to have been given by God. John wanted to be out of this prison as much as anyone, he just didn't want to rely on that escape being determined by a lunatic or some guy in a fairy story. When John was finally contacted by the mysterious Mr. H he found a hope to his prayers.

The crowd gathered once more in the tiny metaphorical pulpit which Father Alan still seemed to own. Talk of this mysterious Ahmet had spread around their complex like wild fire. People everywhere were trying to find out where this Father Alan could be found; some people were even beginning to say, this Father Alan is a new prophet and will help us deliver the true message of God. As it can be with these things a counter rebellion was just beginning to develop; an underground insurrection if you will. Some people were beginning to be more forceful in their atheistic approach to life. There were growing rumours spreading about this religious guy who was starting to get a movement going. Father Alan was fairly clued up on all of the happenings around the base and very much tried to level his approach to the now increased and more varied audience. "Ladies and gentlemen, people of faith I know and the other individuals who I have not yet been introduced to. Thank you all for your presence here at this key moment in human history. Never before had the people of Earth ever come across an alien species and been able to tell the tale, yet now we, as denizens of Complex 63, are here in the flesh and able to experience life with an alien force".
There were some faint cheers and a small round of applause even this early on.
"I know that many of you, including some of my good friends of this small congregation such as Graham and indeed others have started to worry about what our situation as undoubtedly prisoners says about God. I put it to you that humanity has not yet been eternally damned, though that may alas happen to some of us here in this base. It says clearly in the New

Testament, in Romans, "The wages of sin is death", and I would each of you to consider whether we are all now paying the price of our sins and greed and doubt throughout the years".

"Did not the Lord say to Ezekiel, 'By the swords of the mighty will I cause thy multitude to fall, the terrible of nations all of them'. I would hope most of you think that even our nation, the great USA, was not recovered from the state of being a terrible nation".

In the midst of some cheers, Father Alan heard a very clear voice, "That is bullshit Alan; I won't accept this nonsense about America being damned. We weren't the only nation taken over, it was the whole damn world. Plus you make it sound like these people are sent by God, like they were angels or something. How about the idea that these guys are a test to us; I know my Bible too Father and does it not say in the New Testament…" Graham reached for his back pocket and pulled out a small red copy of the New Testament.

'Let nothing be done through strife or vainglory; but in the lowliness of mind let each other esteem each other better than themselves".

"That is a fair point, Graham, but I would argue that if The Bible has taught us anything it's that, well good things come to those who wait".

There were a few laughs at that remark and a small round of applause. "You see friends, I'm a firm believer in God as a compassionate being. A perfect entity of love and mercy; he didn't leave us here alone any more that Jesus was left alone or indeed any of the other prophets".

Franklin politely intervened at this point "Any of the other prophets? I don't think that's right Father."

"Please go on, brother Franklin"

"Right, I was just saying that even though God was with the prophets, he wasn't there to really offer comfort or love I'm sorry to say. He was sending a warning through these people; I mean to Jeremiah he told us "I will correct thee in measure, and will not leave thee altogether unpunished".

"That does indeed sound like the same God I believe in too, testing Jesus for 40 days, leaving even the son of God not fully unpunished".

There was another small round of applause at that point, one guy called out from the back of the assembly 'damn right!'

Franklin continued whilst he had the floor, "I was choosing the most reasonable point first Father, in the same book of Jeremiah, God is described as telling him 'I have wounded thee with the wound of an

172

enemy; with the chastisement of a cruel one, for the multitude of thine iniquity; because thy sins were increased, I have done these things to thee".

Father Alan remained calm and on song, "Indeed, our friend Franklin here is right. We were subjected to more scrutiny by God in the ancient times, he did indeed test the prophets fully. And it was not until his son, Jesus the Christ, who was bought into the world that this was changed. "For God so loved the world, that he gave his only begotten son, that whosoever believeth in him should not perish, but have ever lasting life.

Again there followed a slightly more rowdy set of cheers and calls to praise the Lord. Father Alan felt charged with the love of his congregation, he felt a real blast of affection and understanding sweeping through him.

The next person to address the congregation however, changed Father Alan's life forever in the way that the first sermon he attended did.

A small, Muslim chap intervened at this point solemnly but forcefully to address the congregation.

"I do not think you are wise to offer the promise of eternal salvation to any one, father".

Father Alan's features visibly dropped; something deep in the back of his mid kept quietly calling out to him, 'remember Ahmet Father, remember him now".

"Well, fellow worshippers this is certainly a first for our congregation to have a follower of… Islam, right, to join this sermon".

"Yes indeed, Islam Father, the honour is simply yours however. I feel I should tell this congregation that whilst our entire faith knows and acknowledges brother Jesus as a prophet, before our final prophet Muhammad, he is not seen as the saviour of humanity, as we do not truly have one".

Graham intervened this time before the father could reply, "Now look here friend, we are here to welcome you but you can't go round denying so many people there beliefs. It ain't right, you know I ain't going be able to say to you 'sheesh sorry pal but that chap Muhammad was no prophet".

It was a good thing he good thing Graham got there first, there were some calls emanating from the crowd including 'terrorist' and 'demon'.

The stranger continued.

"You would be in your right to say that. I understand your emotions, but a voice of questioning here seems required. Our religion says that though Jesus was blessed with the holy spirit he himself was to be no more valued

173

than Moses or indeed prophets such as Jeremiah".

"What is your name, sir?" Father Alan politely inquired.

"Ahmet".

Father Alan felt his heart drop a thousand feet.

"Interesting, right, a pleasure to meet you".

"I should tell you our religion also believes 'God doth not command you to take the angels or prophets as lords"

Despite some of the murmurs from the audience, Father Alan addressed them again.

"Right, indeed of course not. Apologies, I think this is the end of our sermon for today. Just as the congregation was beginning to leave, Father Alan chanced a meeting with his latest member.

"Ahmet, may I speak to you in private?".

"Yes of course".

Both left the main assembly area of their zone and took off the short distance to Father Alan's quarters.

Franklin couldn't sleep that night. Father Alan wasn't the only person to feel both shocked and a big scared by the arrival of Ahmet. He still didn't believe in this new saviour story, it was too similar to the last time, but all the same the arrival of this stranger had disrupted him. He had to be called Ahmet, didn't he? Alan had probably known about this guy having checked the records for Muslim inhabitants or something; he probably told us all that bullshit about a new saviour so he could keep that gaggle of followers he had totally in thrall to his every word. Franklin was a believer in God alright, just not really in the manner of Father Alan or indeed guys like Ahmet. He knew about the power and potentially devastating impact that religion and saviour prophets in particular could have on average people. They were all looking for answers; all of these congregation members were simply looking for a word or a line reassuring them that this damned hell hole we had to share wasn't the beginning or end of existence. People would follow guys like Father Alan as if they were Jesus himself. The work of one guy could prove to be disastrous, people would suddenly find themselves praising Jesus at frequent intervals during even the most mundane or serious of sermons. Franklin had a secret though; he did believe in the salvation of Jesus. It was that which really scared him all along; this idea that for all of the denial of fat and blood, for all of the restraint and burnt offerings, deep down the idea that one man could wave his hands and in a flash redeem a sole of all of his sins put the fear of God into him. He couldn't help but ruminate on the idea that if this was the case, and a single great person could redeem the worst sinners, then what is the point of morality? Surely with the total redemption of Jesus the Christ people would no longer worry about not stealing, about not praying to one God, about respecting parents. Guys like Jesus, they had the raw power to change order; they had the innate ability to turn society on it's head, and the worst part, the worst part still remained that Franklin was drawn to this. The release it offered, the gift of salvation; he knew enough though to remain serious and not totally accept all of the tenants that followed. The God he believed in was more about destruction and wrath rather than compassion or mercy despite the hysteria of the assembly; Franklin still had his own beliefs about the true nature of God. The treatment and deification of Jesus may be able to raise cheers and help the damned to hope, but it was still a potentially dangerous precept. The notion that one could save all could lead to an abdication of morality. The fear also still remained that, well if all of the beliefs about Jesus Christ were true, and more than enough people did truly believe this, then could he be more moral than God? He didn't believe so, but it was still a dangerous notion that occasionally underlined certain sermons. Franklin struggled with his own faith more than many others. He still believed in the single God, who indeed asked people not to worship false ideals, he still believed in God as the person who threw out Adam and Eve and the same God that sent the plagues to Egypt. Truly indeed the same God who promised a holy land to his people. Franklin couldn't help feeling cheated really; for all that he had believed, for all that he had sacrificed and denied others, it all felt wrong. Stuck underground, damned and waiting for judgement, he felt a rare surge of very real anger. The people who had put him in this position, this life of crushed damnation would pay for what they had done.

The letter from Mr. H was lying on his desk. John carefully tore open the envelope side ways on and began to read.
"Mr. Phillips,
I represent a movement that has been here in the compound from the very first day of our imprisonment. We as an organisation have been utilising all of the resources available to focus on the long term infiltration of the Apolites, with the long term aim of ensuring the full and forced release of

the human race. I should state that we are not an organisation that is seeking to negotiate of discuss matters with these aliens; far from it, we are agents of force seeking to fully ensure the freedom of our species to ensure a long term survival of humanity on Earth. We have contacts on the Apolites side, and every piece of intelligence we have received has indicated that our alien captors have no intention of returning us at any stage to the surface. They believe that we are being sufficiently well kept. I should also say at this stage that we have received no strong evidence as of yet to indicate that the humans being held underground are to be killed. Our research so far has indicated that the Apolites have not yet developed any plans to see the destruction of human inhabitants. Our contact within the Apolite high command, has indicated that the current maintenance of human life is to continue as planned and that activities would only change to increase levels of solitary confinement; they have given no indication whatsoever that we may at any time return to the Earth's surface. This as you may not be surprised to hear Mr. Phillips is very much unacceptable to us; the manners of the Apolites are insufficient to counteract the sheer oppression of our treatment. You have been selected for our boldest attempt yet to destroy the Apolite high command. We want you to plant a small but devastating explosive device in the central chamber of communication used by the aliens. We have already established a cover for your arrival at the central chamber; you are there to discuss improving the nutritional situation of the human inmates and to discuss increasing the numbers of internal greenhouses to increase the levels of internal food production. The device is no bigger than an envelope, and is to be placed in the corner of the chamber by your chair; the device will be planted in your left trouser leg and is to be dropped at the very end of your meeting. This is the first time we have attempted such espionage Mr. Phillips, and as such your total commitment is required. Indeed only I know of your presence and identity as the planned infiltration individual. As of now, only you and I know of your mission and name; the leadership of our movement has placed their trust in myself and I am doing the same to you. This uprising has began as a last resort; we have tried using our contact within the Apolite high command to try and initiate a return to the surface for our people. The approach was routinely condemned, and I quote from their leader, "humanity does not deserve another chance yet to ruin the Earth". They have taken over our planet and have dismissed all of our works, you are to be the key man Mr. Phillips in destroying the high command. We have already got in place another infiltrator to open the main gates of the compound. This is a carefully planned operation Mr. Phillips with others in charge of objectives even I am not able to know of. Our movement has waited long enough to strike back against our captors. With your help we should be able to halt the Apolites for long enough to ensure the escape of the members of our compound. We shall be the first to escape should this operation go to plan Mr. Phillips so I need not tell you of the severity of this mission. Once free we are to return to the surviving buildings in the city and to then try and reconnect with military hardware with the view of liberating the other compounds.

Good luck,

Mr. H."

John felt both scared and exhilarated by the prospect of the task ahead; he felt another moment of feeling pleased with his non religious stance. The moral implications of blowing up a room full of alien beings wouldn't affect his conscious in the same way that it would affect guys like Father Alan. He knew he was meant to be the guy to do this job. Had he found the word he would have called it destiny.

The Commander was feeling energised; his plans for the attempted military coup to regain control of the Earth seemed to be proceeding effectively. If not perfectly frankly. He had selected his team for the operation nearly a year ago and all were now clued in on the key aspects of the operation. The conference in the central chamber was to be initiated by Howard Jones, the explosion would be set off by Franklin Davis, the leading tech men Unger and Thornill would then be sent to the central mainframe operating room to release the gates whereby Graham Sears and Paul Frost would roll out the two largest terrain vehicles owned by the Apolites. Frankly he wasn't given knowledge by the Apolites about the state of the Earth's surface. The leading scientists he dealt with reassured him that there was no chance of nuclear waste being a problem although much of the terrain may now be a desert leading to potential problems of growing food. This would be a necessary challenge in order to reclaim the Earth's territory from the largest oppressors ever seen. He was aware of the religious orders within the compound; he had heard about the rumours of some prophecy being enacted involving one of the aliens and a guy called Ahmet who was the descendent of an Egyptian involved with these same

Apolites thousands of years ago. Truthfully The Commander had never been a religious man and all of this talk of an Ahmet to him simply provided a smoke screen for the people down at the bottom. Anything that shielded their eyes from the scorching truth of a seared Earth could prove to be incredibly useful. The Commander hated the idea that these aliens had defeated the full technology of the Earth. Something deep inside him was slightly impressed with the effective colonisation of our planet. They put the US efforts in Iraq, Vietnam and Afghanistan to shame and the damn hippies did it without firing a single shell or killing a single soldier. They didn't even kill the guys who were trying to pilot their crafts into the space ships, they literally used their damn technology to re-land our own planes! That part really got to him; the easy use of such powerful measures to control all of our military might. The nukes should have done some damage, any damage given the sheer weight of mega tonnes involved but not these guys, no the surface of their giant crafts were not even scratched. There must have been some force field not that that mattered any more; least not till he himself got hold of some fighter crafts and some more damn nukes. This infiltration fighting felt deeply wrong on a principle level to The Commander; he'd spent so much time fighting guys who used this type of approach, it was cowardly really. There was no choice though; to regain any semblance of the Earth's system the main operating room would need to be temporarily regained. He just prayed that the point man, John would get out in time having dropped the letter bomb. He would have done this himself but too many parts of the operation needed co-ordination.

Father Alan sat Ahmet across from his desk. As he was getting comfortable Father Alan set the coffee machine on and went to get cups whilst the contraption slowly began to whir into quiet life. The smell began to fill the air as the two men began talking to one another.

"Thank you for joining me, Ahmet, right?" He knew it was right of course. "Yes indeed. Ahmet Al-Sahih. Thank you for your time, and coffee. I must say fresh coffee is truly a great luxury!"

"You're welcome, it's one of the privileges they give to those who co-operate with the Apolites from time to time. I'm used like many others to maintain high spirits and to address those people who believe to keep believe. I don't tell everyone I meet due to potential jealously but it's no secret. I mention it during the occasional sermon; I don't want people to feel the Apolites are an enemy".

"I wasn't aware of that deal, thank you for your honesty".

"No problem. How do you like it?"

"Excuse me?"

"Your coffee Ahmet".

"Ah, black with one sugar if you have any"

"Of course"

Despite the pleasantries and the formalities Father Alan could still feel a restless force coursing through his veins, as if he were possessed by a ghost or perhaps as if he were being spiritually plugged into a giant metaphorically divine power grid. He composed himself to stir in the sugar and to pour his own before handing the hot rare drink over.

"Thank you"

"That's fine no problem. I appreciate you coming down to hear my sermon despite our obvious differences"

"The differences are less obvious than you think Father Alan"

"Well I suppose so, the stuff about your faith denying the divinity of Jesus is pretty unchanging though isn't it?"

"Yes with regards to the existence of Jesus, yet I think you know that isn't the single reason for the success of your faith"

"For once I'm going to have to disagree with you sir. I think he is the only reason our faith is as it is; I could no more deny that Jesus is the son of God than you could deny that Muhammad is the final prophet".

"Peace be upon him. However despite our differences Father I think you should acknowledge how much things have changed. If Jesus died for our sins, then why are we now being punished by God?"

"Well that is where we differ. I don't believe that this is a punishment from God but the start of a new life of liberty and prosperity"

"What with the entire population of the Earth living under the ground? It seems easy for you to be positive about these aliens whilst they are kind to you. Others are not so forgiving".

"You're a smart man Ahmet, you should know that one of the core pillars, if you pardon the coarse analogy, of our faith, Christianity, is that of compassion and forgiveness. 'Let he is without sin cast the first stone' and so on".

"I appreciate that sentiment Father, but I feel you need to consider some other teachings. We are warned of the importance of signs in The Koran, you should perhaps note that according to Muhammad, 'As for those who believe not in the signs of God, God will not guide them, and a sore torment doth await them".

"Do you foresee sore torment for myself Ahmet?"

"I would hope not Father Alan! Alas it could be the way for some of your congregation. I felt inclined to meet you sir not because of what I have heard of you, far from it, but rather what I have heard though word of mouth about what some of your followers think. Have you heard those rumours?"

"Please enlighten me, I've heard some whispers"

"Some people believe you are God; which I think you'd understand if I disagree with"

"I wouldn't claim to be myself!"

"Indeed, that doesn't surprise me. Your talks though, especially the rumours of a new saviour to rescue us have spread far and wide".

Father Alan swallowed some air accidentally, he felt himself worry that Ahmet had heard his name and was about to tell him that his claim was true, or worse that it was absolutely untrue.

"What is your opinion?"

"I don't believe either one of us is this prophet you mention Father Alan, and besides I think you know that my belief really begins and ends with Muhammad as the final prophet"

"Here is where I may correct you perhaps Ahmet, you're faith contains more than just the teachings of Muhammad"

"I would disagree with your assertion this time Father"

"Reasonable enough, however I feel you are ignoring the extent to which your faith and The Koran acknowledge the importance of other faiths including Christianity and Judaism"

"I am aware of this point, 'We have our works and ye have your works; and we are sincerely His'".

"Yet you would doubt our beliefs in Jesus Christ"

"Only to an extent; we acknowledge him as a prophet and as one of those 'with near access to God' yet he is very much not seen as a figure who can rescue us from the flames of damnation set by God. For your comfort I should also direct you to the quote 'If the God of Mercy had a son, the first I would be to worship him'"?

Father Alan felt a strange sensation flowing through him; it was a strange heady mix of fear, nausea, elation, doubt and arousal. It confused his mind whilst Ahmet was speaking. He felt he was to be in the presence of a descendent of the original prophet. Father Alan decided finally to question this new stranger on his knowledge of ancient religious history.

"Are you aware of any references to the Apolites in the Islamic faith Mr. Al-Sahih?"

"The Apolites themselves?"

"Yes"

"Well, I've thought about this point too Father Alan. There were references in The Koran to a day when 'the heaven shall give out a palpable smoke which shall enshroud mankind: this will be an afflictive torment"

"I see. That does sound fairly accurate"

"I am sorry to agree with you Father"

Sensing he was not going to receive the answers he was looking for from Ahmet Al-Sahih for today, Father Alan politely collected his cup and politely sent him on his way.

"Thank you for your time, Mr. Al-Sahih"

"Ahmet is fine"

"Right, Ahmet it is".

After sending Ahmet off, Father Alan sat down and began to ruminate on what had just happened. His mind was coursing with questions and problems; could he really be the new saviour? Could it truly be true that a man who questioned the divinity of Christ is actually the future saviour of the human race? Was this guy right personally in his assessment that we are indeed all damned by the 'smoke' of judgement as it were from God. Father Alan switched off the coffee machine and went about his normal business of reading The Bible, searching for inspiration and reassurance about God and Jesus Christ. It felt like harder work having met Ahmet, the forces surging through his body had energised him whilst meeting the man, but he felt exhausted now in the aftermath. If he was wrong about Ahmet, could he be wrong about Jesus? The potential for error made Father Alan look at The Bible with more trepidation and nerves than ever before.